RULE

ONE

TWENTY

Author: E. A. Padilla

To Laura,
   It was great to see you at
your wedding & Bob's birthday!
I hope you enjoy it!
          Sincerly,
E. A. Padilla (AKA - Andre')

Rule One Twenty
E. A. Padilla

EAP Publishing

eappublishing.com

Copyright © 2015 E. A. Padilla

ISBN 978-0-9964818-0-9

First Edition 2015

PUBLISHER'S NOTE

Dedication

A special thanks to my family and friends. For my family's constant support and encouragement throughout my life and through this entire process to publish my first book.

To my parents and other family members- Clara and Robert Neebling, my sisters Lisa, Gordi and Suzanne, my stepson Michael and my son A. Michael. To my friends, Patrick Gleason, Edward Stevens and Rebecca Gutierrez, who read the manuscript and provided valuable feedback.

Contents

Cost of Freedom

They veered off of Highway 17, a main road connecting the Bay Area to the quiet Santa Cruz and Monterey County beachfronts. The Agency used this mountainous area as one of its dumpsites.

As the population of the San Francisco Bay Area continued to increase, disposing of bodies on the ocean became more and more risky. Increased traffic of oil tankers, cruise ships, and personal vessels made suspicion and detection a real possibility. The practice of leaving a body submerged for the sharks had been abandoned years ago, something that the convicted murderer Scott Peterson had discovered.

The unmarked brown van slowed exiting off onto the dirt shoulder of the southbound lanes of Highway 17. The driver followed Agency protocol. Scanning his rearview mirror, he was looking for approaching headlights. The Agency's preferred time to dump a body was at night. Only on extreme occasions were dumps ever initiated during daylight hours. Nighttime not only presented less traffic but also provided its most obvious advantage—avoiding visual detection.

A single white GMC Suburban appeared in the rear view mirror. It was the only other vehicle present in either direction. The van slowed, allowing the Suburban to pass. After the oversized all-terrain, behemoth-like station wagon rounded a sweeping curve, the agents simultaneously powered down their windows. Only the rumble of their V8 engine could be heard.

The driver exited the paved road and slid onto the dirt shoulder. Rotating the plastic-coated ignition key, he killed the engine. They sat the required twenty seconds. Every detail had been planned. Over the years, the Agency procedures had been honed to perfection. They had developed into a dynamic yet predictable set of choreographed events. Each phase of the procedure had its own set of contingencies. The bodies were never taken back to the Agency. No physical evidence linking the government to the murdering of its citizens would be risked. Although they recognized the efficiency of the idea and had contemplated it many times, the dangers were just too great.

The silence of the vacant road was eerie. The night enhanced the absence of typical road noises—from the roar of combustion engines, the unique rattles and clanks of vehicles in tow, to the distinctive whirl of rotating rubber tires gripping asphalt. The men continued to wait.

After the allotted time had passed, the driver restarted the engine and smashed his foot down onto the accelerator, maneuvering the vehicle along the shoulder of the highway. At the next road, the driver careened the van onto Old Glenwood Highway. This section of road was a perfect disposal location. It offered two points of entry, a direct marking post along the highway and a nondescript parallel dirt frontage road.

This double access allowed the Agency plausible deniability. If they were forced to delay the dump, they had an easy alternate route back to Highway 17. Such action would only be undertaken if they had any reason to believe that their cover had been blown. At this particular location, the presence of several large sweeping curves in both directions decreased the possibility that anyone could detect the presence of a vehicle driving down that road.

Typically, the bodies that the Agency disposed of were unique. In every case, the targeted individual represented a threat to the national security of the United States of America. As such, the circumstances surrounding their disappearances could never be revealed or acknowledged. These corpses could never be found. However, if by some chance they were found, they could not be identified, in which case, the condition of the DNA needed to be purposely degraded so that the identity of these poor souls could not be matched.

For these reasons, the Agency had protocol and standard operating procedures that had to be followed. From the transportation, preparation, and disposal of a corpse, the Agency established contingency upon contingency.

To date, since the initial disposal in 1958, none of the Agency's disposals had ever been positively identified. In total, only four bodies had ever been unearthed. In each instance, the skeletal remains and bone fragments had led local law enforcement nowhere. The common conclusion in each case was that the bones were human. Neither foul play nor natural causes could be ruled out. All of these cases were abandoned and remained open unsolved cold cases. They were never identified. The deceased were believed to be drifters or one of the many homeless Americans falling into obscurity to die alone, where they were laid to rest at the designated potter's fields. The true identities of these high-profile missing persons remained unsolved. No suspicions were raised.

The van settled on Old Glenwood Highway. They had reached the predetermined physical location that Agency protocol recognized as the point of no return. In each case, depending on the circumstances, it was located a specific distance away from the Pre-Team Landing Zone, or PTLZ. If anyone entered this area and it was determined that they may have witnessed any of the Agency's activities, the unfortunate onlookers would be eliminated. There was no turning back.

To assist the drop team, the Pre-Team had installed a sophisticated surveillance system along the highway. The system allowed the drop team the ability to determine in real time the presence of any vehicle traveling within three miles in either direction. This six-mile zone gave the drop team enough time to safely enter the PTLZ. The portable surveillance devices would be extracted seven days after the formal disposal. These devices served a dual purpose by gathering the driving trends to determine the best time to schedule the dump during the time period that represented the least number of vehicles driving the roadway. It also provided the team with a warning system for oncoming vehicles in both direction of traffic.

"Go ahead and activate it," instructed the driver.

Sitting in the front seat, the passenger reached up and pulled down the overhead visor. Hidden behind the visor were five buttons embedded into the roof of the Agency vehicle. After depressing one of the buttons, all the switches lit up in unison. A bright green console panel illuminated the interior of the van. The Global Positioning System displayed the exact location in a bird's-eye, computer-imagery fashion. The interior of the van illuminated a soft mint green, as if a small candle were burning. The GPS did its magic.

A small keypad was built into the compartment door. This miniaturized desktop computer was embedded within the glove compartment itself. After the agent entered his personal password, the miniature monitor pinpointed the exact location where the Pre-Team had prepared a hole. The location of the hole stood in deep contrast to the mint green. A bright white cross began blinking on and off and would continue to do so until the closing code was keyed into the system. That code would be entered only after the bodies had been disposed of and when the van had exited the six-mile surveillance perimeter.

In the event a drop team failed to enter the assignment code within four hours after the GPS location had been pinpointed and activated, protocol dictated that the Agency would initiate an immediate follow-up team. Such delays could only mean that there was a problem, one involving additional bodies that now needed disposing.

Even with contingencies, planning, protocol, and standard operating procedures, there was always a possibility that additional unforeseen casualties would be required. It was a mathematical certainty. Each agent knew the odds. The domestic team understood the *One Twenty Rule*. In the law of large numbers, an urban inner-city disposal resulted in additional casualties every twenty drops. In contrast, rural areas had a smaller likelihood of detection: one in every one hundred drops. This would be a rural drop, where the *One One Hundred Rule* would apply.

The miniature screen looked similar to a treasure map. In some ways, each tomb was a treasure—a treasure of evidence. But to reap the benefit of each treasure, the discoverer would first need to prove beyond a shadow of doubt the identity of its occupant. Then, if by some miracle the interred body was identified, the first connection would need to be made. Exactly how and for what reason did this person die?

Then, if all of these obscure connections were made, the discoverer would still need to unravel what he or she knew or could prove justifying the individual's assassination. Finally, only after all these interrelated mysteries were solved could the true rationale behind the person's demise be fully comprehended. In most cases, these individuals never completely appreciated or understood the obscure connection their lives played in the Agency's twisted thought process. The only true result was that the person died. They were murdered. Seldom did these individuals appreciate the impact of what they knew, witnessed, or could prove. Rarely did they themselves make the connection as to why they were being eliminated.

Elimination was always a last resort. Extreme measures required a complicated and detailed decision-making process. Even within the hidden operations of secret agencies, murder is a serious matter, requiring proper authority. Rogue warriors had no place in the Agency. The only green light in terms of lethal force was during the disposal of bodies.

If the Agency wanted a public assassination, such an orchestrated event took unbelievable planning and thus were very rare. The first truly organized and high-profile public assassination occurred in the Kennedy assassination. In most cases, the only unrehearsed public killings took place when someone unexpectedly witnessed a body disposal and also had to be eliminated. The fear of additional unexpected bodies to dispose of, and more tracks to cover, was an ongoing concern for the Agency. Consequently, the preferred means of killing were well orchestrated and preplanned.

Earlier that day, a team had prepared the area. Posing as a Pacific Gas and Electric construction crew, the Pre-Team had researched and confirmed that this location was now ready and safe for use. These Pre-Teams were constantly locating and preparing such areas. One of the principle prerequisites for site selection was that the area had to have at least a five-square-mile area free from logging, camping, buildings, or any form of surveying activities for future development. Otherwise, it would be ineligible for consideration.

Once the Pre-Team located a potential sight, they would prepare the area as a future site to dispose of a body. In this case, the Pre-Team disguised themselves as a PG&E crew. This disguise allowed them the option of taking light and heavy equipment into the remote location without drawing unneeded attention. It also offered a significant backdrop to protect their activities from being viewed by casual passersby.

The Pre-Team had located the area, dug an eight-foot-deep and two-foot-diameter hole. Inside the hole, lye, sulfuric acid and false evidence stood ready, awaiting the arrival of the drop team. Hair had been collected from a local salon, jewelry purchased from a local jeweler, and teeth taken from scientifically donated cadavers. The materials were then placed at the bottom of the pit, and the bagged items and containers were stored inside the tomb. The opening was then covered with sticks and leaves.

Exactly twenty-five feet in front and behind the hole, small white reflectors were fastened to tree trunks, thirty-two inches from the ground. The location was in the same line of sight as where the headlights of the drop team's van would be pointing. The coordinates of the reflectors were entered into the Agency's master GPS library. With these tasks accomplished, the Pre-Team vacated the site. Under no circumstances would a Pre-Team ever return to a site once it had been prepared and its location entered into the GPS system.

* * * * *

The cold coastal night was brisk. As the van approached the second Bean Creek marker, the agents exchanged eye contact with each other, acknowledging that they had just passed the point of no return. Detection by any person would require lethal action. Protocol now included the use of the *One One Hundred Rule*. "What's the exact GPS location?" asked the driver.

The passenger clicked away onto the keyboard. The green console came back to life and lit up the coordinates. "It looks to be about one-tenth of a mile away." They continued to scan to the right of the road. The markings for the PTLZ should be located in that direction. Their mission included the disposal of the body, then to remove the reflecting markers and return to the Agency Headquarters. The agents were looking for Mountain Charlie Road. During their exit from the dumpsite, they would double back on an alternative roadway, driving north and avoiding Highway 17 altogether. It was Agency protocol. Never enter and exit from the same road.

The driver slowed the van and began scanning the roadside for the reflectors. As they neared the location, the console let out a high pitched "beep," letting them know a vehicle had just driven by their first sensor on Old Glenwood Highway. There was a distinct clicking sound as he punched the miniature keyboard to determine from which direction the vehicle was traveling.

"It's traveling southbound. Based on standard speed predictions, we can expect to see the vehicle in three minutes," reported the passenger. Both agents contemplated the *One One Hundred* scenario. There was plenty of time to locate the reflectors, enter the brush, and shut off the van. Their concern was that the oncoming vehicle may have seen the van's headlights. The van continued forward.

Given the terrain, if the oncoming vehicle was traveling thirty-five miles per hour, they had at least three minutes. The agents had plenty of time. The driver continued looking forward and to the right. The oncoming headlights could not be seen nor its engine noise heard. Fifteen seconds after hearing the beep, the agent riding shotgun saw the reflectors. The van's headlights began to shine on a single bright white reflector that twinkled just to the right of the road. The Pre-Team had created a nondescript passageway through the woods and bushes.

The van pulled off the road and continued along the narrow temporary pathway. The area was thick with brush and pine trees. As the van pushed deeper into the woods, the debris and low lying bushes scratched the van's sides. After traveling a short distance, the driver parked the van, switched off the ignition, and turned off the lights. The passenger reached up to the ceiling and deactivated the interior dome light. Only then did the agents exit the van.

Each man shuffled along the sides of the van and pulled out his silenced forty-five-caliber pistols. The passenger slunk back along the fresh pathway, ducking into the brush carefully to avoid the unnatural opening back onto the main road. After locating a specific eight-foot evergreen tree, he reached from behind the tree to remove the reflector. As his hands made contact with the cold metal object, he tightened his grip, rotated his wrist and pulled, detaching the reflector from the tree.

* * * * *

A white Jeep Grand Cherokee sped along Old Glenwood Highway. The steady jolting and whir of the four-by-four tires echoed off the roadway and nearby trees. The unique staccato sound reverberating through the forest became louder as it approached the PTLZ entrance. The driver's face lightened with a tired smile as he watched his wife. Her cheek was resting against the headrest. She continued to sleep as her husband maneuvered the vehicle through the mountain pass.

Soft jazz music from Kenny G's latest CD filled the interior cabin. The couple's two children had long since fallen asleep in the back, strapped into their car seat boosters. The Sinclair family was returning from his sister's twentieth-wedding-anniversary party in Citrus Heights, just east of Sacramento. Both Richie and his wife were born and raised in local Scotts Valley. They had driven this shortcut countless times before. It was used by the locals to bypass the meandering Highway 17. Richie had no clue as to the danger in which he had just placed his family.

Richie tightened his grip on the leather covered steering wheel. The Jeep banked the familiar sweeping curve. Richie thought he noticed something out of place. Something was different about the landscaping. It was as if some of the trees had been removed. He even thought he noticed fresh exposed earth leading into the woods, even though the bushes seemed overgrown. He couldn't recall any construction being done this far back off the main road, especially near Old Man Blythe's property line.

For a brief moment, he lifted his foot off of the accelerator and considered applying the brakes to get a closer look, but his thoughts were interrupted when his 300M Triathlon watch chirped. It was exactly 2:00 a.m. He forgot about the distraction and concentrated on getting his family tucked into bed in their own home. He reapplied pressure to the accelerator, doubling his efforts at concentrating on the road ahead.

As the Jeep passed in front of the PTLZ, out of the corner of his eye something else caught his attention. As he approached the fresh tracks along the road, he thought he saw a hand. He blinked hard and kept his eyes on the dirt road ahead. It was late. His eyes had to be playing tricks on him. Without giving it a second thought, he continued pressing his right foot on the

E. A. Padilla

accelerator pedal and never looked back. He just wanted to get home.

* * * * *

The agent pulled his hand back from around the base of the tree. He was sure that the reflector had been removed from sight before the *Jeep* came into view. The SUV's head lamps danced across the PTLZ entrance. Both agents had their backs against separate pine trees. They stood close enough to look into each other's eyes. With the lighting from the Jeep, the agents were able to make eye contact with each other. Protocol required that if there was any evidence that their presence had been detected, all potential witnesses were to be eliminated.

The passenger agent watched the vehicle continue on the dirt road. His eyebrows squinted as if trying to increase his visual concentration. This agent had to determine if the driver showed any indication that he detected their presence. The Jeep continued on its course. The brake lights never came on. The vehicle didn't appear to reduce its speed. In his judgment, they were not detected. This same agent placed a call instructing the South Exit Team to let the vehicle pass.

Both agents remained frozen hiding behind a tree. They listened to the sound of the departing vehicle. The engine's roar continued to drift, fading off into the distance. As the night returned to calm, the sounds of crickets began to blare as a single electronic tone simultaneously sounded in their earpieces. The vehicle exited the three-mile perimeter. The agents stood up and stretched out of their crouched stances. Their blood flow began to return to normal as they strode back to the van. It was time to unload their packages.

* * * * *

As the tank dropped loose and the last of the acid dropped into the pit, the agents removed their gloves, surgical masks, and

10

hair nets, placing them into the agency-issued stainless steel bowl. These items were designed to quickly dissolve. The driver stirred the mixture. The items melted away and dissolved into a soupy liquid. With the body parts properly prepared and the DNA-compromising solution applied, the soupy mixture was dumped into the hole.

After the items were drenched with distilled water and wiped clean, the bowl was stashed away in a duffel bag designed to hold all of the dismembering tools. The agent then disguised the duffle bag by placing it in what would appear to be a first-aid kit. This kit was designed so that once closed, it could be reopened only at the Agency. Other than it being blown apart with high explosives, only a digitized radio wave would allow the kit to be opened.

This disposal was an easy dump. After destroying the identification markings on the bodies, paying close attention to the teeth, fingers, palms, and footprints, the agents removed their night-vision goggles. The victims' jaws were also removed in their entirety and then brutally pulverized until every tooth was detached from the bone. Of all the body parts, the teeth were purposely left in the bottom of the bowl, allowing the greatest exposure time to the caustic solution. Once the agents had prepared a body, if it remained undisturbed and away from scientific eyes for at least six weeks from that date, the highly concentrated solvents would prevent an accurate DNA analysis from ever being made. After a twelve-month exposure, even the bone fragments would vanish.

This disposal was going according to plan. Each part of the mission followed the protocol and procedure manual of the Agency. The final touch involved filling the hole with dirt and an overt misdirection—a false distraction was used.

"Is it ready for the sign?" asked the driver.

The passenger patted the hole with an Agency issued shovel. Like all of the rest of their equipment, not a single identifying manufacturer, label or insignia could be found. The fact that their equipment was devoid of this information in itself could draw attention. But because everything they used was literally generic and nondescript, if any item were accidentally left behind, it would be impossible to track back to the Agency.

Looking up, the agent grunted. "Ready as it'll ever be."

The driver pulled out an Agency issued Phillips screwdriver and scored the front of a plastic covering and pulled it away, exposing the bright yellow, clearly visible sign, "Digging Forbidden! PG&E Power Lines Present." The hum of the cordless screwdriver pierced the silence of the moment.

The other agent readied a large sledgehammer and hurled it through the air. The heavy object ripped through the night air, thrusting air outward toward the agents, and then, with a dull thud, the metal head smashed the post deep into the dirt tomb. The sign was authentic PG&E signage acquired by the Pre-Team. Nothing was left to chance. Everything the A-Team left at the location had to be authentic. Nothing—not even the signpost—could draw unwanted attention that something was out of the ordinary.

Within five minutes, the hole was filled. For a brief moment, the agents stood motionless and evaluated the area. Everything looked normal. The sign was installed as indicated in the PG&E manuals. The agents turned their attention to the tools used in the dismembering process.

After all the tools were dried and bagged, one of the agents entered the van. He slid the door shut and opened the false bottom of the van's floor. The bag was stored inside a triple-ply bag designed like a giant zip-locking sandwich bag. As protocol required, each layer of zip lock was inserted inside of the other bag so that the zip seal would be placed at the bottom of the next bag. Only after all three layers were zipped shut was the bag stored in the secret compartment.

The agent yanked the carpeting back into place to conceal the compartment. Once the carpeting was fastened to the Velcro attachments, the agent leaned forward into the driving area and wedged himself between the front bucket seats, settling into the passenger seat. It was almost time to exit the PTLZ.

During this entire time, the driver remained standing outside of the van, surveying the area for any oncoming vehicles or unsuspecting persons approaching on foot. The *One One Hundred Rule* was always on their mind. Once the driver saw the passenger begin to re-engage the computer, only after he saw the mint-green glow from inside the van did he begin to relax. That light was the signal for him to re-enter the van. As his hand gripped the chilled door handle, his thoughts turned away from the package buried in the hole. His only thoughts were on reporting back to headquarters and closing out the GPS notification.

The driver reached for the ignition switch and broke the silence. "There were no unusual noises. No signs of any vehicle lights coming in either direction," he reported, for the benefit of the onboard recording system.

It was similar to the black box on commercial airlines. Every aspect of a dump was documented. A CD would be burned and stored with the file. Only one physical hard copy of the event would be kept. No duplication of the file would be made. Everything was to be kept in its original format. The Agency held true to the belief that a single encrypted physical record was the safest form of documentation. Nothing would be stored in any form of data that could be compromised for later viewing. The only way to review the records was through a unique decoding computer system that randomly generated characters unique to that file. The encryption, codes, and documents were all customized for a one-time use specific to each file.

The Agency was a huge organization that was kept isolated into separate independent agencies. Each Zone within the Agency maintained independent isolated unique computer systems. The isolation was designed to keep the files and documents specific to that Zone. Even the vendors used to assemble, create, and maintain the equipment were unrelated and independent from each other.

There was no sharing of anything to do with the storing of this data. These systems were intentionally different from Zone to Zone. They were isolated, stand-alone creations. As a result, the data within the Agency was so sensitive that it could be reviewed only from that particular Zone location. This data was beyond Top Secret. The primary objective was for the activities of the Agency to remain beyond the purview of the rest of the world. The files never existed, and the Agency possessed no knowledge surrounding any of the events leading up to anything to do with these missing persons.

After nodding to one another, the agents began to relax. Their efforts to remain at a heightened state of attention began to subside. The driver closed his door and turned on the ignition switch. The grinding of the engine starter preceded the rumble of the V8 motor. These noises cut through the still night air.

The mint green lights from the monitor did not affect their night vision. It was still intact. The last exposure to high incandescent lighting had been over forty-five minutes ago, when the Jeep had passed. The Agency dump teams knew their jobs. Thoroughly disposing of the package was the game. The planning that went into the process was layered to the last detail. Although textbook cases rarely took place, perfect adherence to standard operating procedures was the focus. Each dump had the goal of remaining flexible.

Given the numerous factors that go into completing a successful assassination, remaining flexible and adhering to these variations was how each team and each operation was graded. Ironically, even in the business of murder, humans still maintained that desire to excel and reach their maximum potential. Humans needed to be recognized for their efforts and complimented on jobs well done. So the success of an operation went beyond getting rid of the evidence. Each team had to debrief Headquarters. And like it or not, these agents were still employees, who looked forward to advancement, recognition, and salary reviews. It was their career. They wanted to do a good job.

In this particular case, from the time of the actual assassination, from the Pre-Team's arrival, only a brief four hours had transpired. Since disposals were an ongoing event, drop sites were constantly being found and prepared. Each Zone typically had six predesignated drop areas ready for use at a moment's notice. Factors such as weather, roadwork, and construction delays made dump-sight acquisition and preparation a full-time job with a separate ten-person department within each Zone. Flexibility and preparation were the mantra.

As their eyes had not been affected by any form of lighting since the encounter with the Jeep, they maneuvered the van, without the use of headlights, backtracking through the makeshift path created by the Pre-Team. Once they re-entered the van, use of the night vision goggles was strictly forbidden. At this phase of the operation, should they be discovered in any way, they had two options. Dispose of the unfortunate passerby or abandon the site and leave the area under the cover of night. This night would prove to be uneventful. Within forty-five seconds after starting the van they had reached the paved road leading back toward the South Bay.

The rules of engagement now changed. From this point forward, at no time could lethal force be used. The assumption was that locating the PTLZ was by design unlikely. The last thing the Agency wanted was to overanalyze the risk of discovery and create an unnecessary situation that would call attention to their activities.

The brown van accelerated along Mountain Charlie Road. The road was covered by worn asphalt but was still in fairly good shape. After traveling about a quarter of a mile, the driver turned on his headlights. Exactly three miles after reacquiring Charlie Road, they saw the Pre-Team's exit reflectors on the right side of the road. The passenger toggled the keyboard, and the console once again illuminated the interior with a splash of mint green lighting. The passenger entered his password, and the computer transmitted an encrypted message to the Agency satellite above: "Mission complete—heading out." Once the message was received by the Agency, it triggered a sequence of events that involved four different departments. The assignment was preparing to close out its file. Their mission was almost complete. Everything was going as planned.

The driver reached back and reactivated the dome light. Their final task was to deliver the van back to the Agency Zone Headquarters, where another team awaited their arrival to properly sanitize the van, download the data and remove the CD recording to properly document the case with the only hard copy of the file.

* * * * *

The old man couldn't help but hear the van coming up through the center of his kingdom. Blythe had owned this stretch of land since World War II. It had been seized from a Japanese family who was interned in a concentration camp after the bombing of Pearl Harbor. Gerald Blythe had purchased it at a bargain price when it was auctioned off. Since then, Old Man Blythe had sold ten different five-acre residential parcels. He was considered by the locals to be fairly rich. Blythe still owned over 300 acres of that stretch of Highway 17.

Blythe's tired hand wrestled with the curtains. He was just in time to see a van driving on Mountain Charlie Road. It was about three in the morning. He seemed more interested in who it might be than annoyed at the sounds disturbing his privacy. It didn't appear to be any of his neighbors' vehicles. It had been at least six months since anyone had been using that stretch of long-forgotten dirt path. He thought it somewhat odd that it was only a short time ago when a PG&E crew had been working in that same area. He continued to watch the van pull onto the main road when he noticed the van's headlights turn on. He couldn't understand what he was watching. *Why are they driving without headlights?*

The old man shuffled back to the kitchen. His elbows ached as he set the glass of bottled water onto his granite countertop. His mind wandered as his hand unconsciously stroked across the cold stone. His fingernails scraped the surface as if to polish the ends of his nails. His wife, May, had picked out the countertops. She had passed away three years earlier. Driven by habit, he relived the good times they had shared together.

He had to force the pleasant thoughts out of his mind to come back to the present. Old Man Blythe urged his shriveled legs to muster the energy to cross the Berber carpet. The scraping from his fuzzy slippers echoed off the cold empty walls of his 3,500 square foot home. He reached his bedroom. As if on auto pilot, Old Man Blythe fell into his king sized bed, hid under the thick goose down comforter, and closed his eyes. Taking a deep breath, he started his lonely routine, knowing it would be another long, sleepless night. He checked the clock on the end table and couldn't wait for the first signs of sunlight to peek over the mountain top. He had long since forgotten about the van, as it disappeared over the horizon heading toward the highway.

* * * * *

The van merged onto Highway 101 heading north. Breaking the silence, the passenger began to type away on the miniature keyboard, communicating with the satellite. He updated their GPS location and reaffirmed his initial report that no apparent witnesses or problems arose during the mission. He signed off and closed the glove compartment door. The driver settled into his bucket seat, preparing for his drive up to the San Francisco Headquarters, where all of the vehicles were serviced. As protocol required, any vehicles involved in a dump were required to have their equipment scrubbed clean.

The local KFOG radio station blared through the cabin. The passenger pulled out his silver Agency-issued thermos and offered the driver a cup. It was strange how an operation started and ended in total normalcy. It was only minutes earlier that they were dismembering and burying a body off of Highway 17. To anyone else, they simply looked like any two men one might see on the freeway. It's funny to think that no one really knows the character of an individual they may have cut off on the freeway. No one truly appreciates what any individual or organization is capable of doing.

Unknown to the men, the South Exit Team had a different opinion of the exposure that the white Jeep Cherokee posed. As such, the Exit Team was still busy finalizing the staging of what would later be reported as a solo car accident with four unfortunate fatalities. The manufacturer's engineers would be facing a new lawsuit from California for a steering column failure that would trigger unjustified scrutiny.

The ripple effect that the Agency caused from a killing had exponential reach in the number of individuals and organizations that would be impacted. To the Agency, such reactions only acted as a positive reinforcement for their efforts to conceal their true activities. Some things are just more important than individual rights and liberties. The Agency was protecting the national security of the United States.

Life's Lessons

"Hey! Hey you, Curt! What the hell are you doin', anyway? Get your butt down from there before the inspector arrives," yelled the foreman. "I thought you had this house wired and cleaned already!"

"I do, I'm just finishing this last connection," Curt replied, as he adjusted the acoustic ceiling grid back into its original position. "Besides, you wouldn't want me to accidentally ground the wires and torch this puppy, now, would ya?"

Brunanski retorted, "Yeah, yeah, you berserkly freak. Why don't you get a real job? What the hell you doin' wiring subdivisions for, anyways? I thought engineers worked in offices downtown, not shleppin' wire and tinkering with subcontractor work. What happened? You barely fuckin' pass, or what?"

Bru and Curt were lifelong friends. They had met when Curt moved into Bru's neighborhood in a predominantly white, middle-class section of town. Although by nature Curt was shy, being an only child and a military brat had developed his skills at making friends. It was either get over being shy or learn to be lonely. Moving every three years teaches kids that if you're too slow at making friends, you may have to wait until the next transfer to make any at all.

Curt learned that one the hard way. In his first move, he discovered that once other kids found out someone was leaving, they instinctively began to distance themselves from that person. Even at that young age, the adult influences somehow get filtered to the kids, that getting emotionally close to someone who'd be leaving in the near future didn't make sense. After that tough lesson from the school of hard knocks, Curt learned to restrict the subject of moving to discussions with his parents. He only told his friends the last week before they bugged out.

The constant moving from place to place also meant being the "new kid"—the outsider. To survive, the operative skill was to adapt and be assertive. Being an only child, Curt didn't have the luxury of a brother or sister to play with. It was pretty simple: Make friends, or learn to be a ventriloquist so he could hold a conversation with himself in the bathroom mirror.

Of course, Curt knew that the other military kids he met on base would also be moving on to their next assignment, just like his family would. He also understood that to be afraid of liking someone because of the emotional pain and emptiness one would feel later on, was a learned response. Being the one leaving helped change his perspective on such prejudices. Consequently, Curt made it a point to extend the hand of friendship to the new kids who arrived. He knew he liked being accepted and hoped that someone would repay his kindness when he had to make that inevitable relocation every three years.

Curt's father, Wayne Anderson, made his career in the U.S. Air Force. His family had learned the routine: multiple homes and short-term friends; acquaintances, really. They had no real roots. They were modern military gypsies for hire. The constant moving made keeping in touch with those special friends difficult, if not impossible. The inevitable contacts would dwindle from weekly phone calls to once a month to holidays to an annual Christmas card. After the years of similar disassociations, Curt's family learned it was easier to say your good-byes and never really look back. It was a clean break. But when Curt met Bru, that all changed. Mr. Anderson's sudden death was an ironic twist of fate that ended their gypsy existence.

His parents had married in Tupelo, Mississippi. Curt and his mother stayed with Wayne's relatives while he was stationed for a short tour in Seoul, Korea. Keeping the family intact meant going to the closest American base that had family housing. In this case, that meant Okinawa, Japan. However, given that the assignment was for only a short six months, it didn't make sense to move and upset the family when they would have to move again almost as soon as they unpacked. They all agreed it would be best to have a short separation. His mother would stay with Wayne's relatives in nearby Birmingham, Alabama.

When they returned from Japan, they were temporarily reassigned to Fort Rucker. For the next year and a half, the Anderson family planted roots, but only in a portable pot. With the rank of Major, Anderson was offered an opportunity to cross-train with the Army. After Fort Rucker, they were transferred to Europe. It was during those early years of their marriage when Wayne's wife, Janice, grew more and more depressed. Coupled with the constant moves, she was unable to conceive a child. She began to feel more abandoned and isolated. They began to consider adoption. Although Wayne wanted to father his own child, he understood the loneliness Janice had to endure. He agreed to pursue adoption but preferred to wait until they were stateside.

As luck would have it, a young, single German civilian woman who had been working on base had died during childbirth. The only surviving relative was the woman's widowed elderly father, who also had ties to the base. The Andersons had been having conversations with the Chaplain and making formal inquires into the adoption process; so when they learned of the situation, arrangements were made and the child was legally adopted by Wayne and Janice. They named him Curt Anderson.

They had met the grandfather and learned that during World War II, he had served in the German military. He was pleasant and seemed very intelligent. He promised not to interfere in the way in which they chose to raise their adopted son. He wanted them to understand that revealing to the child that he was adopted was their decision. In his desire to show his appreciation, the grandfather offered to assist them in any way he could; after all, their adopted child was still his daughter's own flesh and blood, as well as his own.

Before the adoption had been finalized, Janice and Wayne met the grandfather for only a brief moment. They were grateful and expressed sympathy for the loss of his daughter. They exchanged information and agreed they would contact him if they needed anything. Although Curt's biological grandfather never missed sending a Christmas or birthday card, neither Janice nor Wayne had the opportunity to speak to the old man again. It was only while Curt attended college that he got to truly know his grandfather.

When Curt was in the middle of first grade, his family was again transferred—this time, to Mather Air Force Base in Sacramento, California. Then, following Curt's fourth grade year, they moved to Moffett Air Force Base near San Jose, California. It was unusual to be transferred within the same state. Early in their military career, before they felt like gypsies, the Andersons had been excited about the opportunity to travel abroad. That all changed.

As a child, Curt grew cynical. The constant moving and loss of friends affected him. In fact, in Sacramento, Curt began to have behavior problems during pleasure reading. He was upset having to read the "Dick and Jane" series. It was only later that Curt realized it wasn't the reading he had disliked. Rather, it was the subject matter. Where were these perfect homes with little white picket fences? Curt had always lived on base housing. Why didn't those childhood stories ever discuss Base passes, TDYs, or those infamous ready-to-eat MRE meals? The harsh reality of military life was that it just didn't match the storybook version retold in school.

Curt's mother, Janice, was shy and introverted. Curt loved her very much, but he never understood why his father continually left them alone. Curt never knew his father, at least not in the way he wanted to know him. The truth was, Major

Anderson not only flew F-111s but also was essentially married to them. Curt remembered his dad being tired after completing his flights, too busy preparing for the next mission to be bothered with either him or his mother.

As a child, Curt prayed that his father would not reenlist. Unfortunately, like so many other career military, Major Anderson dreamed about the day he could be a civilian and work in the "private sector." Then he could "double dip" and receive both a military pension and private-sector income.

If Major Anderson could have held on just four more years, he would have had that full military retirement. To be eligible for a military pension, the Andersons would have had to be military gypsies for a total of twenty years. They would have had to put their lives on hold until Major Anderson had put in enough time to double dip. To do anything less would have been a waste of all the years they had already put in. Curt and Mrs. Anderson knew that the extreme cost in human happiness was too great. To the two of them, at least, it just wasn't worth it.

Major Anderson was kind to both Curt and his mother. Curt was never physically abused, but the Major never really took the time to develop a father-son relationship. The stresses of the military rarely left the Major with enough energy to play catch, go to the movies, or play miniature golf with Curt. Eventually, Curt just learned to avoid his father. Major Anderson needed his rest, and Curt couldn't handle the rejection.

As the years passed, Curt wasn't sure that his father remembered or cared about their special occasions. It seemed that only civilian kids celebrated those things. A military family had to make sacrifices. Military families were expected to appreciate and endure. Marrying into the military had no hidden agenda. The purpose of the military was to protect, defend, and preserve America. And serving one's country required a special person and commitment.

The more Curt was forced to forgo his happiness for his father's career, combined with their separation from him for such long periods, the more Curt lost respect for his father. Curt began to see his father as selfish and uncaring. It seemed as if the military always came first.

* * * * *

Major Anderson died during a routine stopover at the El Toro Marine Air Station in Tustin, California. The Andersons had just received their new assignment to Billings, Montana, but because of his death, they never made the move.

Major Anderson's death affected Curt differently than even Curt expected. "Major Anderson" was the man Curt knew. Although he missed that person, it was more like mourning the loss of a father he would never get to know. He missed Major Anderson, but the pangs of loss were greater from knowing he would never get the opportunity to see what it would be like to have a dad.

It was ironic that his father had died in early January. The investigation concluded that it had been human error. Jet fuel is stored in the wings of the aircraft. Apparently, the ground crew had filled one of the wings. The uneven weight distribution within the wings prevented a normal liftoff. As the jet began to lift off the tarmac, Major Anderson's jet began to lean uncontrollably toward the aircraft's heavier side.

The official report could only speculate that the Major had attempted to gain control. Even if he had reacted at the exact moment the jet became airborne, it would have been too late. Ejecting was only a theoretical option. The speed at which the jet rolled would have prevented Major Anderson from surviving, even if he had ejected. The exploding canopy system would have projected him into the solid asphalt tarmac. The Air Force concluded that the only way the accident could have been prevented was if the problem had been identified during the preflight check. Once the decision to go to the air was made, the crash was not a theoretical possibility but rather a physical certainty.

During his parents' fourteen years of marriage, Curt had never understood why his mother was always sad and lonely during the weeks following Christmas. On Curt's tenth Christmas, he waited until after midnight to sneak out of his bedroom to steal one of Santa's cookies. As Curt crawled through the thick brown shag carpeting, he saw his mother sitting on the living room sofa. The television sat silent. She sat motionless—alone.

As Curt's eyes focused in the dark, he saw tears trickling down his mother's shiny cheeks. Mrs. Anderson was admiring a faded crushed red rose preserved inside the worn family photo album. Mrs. Anderson glanced between the flower and her wedding ring. At that time, Curt was too young to understand the significance of January 8 and what it meant to his mother. As a ten-year-old, Curt was too scared to ask his mother what was wrong. He was afraid of getting in trouble for being out of bed.

Three years after Curt's father died, Curt realized the significance of that day. His father's funeral had occurred on his parents' wedding anniversary. In a twist of fate, due to remote TDYs, schools, and missions, Major Anderson had missed every one of their fourteen prior wedding anniversaries. Yet, in fifteen years of marriage, Mrs. Anderson would finally be able to share this special occasion with her husband—the first time the day they married, and the second time the day of his funeral. It also marked the first time Curt discovered that he had been adopted.

How strange that Mrs. Anderson felt some satisfaction that the military hadn't prevented their being together for their fifteenth wedding anniversary. They would not be separated this time! She had hoped the funeral would be like their wedding, which had been a personal church ceremony, where no military uniforms were evident in the wedding party—every one of the men had worn black tuxes. But the death of a pilot is a serious matter in any military branch. It went without saying that the military had to orchestrate the proceedings. After all, it was military protocol.

* * * * *

Curt looked back up at the acoustic-ceiling grid, admiring his hidden surveillance system. Hearing Bru yelling at the workers, Curt began to think back on how Bru came to be his boss. At 28 years old with only his high school diploma, Bru had followed in his father's footsteps—the construction trade. Bru had mastered his hammering skills by the age of thirteen, where he could hammer a framing nail into place with one solid swing. Mr. Brunanski knew one day his son would be not only a skilled carpenter but a good boss. Young Christopher Brunanski was a working man's man. Bru was being groomed to take over Brunanski Construction Company when Old Man Brunanski was ready to retire.

* * * * *

Bru was a lifelong friend. He wasn't just Curt's boss. Bru stood five foot two, weighed 180 pounds, and had forearms like Popeye. Ever since Curt could remember, Bru had possessed an intimidating demeanor, always acting the tough guy. Upon Curt's return from studying abroad, though, that all changed. Everyone noticed something, as if Curt possessed a new inner confidence. Bru had once been the tough guy, yet the subtle body language and facial gestures switched places between the two men; those dominant alpha male characteristics had somehow been transferred to Curt.

At first, Bru attributed this change in status as a feeling of jealousy that Curt had attended college, studied abroad in Germany, and traveled the world. Curt had lost his father and then his mother to cancer and was forced to face his life alone; these were experiences Bru had yet to face. Bru tried to appreciate Curt's new maturity. He failed to coax Curt into sharing those experiences, dashing the hope that he could gain experience from the retelling of those moments. No matter how hard Bru tried, Curt always dismissed those events as the same old crap, just on a different continent.

Two specific episodes remained buried deep in Bru's psyche, and these events forever changed his attitude toward Curt. After Curt's return stateside, Bru was helping him prepare for a poker party in Curt's apartment. As he searched the carport storage cabinet for the poker chips, he found a thick fabric bag. Inside he found a well-worn passport and an oversized blocky cellular phone. The phone had a bendable antenna and appeared very durable, as if it were designed to resist a severe impact.

Thumbing through the passport, Bru saw countless stamps from Czechoslovakia, East Germany, Croatia, and the USSR. Curt had never mentioned these excursions. Hearing an upstairs door slam shut and the distinctive sound of feet jogging down stairs, Bru turned his attention away from the passport and phone. Feeling as if he had invaded Curt's privacy, he shoved the items back into the bag and returned it to its hiding space.

Bru turned toward Curt. "Hey, where are the chips?" Reaching above Bru's head, Curt pulled out a tattered cardboard box.

"Here they are, you doofus! That's what you get for being vertically challenged." As they began to laugh, Bru had the distinct impression that Curt had glanced toward the area where he found the fabric bag. After closing the cabinet doors, Curt studied Bru with a different focus. For a brief moment, Bru had the impression that Curt was contemplating whether Bru had discovered the bag. Breaking the awkward moment, Bru turned away, heading back upstairs and yelling over his shoulder that he needed some beer. Brunanski never brought up the fabric bag, and Curt never told anyone he had visited those countries.

Another event took place at a fraternity party he attended at Curt's college. After endless drinking games, most of the attendees were well beyond the legal alcohol limit. A kid from a rival frat house had been putting the moves on Curt's girl-friend, Melody. The young man was too confident and became physical and aggressive in his pursuits. As the party broke up, this same guy had some how slipped on the front porch stairs and was found lying unconscious in the shrubs.

As the hosting members learned of the incident, Bru began looking for Curt and found him some time later. Curt offered Bru an unsolicited explanation that he had gone to his van to get his cigarettes. As they started walking back to their car, Bru could have sworn he saw Curt glance over the porch landing at the precise location where the boy had been injured. To his surprise, Curt appeared to be smiling.

* * * * *

Descending the ladder, Curt shifted his weight, causing the metal legs to scrape the concrete and emit a high-pitched screech. The noise tore Bru from his thoughts. Those events had reshaped his feelings. Although Curt was his best friend, he more than respected him; he feared him.

Climbing down the aluminum ladder, Curt clutched the cold rung of the ladder. The cold sensation dredged up a stagnant memory that only a child's mind would lock away. The unexpected release of memories catapulted his thoughts back to the day his father's body was flown back home. Curt's face contorted and his body recoiled as the memories came flooding forward from the permanent record in his subconscious.

* * * * *

Curt held his mother's hand as Major Anderson's coffin was lifted out of the C-130.

A typical airstrip is deafening with the roar of jets, but not this day. No aircraft, other than the C-130 carrying his father, was allowed to taxi or land. The fallen pilot had to be properly received with full military honors.

The loved ones looked on from their cold-to-the-touch aluminum folding chairs positioned according to the diagram prepared by the officer on duty. During that brief silence, only the echo of the pall bearers' shiny boots slapping against the tarmac could be heard. Curt's tearful eyes pried away from the coffin, his head tilting upward as the roar of his father's squadron appeared overhead. The distinct smell of exhaust fumes filled Curt's small nostrils, and his white dress shirt fluttered from the jet wash. As the squadron flew past, Curt noticed a missing spot within the formation. Later that day, Lieutenants Kellar and Thiel explained the significance of the missing jet. It was the missing man formation and represented the loss of his dad.

Years later, as an adult, Curt learned that this type of formation was simply a required part of the military ceremony. Such honors were bestowed only on important personnel; those who had attained that certain level of authority, which included pilots who died in action. It was protocol.

That ceremony symbolized not only Major Anderson's ultimate sacrifice, but also that of Curt and his mother. It was appropriate. A perfect conclusion to their military lives. Everything took on its proper perspective. The ceremony and their lives adhered to military procedure and its etiquette. On January 8, Major Anderson's funeral went according to plan. It was orchestrated by the military while the decedent's loved ones and his chain of command watched on as spectators.

The thunderous roar of the jets faded away into the afternoon sky. The contrasting silence was replaced with the normal air traffic of any air force base. Life must go on. Curt knew he would miss having a dad. But at the same time, he was relieved at being free of the military. Maybe now he and his mom would have a chance at normal civilian lives after all.

* * * * *

Looking back for a final visual inspection, Curt was certain that the future homeowner would never suspect that such a sophisticated surveillance system would be watching their every move. The system was small and undetectable. As the main remote components were hidden deep within the ceiling joist, Curt was confident that this first of many systems would achieve his goal. He couldn't wait to test it!

As he walked out the front door of one of his future neighbors, he glanced back at the kitchen ceiling. He was certain no one would ever know. This home was on the same cul-de-sac where Curt's home was to be built. A cul-de-sac, as opposed to a regular through street, gave Curt a better vantage point and more opportunities to snoop on more than just his immediate neighbors.

* * * * *

Curt was finishing the final touches on the second house in his surveillance scheme. As Curt came down the ladder, he slipped off one of the ladder rungs and caught his balance only after grabbing the top of the ladder. Curt's screwdriver tumbled from the top of the ladder, plunging down like an eagle dive-bombing toward a lake to catch its morning meal. Given the unequal weight distribution, the heavy handle, not the metal point, ricocheted off of Bru's shiny bald head.

"What the...? Dammit, Curt! You're only three feet off the ground, and you act like you're falling off a fucking cliff!"

"Relax," said Curt, as he continued his timid and controlled descent down the ladder. "Shit, Bru, I saved you a Workers Comp claim." Curt looked up at the ceiling grid to double-check his work. The second installation is always easier than the first. It was starting to go like clockwork. The final three homes were going to be a piece of cake. Curt felt a sense of satisfaction with his surveillance scheme and felt superior that he was doing it under Bru's nose.

Curt had graduated from the University of California at Berkeley. Given his permanent dislike for the military lifestyle, he had vowed to do whatever it took to become as well educated as he could to assure a career in the private sector. Although Curt was a gifted student, he underplayed his scholastic achievements. Deep inside, he needed to achieve and be mentally superior, but his grandfather had taught him well: Those inner desires were held in check and controlled. He even joked that his Bachelor of Science degrees were nothing more than "B.S."

While he was in college, his mother died of cancer. At her funeral, Curt met his biological grandfather for the first time. After the death of Major Anderson, Curt's grandfather had begun sending him birthday and Christmas presents. His mom had explained away his absence as a rift in their relationship and never revealed that Curt was adopted. Other than that, neither of his parents had ever mentioned him. They had not encouraged any relationship with this man. As such, Curt never wrote him, but he felt emotional tugs at his heart upon receiving the gifts. At his mom's funeral, Curt learned that his biological mother had died during labor and that he had been adopted shortly thereafter. His adoptive mother, Janice, had been unable to conceive a baby and, as circumstances would have it, the Andersons were ready to love him as their own.

At Janice's funeral, his grandfather took Curt aside and expressed his condolences for his loss. He explained to Curt that he was an adult now and had to make correct decisions that would impact his future. To make sure Curt completed his university education, his biological grandfather paid for the remainder of his expenses until his graduation. He even encouraged Curt to pursue at least one year of his college edu-cation abroad. Curt agreed and attended the prestigious Berlin University in Germany.

Although the ten-month separation from his girlfriend, Melody, had been painful, it proved to be a time of experi-mentation for them both. Their reconciliation had its bumps, but Curt settled back into a steady relationship by their mid-junior year. That brief separation became a topic that Curt and Melody avoided. They had an understanding that this was a time in their lives that was better left unshared between them.

Upon Curt's return to the States, his friends were surprised at how little he spoke about his European adventure. He seemed to downplay that time as if hiding something. Melody detected a much more self-assured Curt. The foreign-exchange-student experience had given him an inner strength, almost an arrogance. Curt had changed.

Most of his neighborhood friends looked up to him. He was the type of person everyone could relate to and envy in terms of brainpower. Regardless of Curt's physical and charismatic shortcomings, in most cases, it was an unspoken understanding that Curt set the standard in terms of intellectual capacity. Had Curt been less a wallflower in his high school interactions, he would have been a shoe-in for the person most likely to succeed. In the social ladders of the high school cliques, he was just a quiet guy in those college-prep classes. He didn't stand out enough to be labeled a geek.

Only the neighborhood kids fully appreciated Curt. In the neighborhood, he was never considered a ladies' man. However, his ability to listen and empathize had a disarming affect on others. People would trust and open up to him. As a result, Curt was almost always a friend—a real friend—to the neighborhood girls.

After graduating from Berkeley, he was approached by Bru upon his arrival back from school. Brunanski and Curt had remained in touch during those years at Berkeley. Curt had kept his mom's home as his permanent residence and always came back there to visit the old neighborhood during every Christmas, Easter and summer break. Consequently, he never really lost contact with his friends. Most of the neighborhood friends did not go onto to college. After high school, they entered the workforce and began pursuing the American Dream.

Brunanski began working for his father's construction firm. During the years that Curt was away, Brunanski took over the business from his father; it was time for Old Man Brunanski to call it quits. Given that Bru had been working side by side with his father since he could hold a hammer, Bru's youth didn't hamper his ability to run the business.

During high school, Curt and Bru purchased computers. With the explosion of the Internet and modems, they were able to remain in constant contact. It became a daily ritual for them to both get home and log onto their local Internet provider and use the latest enhancement that allowed them to speak to each other. As technology improved, they updated their programs to improve the quality of those conversations. By taking advantage of this technology, they avoided paying long distance phone bills. Who needed a telephone when you could piggyback on your Internet provider?

Curt shared his growing knowledge with Bru, and in return Bru kept him in touch with the neighborhood gang. Curt was in charge of keeping Bru up to speed on computer applications, while Bru was in charge of keeping Curt in touch with the local male-bonding rituals. While in college, Curt participated in football and baseball fantasy sports leagues. They had draft nights and meetings at Bru's place and would conference Curt in by way of the computer. It was as good as being there-almost.

It amazed both Curt and Bru how successfully the Brunanski Construction Company had blossomed. Bru was making a very good living. Curt questioned the logic in his own pursuit of education, given Bru's financial success and personal wealth. Although the Bay Area offered a lucrative opportunity in the construction business, there were countless fly-by-night organizations that would be here today and gone tomorrow.

Bru reminded Curt that the construction trade was cyclical. They both believed that in the long run, Curt's college degrees would pay off. The benefits of corporate life in one's later years of life made sense. Bru joked that it would be difficult pounding the streets and building homes at sixty years old. In comparison, an eighty-year-old could still move a mouse or talk into the computer like Scotty in the *Star Trek: The Voyage Home* flick.

Bru offered Curt a deal that he couldn't refuse. In exchange for wiring at least 125 units in this next project, he would get one of the homes in trade. There were five different models, and Curt could have the model of his choosing, with as many upgrades as they could stuff into the square footage. The only restriction was that any upgrade requiring a special order or additional engineering was on Curt's dime, not the company's.

* * * * *

Curt's home would be built opposite this one. He planned on equipping the surrounding homes with the same surveillance cameras. Looking across the street, he watched construction begin on his home. It wouldn't be long now.

Had he known this hobby of his would start a sequence of events that would forever change his life and cause untold misery, Curt would never have installed the cameras. The old saying, "Hindsight is always twenty-twenty," would never be more appropriate.

Melody

Although Curt was given the gift of brains, God had not blessed him with the habit of punctuality and professionalism. Curt was very curious with a tendency to procrastinate, while possessing the perseverance and tenacity to complete a college education. However, during those school days, he had great difficulty completing any subject unrelated to the physical sciences. In fact, he had to repeat English 1A three times and failed his first quarter of Art History.

During Curt's sophomore year, he decided to pledge the Phi Delta Theta fraternity. He hated the useless initiation rites that the pledges were subjected to, but the fringe benefits of organized dating and the use of the previous year's tests offset the pitfalls.

As Curt gathered his tools, he looked outside. At that moment, the landscapers were unloading the rose bushes into the front yard. A group of workers were preparing the ground before planting the roses. As Curt watched the two men adjust their leather gloves, Curt thought back to his embarrassing "Rose Tuck-ins" during his Fraternity years. The "Rose Tuck-ins" was a fundraiser that his fraternity put on. And if it hadn't been for that fundraiser, he would never have met his fiancée, Melody Bergmann.

Throughout the year, all fraternities held fund raisers to help finance their yearly events. The Phi Delts, as a tradition, required all pledges to participate in the "Rose Tuck-ins." Each tuck-in involved a red rose, a Phi Delta Theta pledge, and a contractual obligation to tuck a lucky young lady into bed. Usually, other frat brothers would buy Rose Tuck-ins for each other and hook them up with eligible girls. And even for those tuck-ins that weren't staged, there was still that chance of meeting that special person.

In the recent years, girls began doing the same thing by having their girlfriends arrange Rose Tuck-ins with the guys they wanted to date. Unfortunately, there were still other times when the Rose Tuck-ins were bought as jokes. Depending on the parties involved and their preferences, the joke could go either way.

In any case, because Curt didn't have much experience with women, he didn't want to miss the opportunity to meet that special person. He had dressed in a dark suit and tie and brought a bottle of white Zinfandel wine for the occasion. The pledges were given their assignments during their weekly meeting. The assignments provided the girls' names, addresses, and telephone numbers. On a specific date, the pledges were to meet the person for whom the Rose Tuck-in was purchased and give the girl the rose and tuck her into bed for the night.

The brothers believed that this tradition reinforced the Phi Delt's masculinity while promoting promiscuity. It was never specifically stated, but all the Phi Delta Theta pledges hoped that their assignments would be a beautiful knock out nymphomaniac. In reality, though, these assignments usually resulted in a friendly meeting between a young man trying to establish his self-confidence and a young woman trying to be polite.

* * * * *

A loud thud brought Curt back into the present as one of the landscapers dropped rose-bush containers and ground coverings on the sidewalk. The main area was covered with fresh sod, and the automatic irrigation system was installed below. Pop-up sprinkler heads poked out of the lawn. It was amazing how a bare yard was transformed after a lawn was rolled out onto barren ground. It was like a large jigsaw puzzle. One of the men began digging a hole along the side of the house. Another man lifted the rose canister and carried it to the hole.

* * * * *

It was on a chilly winter night that Curt met Melody Bergmann, the love of his life. She was two years older than Curt and had always wanted to be a schoolteacher. Melody had golden brown hair and clear hazel eyes. She had full lips and an athletic body. Her eyes had a way of engaging another during a conversation, as if no one else existed. It was her subtle beauty and intense ability to connect with people that drew Curt to her.

Early in Melody's childhood, she had earned the respect of her teachers. It therefore came as no surprise to her parents when she expressed her desire to become a teacher herself. Melody spoke of her desire to give the gift of education back to society.

Melody grew up in Groton, Massachusetts, a small town located in the heart of New England, with her three older brothers. Her father was a cranberry grower. That industry took a positive turn when cranberry-juice mixtures became popular. Non-traditional mixtures such as cranapple and even cranrasberry were created. The trend helped revitalize the once stigmatized fruit. It had been twenty years prior when the industry had almost been eliminated from the marketplace when a medical report misidentified cranberries as a carcinogen.

Mr. Bergmann had refused to believe the report and was committed to its production. He reasoned that not a single Bergmann had ever suffered any form of cancer. Based on their faith and perseverance, they remained optimistic and chose to expand their acreage, buying the bogs of other farmers who had given up. Many were unable to weather the storm. Later, the report proved inaccurate and was refuted.

The Bergmanns joined the Oceanspray Co-Op and signed a long-term contract, reaping the rewards of their patience and perseverance. Most of New England was surprised at the cranberry comeback.

As the youngest in her family, Melody was allowed to stretch her wings beyond cranberries. Being the only girl, combined with the cancer scare, she was encouraged to step outside of the family business, like an insurance policy, just in case the report turned out to be true. The Bergmanns would need an alternative means to survive.

The brothers all worked in the family business. As the popularity of cranberries increased, farming became more modern and high tech. During the colder winter months, sophisticated thermostats and sprinklers were used to encourage the freezing of the berries to the vines. This technique protected the berries from direct exposure to the atmosphere. In addition, helicopters became standard vehicles of the bogs. Melody's oldest brother was actually sent to a private flight school so they wouldn't have to employ expensive private flyers. The Bergmanns' self-reliance and family participation added to their bottom line. They expanded their services to include Co-Op pilots for hire.

With New England's deep roots within American politics, it was no surprise that Melody had a certain desire to become involved in politics, herself. The presence of the famous Kennedy family, plus the frequent presidential getaways of both George Bush and Bill Clinton, only added to the notoriety and prestige of New England. After her eighteenth birthday, Melody began to volunteer for re-election campaigns and frequented the New Hampshire Presidential Primaries.

To everyone's surprise, she decided to attend college on the West Coast choosing UC Berkeley rather than an East Coast school. Although she professed that it all boiled down to cost, deep down she wanted a break from her family. Even after factoring in out-of-state tuition, it was less expensive to attend Berkeley than to attend Harvard or Yale. The East Coast students always spoke of how inexpensive it was to attend college in California. But after accounting for all of the flights and long distance calls coast to coast, she probably broke even.

After Melody graduated with Bachelor of Arts degrees in English and Political Science, she earned her California teaching credential to begin her career at Christian Brothers High School in Los Gatos, California. She was the assistant to an English teacher until she obtained her credential. If the faculty accepted her performance, she would be recommended for acceptance at the school. However, she would have true educational security as an educator only after she had gained tenure.

During her teaching-assistant program, the faculty learned of Melody's interest and background in politics. Immediately following her acceptance as a full-fledged teacher, she was appointed as one of the Teachers Union representatives. Melody loved the parties, fundraisers, and polling activities. She began interacting with not only local politicians, but those in the State and U.S. Senatorial races.

* * * * *

The wind blew through the doorframe. Curt had just completed the wiring on the home of one of his future neighbors. He looked forward to finishing the remaining houses so he could work on his. He planned on wiring his house last.

The landscaper added more nitro-humus and fertilizer to the holes he had just dug. Curt inhaled. The smell of roses dominated his senses. Brunanski threw his tattered leather glove across the kitchen. It slapped against Curt's chest, interrupting his thoughts.

"Asshole!" Bru said. "What the hell you daydreaming about, anyway? Taking a shit or what?"

They both laughed. Curt gathered his equipment and took one last glance up at the acoustic ceiling panels. He began walking out the front door toward the next house. Crossing the new concrete walkway, he paused in front of the last rose bush. Reaching out, he caressed a soft rose petal.

The Recruits

The subdivision continued to expand as construction progressed. Curt's contract committed him to Phases 1 through 3. There were still two phases to complete before the entire development would be finished. It was a relief when people began moving in. Fortunately, Curt had long since completed the final touches on his monitor room. He wired the five homes within the cul-de-sac and the house immediately behind his home.

The first house was occupied by an elderly couple. Curt was extremely disappointed. He had a preconceived notion that it was unlikely that there would be much interesting to view. Curt was right. His entertainment was mostly limited to the neighbors' indulging in television watching and their dinner conversations. In a few weeks, Curt had their routine down pat.

One evening after returning form the local Lucky's supermarket, Curt had an awkward face-to-face encounter with the woman. Feeling guilty, he decided to introduce himself. After an abbreviated version of his life, he returned to his home. During that visit, Curt learned their names: Joan and Bret Charles. Joan explained that they had both recently retired. She was once a writer for the *San Jose Mercury News*, and Charles had worked in the periodicals department at San Jose State University.

After that brief visit, Curt reduced his spying on the Charles couple. Surprisingly, he discovered that even the retired remained sexually active after 65.

* * * * *

The next home to become occupied stood across the street. As Curt strode across his living room in his gray sweats, intending to pour a large bowl of Lucky Charms cereal, he saw a dark green Mayflower moving van parked in the cul-de-sac. It didn't really register that a new neighbor had moved in until he heard a high-pitched screech of metal as the ramp was pulled out from its sliding compartment. Curt ran to the kitchen, grabbed a muffin and a glass of orange juice and made a beeline for his closet.

He paused, twisting the front blinds to conceal his activities. Curt now incorporated this maneuver into his standard spying routine. Even though the neighborhood was sparsely occupied at the moment, this habit would one day save Curt's life.

As Curt stumbled into the closet, he slid the heavy mirrored bypass door shut until the closet was void of any outside light. He worked his fingers into the small depression grip concealed in the far corner of the false wall, pulling it back onto its tracks, and slid open the door to the monitor room.

In complete darkness, the single source of light came from the lime green illuminating dot. The distinct hum from his computer dominated the confined space. After crawling into the monitor room, he placed his food on the desk and closed the false door. The double drywall and additional insulation created a barrier concealing the presence of this hidden room. Only a trained eye would be able to detect the loss of space inside of the closet itself. Only a careful observer would ever notice that a false wall separated the closet, shortening the amount of room that one would expect to find, given the outside walls.

As Curt climbed through the narrow passageway, his instincts took over. He knew the routine quite well. His senses had grown accustomed to maneuvering in complete darkness. As he felt along the carpet, Curt reached out for the cold metal leg of the reclining chair. Once locating this landmark, he crawled forward and slid into the comfort of his favorite chair. Tracing his thumb along the lower rim of the smooth green glass shade, Curt tugged on the bronze chain and the light brightened the secret room. As Curt maneuvered the mouse across his Oakland Raiders mouse pad, his oversized twenty-one-inch HP monitor clinked alive. The screen flickered as it awoke from its screen-saving cyber hibernation. Curt began activating the networked monitors so he could access his surveillance program. Activating the center three monitors, Curt began watching his newest neighbors.

Curt began craving his breakfast. With a mouth full of soggy cereal and marshmallow green clovers, he began watching another household. From the initial images he watched a woman unpacking a box in the kitchen. From Curt's vantage point, the woman was in good shape, too. As she bent down to retrieve the contents from the boxes, it was obvious that she dedicated her exercise regimen toward her lower large muscle groups. She looked to be in her mid-twenties, blond hair hung at shoulder length. She was quite attractive.

This voyeuristic hobby would change Curt's life forever. Had he known, he would have stopped playing this dangerous game. It was as if he were starting a tragic unforeseen catastrophe. It was like a plateau that appeared solid and pur-poseful, while in reality it was a reflection, a mysterious illusion, a trap. It became a sinkhole that allowed things to enter below its outer membrane while trapping the intruder from ever escaping.

From a legal perspective, Curt was definitely invading his neighbors' privacy. If these were the only consequences Curt would have to face, he would have considered himself lucky. Curt was about to discover more than just what his neighbors were up to. He was about to stumble on a fifty-year secret that would require every bit of his being to survive.

* * * * *

Dane Phillips was a perfect Agency candidate. He was college educated with a B.A. in Criminal Justice. He had been in the Army ROTC and had served active duty in the first Gulf War conflict. He had always wanted to pursue a career in law enforcement. He had only one speeding ticket and one parking ticket in his entire life. He was a registered Republican and had never missed a vote since being eligible for the privilege. He was Catholic, he had one sister, and his parents were still married. He was six feet tall and possessed a slight build, weighing in at 165 pounds. He was married to his college sweetheart and had recently had his first child.

The Agency was excited about this candidate. Aside from the standard minimum pre-qualifications of credit scores, GPAs, age, perfect twenty-twenty vision, no prior surgeries, scars or tattoos, and excellent field reviews in his current position, Mr. Phillips held two specific skills the Agency wanted. First, he was bilingual in Korean, as his mother was born and raised in Busan, South Korea. His parents had met while his father was stationed in Korea. The second attribute the Agency was interested in was Mr. Phillips' helicopter experience. Possessing the language and pilot skills gave Dane a specialty that few recruits could match.

"This guy is hot. We always need pilots, and he hasn't been slotted for CHP pilots yet. We still have about twelve months before he's eligible; once he's flying a CHP bird, we won't have a chance at luring him."

"Dane is still doing reserve stuff at Moffitt, so we can request interdepartmental cross-training to get a better look at him."

"Our next recruitment vote is in three weeks. Do we have time to get a preliminary eval on him by then?"

"It's just a matter of you saying the word, and it'll happen. We've got Lt. Benson watching this one. He's been eyeballing him since the Academy. Benson knows the kid's old man from the military and has been kind of watching over Dane's career, trying to get him into the Agency."

A knock at the door interrupted their face-to-face meeting. After all the manila folders were closed, Commander Gray replied with a simple "Come in."

"Excuse me. Commander Gray. Here are the other files you requested. Gina, the female candidate we discussed, has the red sticky on the top."

Lt. Colonel Diane Klein looked for any hint of recognition in Gray's eyes. As he panned the stack of folders, he pulled the file with the red sticky note and placed it on the top. In an unexpected gesture, Gray broke protocol and opened the security seal of the folder in Lt. Colonel Klein's presence. The accompanying Recruitment Agent glanced up at Klein, surprised that Commander Gray had opened the seal on the personnel shield with Klein in the room. Being a subordinate, Brooks deferred to his superior. Gray was the man for the West Coast Agency Recruitment. Rumor had it that he was one of the inaugural agents in the Agency. Gray was a living legend.

It was believed that Gray, with his ability to arrange transfers between local and private police districts into the most secret of black operations within the U.S. Government, created political connections that ran deep. He could arrange anything and usually knew more about the big-picture issues than the Agency director. Many times, the field-initiated strategic planning changed because of the type of agents they recruited.

When resources were needed, clearance, training, and indoctrination didn't happen overnight. There was an evolution when creating an Agency Asset. Since Gray was on the front line in terms of developing assets, he could infer the direction of the field agency needs well in advance of any figurehead bureaucrat director type.

When requests for more water and coastal experienced assets were made, Gray would field more requests for Navy Seal–experienced candidates. Likewise, when more demolition and bomb specialists were requested, Gray suggested a move toward a more large-scale terrorist approach. During the recent technology boom of computers, a wave of computer geeks with all the James Bond characteristics was the Agency flavor. The focus of the day had become females and language skills.

Gray looked intensely at the picture in the red-tagged folder; it was an attractive female. Brooks held his poker face as Gray continued this open review of a candidate in the presence of Klein. Although Klein had the clearance to transport the files, she did not possess the authority to review their contents. Gray knew Klein was very interested in this folder. It was her niece's personnel shield, and she'd mentioned seeing her niece come through the initial screening just the other day. She had asked Gray to give her a special look.

"I feel good about this one," acknowledged Gray. With an intense blank stare, Gray looked in Brooks' direction. Without looking at Klein, he blurted, "That will be all, Lt. Colonel."

Klein snapped into action, turned, and exited the room. As she shut the door behind her, a faint smile washed over her otherwise stone face. She had worked with Gray for the last ten years. She had never asked anything of her superior. There was a sense of professional respect that Gray showed Klein. He understood that the backbone of the Agency was the attention to detail. And details were performed by people. Klein was good people. The Agency needed good people.

As the Rolling Stones song goes, "You can't always get what you want," and the adage "Be careful what you wish for" could never have been any more on point than here. In helping Klein's niece, she had unknowingly sealed young Gina's fate. Being selected into the Agency was no doubt the highlight of Gina's career. But her participation and involvement would come at the greatest price of all—her life.

* * * * *

With Curt's obligation to Brunanski complete, he accepted his official role as the cul-de-sac bum and settled into a routine. He'd watch the Charleses' breakfast routine simply because they awoke first. But Curt's focus would change at 7 a.m. sharp, once the Phillips household began to stir. Curt had a growing envy of Dane Phillips' life. The morning romps with his wife came like clockwork. Now that was what marriage was about. Dane would go off to work with the extra high step of a satisfied man.

This morning was different. Normally, Dane's CHP partner Rodriguez would pick him up in front of his house at 9 a.m. sharp. But this morning, an unmarked brown Chevy Corsica was idling out front. Curt, still donning his day-old paisley boxer shorts and a spaghetti-stained t-shirt, was glancing through the window blinds as he watched the morning unfold. Curt's thoughts ran through the possibilities of who these people were.

Two men were sitting in the front seat. The driver was wearing dark field glasses, a gray suit, heavily starched long-sleeved shirt, and a thin black tie. Riding shotgun was Dane's Captain, holding a letter signed by the director of corrections, who had jurisdiction over the California Highway Patrol. Captain Harris was instructed to be present when Mr. Gates explained the reassignment for cross training. This was not a request but an order that they would both accept. Captain Harris had heard of these types of special requests, but until last night he had not participated in one. Harris was forbidden from mentioning this temporary assignment to anyone. No paper trail was to exist. The orders came directly from Director Gamboa himself, from a call that interrupted his evening dinner with the family.

Dane's partner Rodriguez had already been assigned to special detail with another partner and was busied away, too distracted to worry about how his partner would fend.

47

Rodriguez figured he'd catch up with Phillips soon enough, maybe at one of the next roll calls or at the shooting range. He was too preoccupied with his new detail to be concerned about Dane.

Curt eyed the vehicle across the street and instinctively shut the blinds even tighter. He continued to peer out through the small opening at the edge of the window frame. With one eye closed as if looking down the barrel of a rifle, Curt continued his surveillance of the car.

* * * * *

Dane Phillips opened the front door and turned back to give his wife the ritual morning kiss good-bye. As he strode out the front door, he noticed his captain sitting shotgun in an unmarked brown four-door sedan. Something was definitely different today. Before Dane could approach the vehicle, Captain Harris stepped out of the vehicle and opened the back door.

"Good morning, Officer Phillips."

"Morning Cap. What gives?"

"You're due for a little change in scenery and assignments. Take a seat and let's talk."

Dane crouched to enter the back seat and closed the door. Donning dark sunglasses, Dane sat rigidly upright, eyeballing both the unknown driver and Captain Harris.

"Dane, this is Agent Gleason. Agent Gleason, this is Officer Dane Phillips." A nod of respect was exchanged between the men.

"I've got a letter for you from Director Gamboa. It is for your eyes only. Please open it and read it now." Captain Harris lifted the large yellow envelope over his shoulder, passing it back to Dane without turning in his seat. Dane reached out and took the parcel. Turning it over he saw the Great Seal of California insignia embossed on the front. This was the same insignia that graced his university diploma and his CHP graduation certificate. The envelope was sealed shut with a

48

thick transparent tape that had fine, off-tone stenciling within the fibers reading PERSONAL AND CONFIDENTIAL. Dane pulled the exposed tab across the large envelope opening, shredding the transparent tape. He noticed the wording shatter and fracture as the tab broke the transparent seal.

Inside was a single sheet of thick letterhead from Director Gamboa. A single sentence read, "You are hereby reassigned to the U.S. Government's cross-training police division to be supervised by Officer Gleason until further notice." The letter was dated the day previous and had been signed by the director himself.

Somewhat confused, Dane contemplated his situation. He had no idea what the U.S. police division was or why he was being reassigned. He wasn't in any trouble, and by the looks of the VIP treatment this order was getting, it could result in a career-enhancing move. A one-on-one with Cap, a letter from the director—it couldn't be all that bad. And with that, Dane looked up.

"I guess I'm yours, Officer Gleason."

As Gleason jammed the gearshift out of Park and into Drive, he spoke his first words. "We'll drop off Captain Harris, and then I'll take you to the office."

Curt watched the vehicle pull away from the curb. Glancing back at the monitor, he became distracted by Mrs. Phillips' morning aerobic workout and her Spandex tights. This morning offered a little more excitement. Better than watching Joan and Bret enjoying *The Price Is Right*.

* * * * *

The next day, Curt was schlepping some garbage to the curbside trash can when something caught his eye. He saw several people walking up to the house directly next to his. The AVAILABLE sign was still standing tall in the front yard. There were two middle-aged men in dark suits, each wearing dark sunglasses. They were following a woman.

Curt slammed his garbage can lid and hurried back to his house. After entering his house, he slid the patio door and blinds closed, dashed into the kitchen and grabbed a cold Dr Pepper. Sprinting into his bedroom, he sidestepped the bed and craned his neck to double check that he had closed the blinds. Curt slunk into the closet. Once inside, he closed the louver doors behind him and opened the back false wall door and crawled inside. As he wrestled with the door, he concluded that coating the rail tracks with WD-40 had improved its performance. It was getting easier and easier to operate.

With the door shut behind him, Curt jiggled his computer mouse, and the monitor flickered to life. He activated the surveillance programs. As the cameras came on line, the designated monitor began to glow to life, filling the closet walls with a soft glow. Curt's hard drive clicked into action, and one of the monitors began to focus. Three figures began to appear in the center of the screen.

Curt scrunched into his leather office chair and popped open his drink. The only sound that could be heard was the carbonation bubbles erupting in the aluminum can. As Curt settled into the chair, he couldn't help but wonder what these new images would hold. As the first few seconds passed, he became entranced and fixated on the screen. He had already forgotten about his morning ritual. *Regis and Kathy* would have to wait until tomorrow. Curt sat motionless. His glassy eyes burned holes into the monitor. If only he knew who these men were.

* * * * *

They pulled their dark blue four-door Chevy Lumina into the driveway of the vacant home. They were fortunate that this new candidate had moved into a new subdivision. The Agency would find a variety of available homes. The home across the street from the candidate was purchased within hours of receiving their assignment. Writing a check was a simple matter for The Agency. The financial backing from the United States of America made for literally a bottomless pit. And when secret operations were concerned, details were the thing that made the biggest difference.

One would think that purchasing a home in one of the most expensive areas in America would require a lot of reviews by the upper echelons of the organization. But in reality, it was of little concern. No budgetary bean counter would second-guess their expenditures. The Agency had literally no boundaries when it came to the money they spent. They never needed to worry about balancing their checkbook.

"Keith, did you get the telephone turned on?"

They needed a land line to assure that the video feeds were transmitted to the office for proper encryption and storage. Using a wireless transfer for such a sensitive issue was too big a risk. They didn't want someone to accidentally receive an unreliable feed.

"They finished it yesterday afternoon," the driver replied. "What time is the lady supposed to get here?"

"Any minute."

The men waited in the cramped quarters of their four-door sedan. Their postures exhibited neither annoyance nor irritation. If one were to watch them sitting motionless, one got the feeling that they had done this sort of thing before. In unison, each man tilted his head. As if on cue, the whine of an engine could be heard over the soft coastal breeze. It was the realtor. She was right on time.

The woman parked a bright red new GMC Yukon next to the curb and got out. She was a mature woman who looked to be in her mid to late forties. She was wearing a comfortable maroon blazer that hung loosely against her trim figure. She wore khaki Dockers and black leather flats. She saw their car immediately and confidently strode forward in their direction.

The men looked at each other and in unison opened their doors and got out. They met the woman halfway between the house and the sidewalk.

"I hope you found the place okay?" asked the realtor.

"Great directions, it was no problem."

As the woman reached into her blazer and pulled out a key, she continued walking toward the front door. They each heard the garbage can lid shut in the side yard adjacent to the home they were looking at. The sound caught their attention.

"It's just the neighbor," replied the woman. "In fact, he was one of the first ones to move into this cul-de-sac. He's a quiet single man. He keeps his yard in great shape and actually helped build three of the phases in this subdivision."

The two men looked over at the cedar fence. The man had already entered the side yard. The fence and stucco wall outcropping provided a natural barrier so that they could not see him directly. Each man appeared to take mental notes about their neighbor. As if in some sort of Agency innate reflex, they reached the conclusion that he was a non-issue and dismissed him altogether.

They knew they were simply here to observe their newest Agency candidate. This was a basic surveillance job, straight out of the procedures manual. Given that this man was to be assigned to their division, as senior agents they had the final say on who came in. Their years of experience and recruitment proved that more could be learned about a candidate in that person's own environment, seeing how they lived their day-to-day lives, than in any other way.

As the realtor and two men approached the home, the realtor opened a lockbox fastened to the front door. Inside the box was a shiny bronze key, which she retrieved and used to open the house. The Agency had purchased the home outright. No mortgage, which again, was standard operating procedure. No furniture, other than what the surveillance team brought with them, would ever be placed in the home. The expense to actually purchase the home was always a no-brainer. Given the real estate market, the Agency would sell the home and make a tidy profit. The need to thoroughly investigate a candidate outweighed the money spent on the home. The recruitment of any candidate, even one that would actually be passed over, was worth it.

The woman smiled. "We really like this model. It's got a fairly good size lot and has the fourth bedroom too. Many of our families turn it into a den. Continuing with her small talk, she said, "It has Pergo floors and beautiful French doors with side lights." Coyly, she commented, "We were surprised how quickly your company finalized the purchase."

The men stared blankly at her questions. She knew neither of them were going to offer any information. She continued to press. "Did your company just relocate one of you two to the area?"

One of the men replied with a smooth confidence. "No, we are bringing new personnel to our firm. It's part of the relocation benefits. We have the family fill out a detailed questionnaire and the company will take care of the initial housing based on their responses. It works out quite well."

"I see." Another smile. She offered a quick walk through, but both men assured her that they would contact her should they discover anything out of order. She handed each man a card and politely let herself out.

The woman pulled away from the curb. Both men stepped toward the living room windows. From Curt's vantage point, it appeared that the men were watching the woman leave. For several moments after her car had departed, neither man moved. The camera angle was slightly off center, somewhat distorting his view. He finally concluded that they were peering across the street. They didn't appear to be interested in the home, but in something else altogether. These men would keep Curt busy for hours. *What are they looking at? Why didn't they go from room to room? This is weird.*

* * * * *

For the past week, Curt had watched countless dark suited men as they spied on the Phillips house. The only constant was the presence of a tall slender man. He came almost every day but stayed for only twenty to thirty minutes. Curt deduced that this man was their superior.

He was awestruck at these men and their discipline. They exhibited no bantering or unnecessary conversations. They were all business, making full use of the comfortable light-weight metal stools. They sat hour after hour watching the Phillipses through their own monitoring system.

Periodically, their screens fuzzed over as if there were some interference in reception. Curt felt his first sense of fear as he watched the spies' screens fuzz over with interference. He knew it was his system that was causing the problem. After the men adjusted their monitors and double-checked the connections, they appeared content that the interference was a non-issue, attributing it to the overhead high-power lines, and accepted it as part of the situation. There was no doubt that The Phillipses were under constant surveillance. Curt wondered what they had done to warrant such scrutiny. He continued to spy on the spies.

* * * * *

As the days progressed, Curt had reasoned through every possible scenario that would justify the attention the Phillipses were receiving. Initially, he thought it was the IRS. Then he contemplated the possibility that it was the DEA, even the possibility that it was the mafia. After the fourth consecutive day, he concluded that whoever the men worked for, it had to be the federal government. Curt began wondering whether the Phillipses were in the witness relocation program.

Curt found himself afraid of going outside of his own home, but after cooping himself in his home, he reasoned that he had to return to his normal routine; staying inside his house would attract unwanted attention. Sitting in the In-N-Out Burger drive-through lane, Curt decided to step-up his efforts and follow the supervisor. Sipping on his straw and draining his beverage cup empty, he parked his van just outside the entrance to subdivision, waiting to see the familiar brown four-door sedan. Scanning the intersection, looking for the Chevy Lumina, only added to his suspicions. Only a government employee would drive that kind of a vehicle anyway.

Curt shifted his position in the driver's seat, adjusting his shoulders to offset his stiffening back from the long wait. With his girlfriend visiting her parents on the East Coast, he had as much time as he wanted to spend on his new hobby. He contemplated whether to share this new preoccupation with Melody. Curt could no longer dismiss the reality of his secret room and monitoring system. It was not only over the top but also illegal. He decided she didn't need to know about it just yet—maybe never. It would remain his secret.

After adjusting the volume on his stereo, Curt saw the familiar brown four-door pull into the subdivision. It wouldn't be long now. The tall supervisor would usually stay less than half an hour before leaving. Curt's pulse quickened. The Eddie Money song, "Two Tickets to Paradise," blared from the radio, adding to his excitement. He wouldn't have to wait much longer.

* * * * *

The lead agent pulled into the driveway and walked into the house. Two agents were inside and gave him a quick rundown on the day's events. The agency movers had moved the Phillipses' personal belongings into the home. With complete access to the home, they had installed five monitors with full audio capabilities.

They reported that, for some reason, they had a phantom interference, but only intermittently. They continued to run diagnostic tests, but deduced that the high-power lines were to blame. They already tagged the equipment to be checked out after this assignment. Given that this assignment was a low-priority recruitment surveillance and not a third-chance situation, there was no need to be too concerned. The inter-

E. A. Padilla

ference remained a curious annoyance. The agents reported a consistent belief that Mrs. Phillips was attractive and flexible, and that Dane was a lucky man.

The lead agent updated his case notes and started back to the city to work on his other cases. He held his thoughts in check, never sharing his feelings that the daily site visits were mundane and a poor use of his time. Being a career Agency man, he never faltered from protocol. Rules were rules. The lead agent turned the vehicle onto the main boulevard exiting the subdivision, as his thoughts drifted back to Hong and Drakeson. Being preoccupied, he failed to notice a van pull up behind him, following him along the surface streets. The van was almost lost in the crowd of cars traveling onto the 680 interchange leading back to the city.

* * * * *

"Melody, how was your visit to your parents'?"

"Fine," she said to her friend. "I always miss the weather. I know people say I'll get used to California, but I love the seasonal changes of the East Coast." Melody was eager to see Curt. It had been the longest separation from him since last year's graduation.

"Have you seen Curt yet?"

"Not yet, but he's finally finished with his contracting work. His house turned out really nice. But," she said, smiling, "I think its time for him to get a real job."

Melody had the perfect situation. Her full-time teaching position gave her the summers off, where she could remain politically involved for her parents' business. During the summers, she acted as an informal lobbyist for the cranberry industry. She continued her visits and calls, assisting the politicians with their fundraising and polling efforts. The fact that her parents remained one of their biggest contributors didn't hurt. With her family's long-standing involvement and contacts with the New England politicians at both the state and federal levels, Melody became a sought-after commodity with her new California politicians.

She popped in the most recent John Grisham book on CD as her white Volvo pulled out of the mall parking lot. She passed a subdivision under construction and began to wonder where Curt was at that moment. She couldn't wait to see him.

* * * * *

Curt followed the brown Chevy without incident. The agent must have placed the vehicle into cruise control as it maintained a constant pace, never speeding. He was easy to follow. Nearing the city, the lead agent almost lost Curt as he went over the large Bay Bridge that connected Oakland and San Francisco. Curt regained visual contact just before the midpoint at Treasure Island. Curt slowed his van and continued to follow at a safe distance.

The lead agent had no idea he was being followed. He was accustomed to being the pursuer, not the one being pursued. He went straight back to the Agency. After passing a large grassy park, the brown four-door sedan turned into a large, isolated, two-story building. There was a security guard booth, and a large concrete wall encircled the building. Curt reduced his speed as the brown sedan stopped at the security gate. Curt waited until the lead agent entered the facility and the security gate had dropped behind the sedan, before continuing around the block, making a large circle in hopes of a closer look.

What Curt saw only elevated his suspicions. The building had no windows, just a single main lobby entrance. Otherwise, the building was nondescript and boring. It blended with the other buildings and appeared to be designed with the intent of being forgettable and ordinary. Curt pulled his van into the parking lot of the adjacent park and stared at the building.

* * * * *

Lt. Colonel Klein heard the A-Team door open and saw Agent Warren walk through. She smiled politely as he walked through the corridor. Klein's niece had been asking a lot about her work, expressing some understanding that her aunt worked at a very important division of the government. During her military career, Gina had heard many a tale about the secret divisions within our government. With subtle questions and some amateur research, she learned that her aunt was someone special.

Never speaking about her career, but through subtle facial expressions, the Lt. Colonel acknowledged what her niece had suspected: Her position was classified. That said it all. With this vague understanding, her niece had expressed a desire to pursue special operations and asked her aunt to help in any way she could. She understood that working in this section of the government was by invitation only.

Lt. Colonel Klein had made the necessary hints and used all of her contacts to make it happen. With her niece's military and language skills, combined with her education, she knew she would excel at the Agency. She had been able to arrange an interview, but no specific date had yet been made. If her niece made it, she wanted her to work with Agent Warren on the A-Team. It was considered the best spot.

* * * * *

Curt continued his surveillance of the building. The only other arrival since he began this surveillance was the driver of a neon yellow van with the words *Copy Cats* displayed on the sides in large black lettering. It appeared to be a technician. He was pulling a rolling carrying case from his van and proceeded to wait at the building's entrance. Otherwise, there were no other visitors.

Curt sat outside the building, cramped inside his van. He waited until after seven that evening. Only two other vehicles left the back parking area. The building was otherwise quiet.

What is this place? Curt glanced back in his review mirror before heading back to the freeway. He continued to wonder what the building represented. His thoughts were interrupted by the blaring of his cell phone. It was Melody. She must be back from her trip. Curt headed home, still curious about the men and his neighbor. *What's going on?*

* * * * *

"So how is your new partner?" inquired Mrs. Phillips.

"He's not all that bad. But man, is that guy a serious one. I thought the academy made some uptight SOBs, but this guy's the poster child for Serious University."

Dane looked at his bride with the admiration and affection of a newlywed. Dane's drive for success never interfered with his inner peace and contentment. Nor did it detract him from his true love for Suzy. She was also an Amerasian, a Korean-American. The blending of cultures of statehood and military made for a natural intense dedication. The Asian and military influences created an atmosphere of unwavering commitment as part of their character. Dane and Suzy were predestined to make each other whole.

"Today's an important test. Gleason's been hammering us all week about protocol and procedures. He's a control freak, but has a bad habit of jotting notes down on his grease board. I know something's up today. He keeps clearing the block of time from 1:00 to 3:00 p.m." Dane smiled at his wife and reached across their glass-top kitchen table. He let his fingers play soft circles on the back of her hand. Pulling his feet out of his slippers, Dane settled into his academy-issued size-ten boots, and looked up into her eyes. For the last time, he kissed her lips.

Dane strode outside toward the awaiting Chevy Corsica. Without looking back, he yelled, *"Jo Shi Maseyo, sarang he."* Had he known this would be his last day alive, he would have cherished the last look, touch, smile, and gesture toward his wife. He would have savored her every movement. Like so many people, death comes unexpectedly, without preparation and without warning. There are no do-overs.

* * * * *

"So, Gleason, where's the kid at, in terms of getting to the vote?"

"He's almost there. We've got his initial preliminary field assessment coming this afternoon. He's looking good."

The field assignments were handled by a specific department. Folders were created detailing the routes, back-ups, and timeframes. Because this department handled matters of special importance, recruiting and observation evaluations could be orchestrated and monitored with great detail. Only after a candidate passed their screening were they ever allowed to participate, however menially, in the operation.

This rule especially applied to any task involving the A-Team. Everyone understood that the *One Twenty* and the *One One-Hundred* rules still applied, even for candidates and their overseers. If a disposal were somehow witnessed by anyone outside of the A-Team, regardless of that person's identity, short of being part of the executive branch of the federal government, those poor unsuspecting persons were expendable. The standard operating procedure was rote. There were no other contingencies: That person would be eliminated.

* * * * *

A laser printer in the assignment division was developing a glitch. For some unknown reason, the data interface was indiscriminately dropping numeric characters only. The problem became very noticeable when data sheets involving numbers were being printed. As a result, all numerical data reports were re-slated for retrieval the following day, to prevent the likelihood of any miscommunications. The department had believed that no sensitive data had been produced. Consequently, that morning's printouts had not been pulled back and shredded.

Gleason's assignment was one of the fourteen printed that day. The file clerk processed the assignments, just as she had been doing for last two years. She organized them into the appropriate folders. She had no way of her knowing that the reference location had been misprinted, sending Gleason and Dane into quadrant two instead of twelve. The printout had dropped the number 1. This random set of events would send them into a sensitive A-Team drop location rather than the vanilla-coated training exercise in mid-town. The error would be discovered the following day. The glitch started a chain of events that would bring countless people into harm's way.

* * * * *

"So where are we with your current watch list?"

The agent pulled his folder. Each agent maintained physical possession of his case loads. The more senior agents were assigned as lead agents. With this responsibility, the lead agents had the task of supervising a team that would handle the day-to-day tasks of resolving that unique set of circumstances. The lead agent would maintain no more than seven cases at any one time. How the people came to appear on the list was something only the directors would know. Each agent understood that as targets were eliminated, within a week they could expect to receive a new assignment to take its place.

To prevent perpetuating false assumptions about a candidate, the lead agent was assigned the task of gathering his own unique individual perspective. Any information the agent wanted would be made available or obtained. It was the lead agent's responsibility to establish an initial assessment. This process had been adopted after decades of governmental assassinations. The reasoning behind this procedural change came from a natural bias to assume certain facts based on an outside resource. There was no doubt that prior assassination procedures were successful.

In hindsight, just eliminating certain persons wasn't the solution. Information and misinformation was the priority and principle goal of the Agency. Removal of a target left an irreversible consequence. As such, assassination was a last resort. To be placed on the list, a person would have to possess knowledge that, if understood by the general public, would jeopardize the security of the United States of America. The more sensitive the information was, the greater the fear it created within the government.

The controlling factor was the fear. Fear was the primary motivation; it was the most effective means to gain compliance. The fear of discovery, embarrassment, and then fear of the repercussions should someone ever make the connections and have a full understanding; fear of the unknown. Many times, decisions to eliminate people came down to paranoid reasoning. Rational thought focused on the possibility of discovery, rather than the probability of its happening. As such, many targets were eliminated based on only a possibility, regardless of its likelihood.

Getting a person placed on the list was not something that the agents needed to analyze. Their main concern was what specifically did that individual know, and could that information be manipulated to meet their objective? Or was it necessary to prevent that information or event from ever taking place? Ultimately, a decision would be made as to whether that particular person was destined to endure a premature accidental death. This process was the initial euphemism of "Third time's a charm."

The agent opened his worn manila folder. Each caseload was physically maintained by its lead agent. Consequently, the folder took a worn appearance. New folders were provided during each agent's monthly caseload review. However, during those interim four weeks, the folders took their share of abuse.

"Drakeson has his final chance coming up. We're all dialed in. Second chance went nowhere. He just doesn't get it. We're ready to go on him."

Looking up from the folder, the agent raised his eyebrows before continuing. "Do you want any specifics?"

"Only the where and when," replied the director.

"Next Saturday, San Francisco Bay Area, at the New Bay Meadows race track."

The Southern West Coast Director nodded his head and began pounding the computer keyboard. He keyed up his encrypted email program and opened a new message. He typed in Drakeson, next Saturday, San Francisco Bay Area and then hit Send.

The director pulled his hands away from the keyboard and looked up at the lead agent.

"Who's next up?"

"We're on second chance with Hong. Meeting set, all looks good. Still running the A-Team scenarios just in case, but... everyone in the team predicts that it will only take a second chance meeting."

The agent began to flip to his next candidate when the director interrupted. The agent tilted his head and an internal sensor went into high gear. The director wanted more details on the pre-staging phase of Hong's second chance.

"What are the specifics on Hong's second chance?" The director anticipated the lead agent's inquisitive glance. Ignoring it, the director keyed up another email to report. With as little fanfare as possible, the lead agent recounted Hong's pre-stage planning.

"We're planning a luncheon at the Bonaventure Hotel in L.A. A limo ride with agent details at the meal and while in transit. All airline tickets booked, confirmed, and encoded for verification at departure and arrival, coming and going. One-day turnaround, a touch and go. A-Team working throughout. Two elimination scenarios—heart failure at lunch or vehicle accident on the 405."

The director pried further. "Date and time?"

"This Friday, scenarios set for 12:35 p.m. if we take him at the meal or 2:55 p.m. if we take him in transit to LAX."

63

The director keyed in the specifics. Only rarely did anyone get moved up from third chance protocol, but something was up with the Hong case. He knew that the lead agent was fully engaged and awaiting his next order. Before breaking the silence, the director wondered why the orders had come. He considered the recent attention that the North Koreans had attracted with their bold exhibitions over the Sea of Japan.

"Hong just moved up to second chance only. Have the A-Team ready to go. I want to give him every opportunity, so go with the 2:55 time frame in transit to LAX."

Pursing his lips, the agent scratched out the heading on his notes with a black pen and scribbled in "Final Chance." The director moved onto to the lead agent's next case.

"I signed off on your dump in the Santa Cruz Mountains. It's been archived. Good job."

The director and agent exchanged knowing looks. The director wasn't aware how his facial expressions changed every time a dump involved a one-in-a-hundred casualty. The lead agent waited for further instructions. The director glanced at the silver framed portrait of his wife and two children, displayed on the director's oak desk. During the brief awkward silence, the lead agent contemplated the director's career. Not getting his hands dirty in the field must make additional casualties more difficult. The lead agent recalled that the director had just purchased his wife a Jeep Cherokee; hopefully, it wasn't a white one. The director glanced back to the lead agent and blinked his eyes as if to clear his thoughts. Chastising himself for being weak, he remembered that he was the director. Everyone in this business knew the odds. It was one in a hundred, one in a hundred.

"With you watching that new recruit, I'm holding back an assignment. You'll only carry six cases until we make a decision on Dane Phillips. So until Hong and Drakeson are resolved, I'll keep your caseload as it is for now." Your other three are still in the pre–phase one. How's that going?"

"The initial assessments are done. We'll be ready for the team assessments en route to L.A. for Hong. My formal initial report will be available by encryption if you need it before our next review."

"No, no, we're fine. We're fine. Good job."

The director stood, signaling the end of the monthly review. The lead agent exited the large office and noticed the next lead agent awaiting his turn. The director sighed as he noticed the next agent waiting in the lobby. This would be a long day. The director hated monthly reviews. They were too stressful—too much death. As the next agent walked into his office, the director thought about the Agency's motto to serve, protect and defend. As the next lead agent entered his office, the director's steely eyes returned the lead agent's glare.

* * * * *

Agent Gleason pulled his assignments. He had done this countless times before. He accessed the encrypted location codes and received the digitized map for the training exercise. The scenarios changed, but the basic assessment was focusing on the candidate's ability at details. How well would the recruit naturally absorb his or her surroundings? Would the recruit have what it took to be a reliable field agent? Regardless of a candidate's initial assignment, in order to be considered, every agent must be capable of being a field agent.

Although all these agents knew they were being scrutinized, they were never given a formal testing situation like in a classroom. The recruits were under constant sur-veillance and evaluated on their natural tendencies. The Agency sought to predict that recruit's default personality and how that person would react in unrehearsed natural settings. Recruits were like rats in a maze. The recruits had no idea that they were being dissected, living their lives as if under a microscope. Everything—every word spoken, every action analyzed, and each reaction—was being evaluated. Recruits

were never off the clock. Until they were either rejected or accepted, their entire life was open for scrutiny.

Agent Gleason was excited for his recruit. This phase was vital toward Dane's continued involvement. Had Gleason known that a printer malfunction had unwittingly sent them to a drop site that was in progress, his elation would have turned to fear.

As Gleason sat in his car waiting for Dane to say good-bye to his wife, he could barely control his excitement. Dane opened the front door. Gleason heard Dane call something out in Korean to his pretty wife. For a brief moment, he envied the obvious love they felt for each other. After Phillips was inside the vehicle, Gleason gunned the engine, driving off toward their exercise location—or so he thought.

* * * * *

Curt knew something was wrong before Mrs. Phillips did. Without fanfare, the agents watching the Phillips home began packing their gear. Within fifteen minutes, they were gone. It was as if they had never been there.

Curt's routine was shattered. He had been focusing so much attention on Dane and the spies that he hadn't checked on his other neighbors. Without the spies, it no longer held his interest. He was bored. As Curt scanned over the other neighbors, he wondered why things were changing. What had happened? His waiting was about to end.

* * * * *

The kitchen phone rang. Mrs. Phillips walked over and lifted the receiver. It was too early for Dane to call. He usually called as he ate his lunch.

"Hello."

"Is this Mrs. Suzy Phillips?"

The tone of the voice coming through the telephone receiver, combined with the simple question, would strike concern into any military or law enforcement spouse. The main fear of the spouse is receiving *the dreaded call*. Suzy had felt the fear once before, only briefly, when the moving company needed to confirm a pickup time. This time, it was different. She knew it.

Mrs. Phillips' voice was barely audible in her reply. Her strength drained as the telephone receiver seemed to gain weight with every second. "Yes... yes, it is," she squeaked.

"I have some bad news. We'll be sending an officer to you within the next few minutes. Are you at home?"

"Yes" she whispered. Her strength continued to escape her and she sat on the kitchen floor with the phone glued to her ear. Her heart rate doubled as a chill swept over her body.

"Agent Warren will be there shortly. He called in as he was entering your subdivision. He is driving a—"

Just then, a brown four-door sedan pulled up in front of the Phillips residence. Mrs. Phillips interrupted. "Someone is here."

"That's him," the caller replied. "He'll explain everything." The voice on the phone ended the conversation. "I'm sorry for your loss." Mrs. Phillips heard the dial tone blare as the caller hung up.

In that instant, Suzy's world began collapsing around her. Her biggest fear was coming true. The specifics were unimportant. It had happened. Dane had promised it wouldn't happen. He had lied. She knew that he had no control over keeping something like this from happening, but she had made him promise anyway. Now he was gone. The doorbell woke her from her trance. As if by autopilot, she stood and walked to the door.

A tall, thin man in a dark suit stood at the doorway. His facial details were difficult to discern, given the contrast of the sun behind him. The figure took up most of the space in the doorway and began to speak. She absorbed only the words that confirmed Dane's death. Both Dane and his new partner

Gleason had been killed in a random act of violence, an apparent drive-by shooting. Given the nature of their occupations in law enforcement, it was the initial evaluation that it was a result of a gang initiation. Local gangs were being questioned, and Warren was hopeful that something would be found. He promised to find the responsible parties and bring them to justice.

Mrs. Phillips was incapable of absorbing the details. Her mind began shutting down. All she'd heard was the confirmation of Dane's death. He was gone. Agent Warren left Suzy in the doorway. She composed herself long enough to close the door, at which point she sank to the floor, curling into a fetal position. She lay there for almost an hour, crying in huge gasps, unable to catch her breath. Her misery was broken by the ringing of the phone. It was Suzy's mother. After Suzy told her the news, her mother promised to hurry down from Moraga, a small suburb about forty-five minutes to the north.

* * * * *

Curt continued to stare at the monitor. He had no audio sound, but based on the body language, he knew what had just been communicated. He reached out and depressed the button and turned off his computer. He slid out of his secret closet and looked out between the blinds. He could see the tall thin man walking back toward his car. Curt watched the familiar car pull away from the curb.

Dazed, Curt walked back to his secret closet and climbed through the false door. After shutting the door, he sat motionless in the quiet closet. Fear started to set in. What just happened? He knew Dane had been killed before his wife was told anything. *Those men; who are they? They know something. Do they know about me?* Curt's mind began to race. His fear began to change into anger. He had to know what had just happened. He had to get into that building.

The Building

As Curt sat in his white *VW* van, his back began to ache. He rolled the window down just to allow the breeze to cool the now-stagnant interior. His dark Ray-Ban sunglasses kept his eyes covered. Curt continued to watch the busy intersection and waited outside the large building.

Curt had chosen a high-traffic location, a discrete spot in the parking lot of a large grassy park. It had two baseball diamonds and a large pond with domestic ducks and geese. Benches and picnic tables were numerous, and a spacious concrete walkway meandered through the park. At any given time, dozens of skaters and joggers could be seen along the maze. The park occupied several city blocks.

The parking lot ran along a frontage road that paralleled the building. The opposite corner at the end of the park held the city's financial district. Consequently, many city employees and government workers took their breaks and lunches at this park. The high traffic allowed Curt to observe the building from his location, without fear of discovery.

Curt opened his duffel bag and pulled out his Bushnell binoculars. The last time he had pulled them out was during an Oakland A's game over two years ago. From this vantage point, Curt chose to pull the van up at an angle to the building; he didn't want to be too obvious. Then he slid into the back of his van. His dark tinted windows worked out well. The van had a clear view of oncoming vehicles. If another vehicle approached, he would know well in advance. He could relax, knowing he would be undisturbed.

For three hours, he sat and watched the building. It was an isolated two-story, brown, stucco-sided building and looked like any other building in the City except for a few distinct differences. The parking lot was encircled by a large concrete wall. It also had a security guard with a toll gate. The only cars to come and go were somehow similar. For starters, they were all four-door sedans or SUVs. There were no bright colored ones, only white, tan, gray, green, dark blue, or black. There was not a single red, yellow, or orange vehicle in the lot.

The other subtleties were the cars themselves. Not a single foreign car. There were Ford Crown Victorias, Tauruses, and Explorers. There were also Chevy Luminas, GMC Suburbans, Yukons, and Dodge Intrepids. There was not a single Nissan, Toyota or Honda. Another peculiarity with the building itself is that it didn't have a single window. And the most troublesome issue was that there was no address number on the building and no building name.

Hunching into the back section of his VW van, Curt adjusted his binoculars and scanned the building. There was very little activity. He noticed a garage in the back corner section of the compound. As the toll gate opened to allow vehicles to enter and exit, he was just able to see into a small section of the parking compound, where a brown van looked to be undergoing a total detail job. The carpeting had been removed and was strewn out onto the ground. Curt could see another man kneeling on the ground and vacuuming the carpet. The hood was also open. Another man was hunched over at the waist, leaning into the hood opening and adjusting the fuel injection system. Curt continued to wait for another vehicle to go through the gate, for another chance to see anything else.

* * * * *

The receptionist at the Agency could have been up for the Miss America title in her younger years, but something about her demeanor let you know that she was anything but just good looks. She had ten years of prior military service, and her specialty was counter-terrorism. She was an expert marksperson, the politically correct nomenclature for modern warriors, and had proven lethality with her bare hands. Her dark complexion stood in contrast with her bright blue eyes. Her mature beauty kept people off guard. It also allowed her to be used as an unsuspecting tool during the '80s.

During those years, the United States was just beginning to appreciate the differences between the Middle East and Western cultures. As time went on, she was able to expunge more information from her assignments than most of our covert missions ever uncovered. As with most men, even the Middle Easterners had misjudged her capabilities. Her feminine charm and silky voice were perfect disguises.

Initially, she was given non-classified duties at the Saudi Arabian U.S. Embassy. They involved basic office duties that any executive secretary could have done. However, the Agency had wanted to determine what initiative she would have shown if offered the opportunity to obtain information for the U.S. without being asked. Her first test was to discover the politics behind the politics.

She was given no specific instructions other than to work as the direct assistant to the Saudi Lt. Ambassador. There were some initial concerns about his affiliation with the Iraqis and Russian underworld. It was decided that, before implementation of Desert Storm, the perceived alliances with these countries had to be tested.

A single truth about men in general, and especially of those in power, is that they seek recognition for their achievements and are susceptible to flattery. The way men gain respect is through recognition and distinction; they wish to be acknowledged for their success. Unfortunately, the road they travel to succeed, at times, requires secrecy. But to forgo sharing his success prevents him from receiving the reward he truly wants—to be recognized and viewed as a successful person, to be considered someone special.

This basic desire is the root of all "loose lips" and the downfall to most secrets. A secret, regardless of its importance, has no value to the secret-holder, unless the secret is shared with another person. Once the secret-holder knows that someone else—someone he respects—recognizes and acknowledges the importance of knowing this insider information, that is what establishes the value of divulging secrets. This simple exchange of information is the key. Without sharing the information with someone else, the holder is unable to receive the recognition he or she strives to obtain. Without divulging a secret, the secret-holder is unable to feel important.

In today's world, whether women's libbers like it or not, most modern leaders and secret holders are still male. Although these secret holders don't share their treasure exclusively with women, the power beautiful women have over men in general is the avenue most exploited. Although the ultimate desire of such men is to establish a physical connection, a feeling that they are wanted and desired, men achieve this feeling by establishing their importance—building their egos.

Women who have gained this important insight have mastered the art of listening and understanding the differences between themselves and men. Men of power need to feed their ego. Not all achievements and statuses are considered the same to every man. Some men value power over others, while other men pursue the accumulation of wealth or knowledge.

Women who understand these motivations and are able to identify what makes a man tick tend to be good spies. They gain access to a lot of privileged information. Many such women are criticized the world over. But the simple truth is that these women truly understand men. They understand how men think and behave, and what motivates them. This understanding is a universal Achilles heel for most men of power.

Whenever the Agency recruited agents, this Agency receptionist was assigned the task of analyzing and providing feedback to the interviewing panel based on the observations she made while the prospect was waiting in the lobby. Each candidate was placed in the same physical environment. The interviews were all scheduled at the same time, 2:00 p.m. And each candidate was made to wait fifteen minutes.

Interestingly, a lot about an individual's personality can be revealed. Great consideration was placed on the candidate's behavior during the time before the interview. How did they introduce themselves to the receptionist? What did that person share with the receptionist? Where did the person sit? What magazines did the person look at, if any? How did they respond to the 15-minute delay? And so on.

* * * * *

After another hour of spying, Curt saw that he wasn't going to learn anything this way. He had to get into the building without being detected. But how was he going to do it?

Just then, something unusual happened. A bright red convertible Mitsubishi Eclipse pulled up to the curb of the Agency. He hadn't noticed the parking space until that moment. In front of the building, there was only one single parking space. On the curb, in large white letters, the word VISITOR was painted.

An attractive woman stepped out of the car. She appeared to be in her late twenties, fit and sexy and athletic. She was dressed in a dark blue suit, black heels, and a white blouse. Exiting her car, she slammed the door shut, reached over the open canopy into the back seat, and pulled out a leather briefcase. In a confident stride, she walked to the glass-windowed door and entered.

During the entire six hours of spying, this woman had been the first person to enter the front of the building. Interesting. He struggled back into the front seat of the van and returned the binoculars to the duffel bag. He took one last look at the building before pulling away from the parking lot curb. He knew he had to find a way into the building.

* * * * *

Waiting in the Agency lobby was a potential recruit. The initial lure to steal her away to the private black ops was, of course, money. But that was never the only bait used, even though it was the most effective. It seemed that these people typically had to engage their intellectual needs, to expand their mind and maximize their skills—skills they had painstakingly committed most of their adult lives to mastering.

The Agency had learned long ago that the characteristic most common to all successful black ops personnel was their need for constant intellectual challenges, internal competition, and the exercise of their innate sense of danger. The money was just a means to help them overcome the military brain-wash regarding military retirement benefits. Each military member understands the price of leaving the military prior to fulfilling their twenty-year threshold for retirement. After making this decision, in almost every case and regardless of the level of their new private incomes, many individuals still enlisted as a reservist to continue their pursuit of that twenty-year plateau.

The government did something right when they instituted that benefit. They must have installed some chip during basic training that caused these highly skilled people to remain associated and available, well beyond their initial military commitments. In exchange for minimal benefits—entitlements, actually, not insurance—BX access, and a modest retirement income, the U.S. Government had glorified the package. Eighty percent of all ten-year veterans willingly exchanged their time, freedom, and, for some, their lives, to obtain these benefits.

The real exposure to being upgraded to active duty, the additional weekend time, and the annual two-week mission made it unimaginable how obtaining such benefits warranted such a risk and sacrifice. If only corporate America could instill this same dedication and loyalty within its personnel.

This female recruit possessed superior linguistic skills in Russian and Spanish. Given the upheavals of the former USSR states and most of the Spanish-speaking parts of the world, such skills were a sought-after commodity. She had just transferred in from the Monterey Military Language School to Moffett AFB. The Agency still had ties in all branches of the military.

When the Agency had specific needs, the military made sure that certain people holding those much-needed qualifications were somehow assigned to a base near one of the Agency locations. In the United States, the main recruiting bases were Pearl Harbor in Hawaii, Eielson AFB near Fairbanks, Alaska; McChord AFB in the state of Washington, Alameda Naval Air Station in California; Fort Carson near Colorado Springs, and Luke AFB near Phoenix. As for the Central and Eastern Time zones, those bases were Carswell Air Base near Fort Worth, Texas, Glenview NAS near Chicago, Andrews AFB near Washington, DC, and Cape Canaveral in Florida. Given the large population of California, the Agency chose to allow a third recruitment location to be in San Diego, which was conveniently located near the San Diego Naval Base—home to the Pacific Fleet.

The Agency also maintained a two-time-zone configuration. This philosophy meant that for each time zone, the Agency maintained two separate agencies. It made sense that the Agency Branches were located near large military installations. The other consideration was to split the time zone into two separate areas. Given that time zones are divided longitudinally, the Agency zones were divided into northern and southern squadrons.

In most cases, the Agency established its camps near these main military institutions, which allowed the Agency a steady flow of superior candidates. In addition, the specialization of these different bases created unexpected regional strengths determined by the type of base nearest the Agency. For example, in Alameda, because of their frequent participation in the Pacific Fleet, combined with the language school in Monterey, there were an unusually large number of Asian-speaking personnel.

In addition, due to the strong overall military presence in California, almost all forms of computer, electrical and mechanical technicians could be had. In many cases, these technicians were so far removed from the actual black operations that they genuinely had no clue as to how or against whom their toys were being used. In these situations, the Agency kept it that way.

The Agency's U.S. structure was run as if there were ten different isolated and distinct organizations. Only the top two agents in each office had any appreciation or understanding that other such entities existed. Each separate location was led to believe that it was the only office of its kind in existence. If additional resources were required, the top agents were allowed to communicate with a single source. That contact was initiated via electronic communications only. The communications outside of the Agency were strictly monitored. No such written communication was allowed or tolerated. Working files were not allowed to leave the Agency walls. All photocopy machines were monitored. Each copy made was catalogued and designated by agent's identification and file number.

In fact, this technology was later released to the public and came into widespread use in law offices around the world. Such innovations helped finance the various Agencies' needs. Funding for these independent organizations created in 1952 as legitimate governmental entities, was later deemed unconstitutional. So each division became a self-reliant, self-sufficient organization. The Iran-Contra Affair almost exposed the Cape Canaveral Agency.

As the young woman walked in, she gave Lt. Colonel Diane Klein, her aunt, a subtle smile. The Lt. Colonel was never given the heads up on who the next recruit would be. Her role was to render her professional opinions and perceptions about the recruits. She knew that during this particular evaluation, she would have to clarify in the remarks section her personal relationship to this candidate.

As expected, Gina stuck to professional military protocol. She understood the importance of this opportunity and was leaving nothing to chance. Relative or not, she maintained a professional demeanor. She exuded confidence and introduced herself to Lt. Colonel Klein, who confirmed her appointment would begin within the next 15 minutes. There was no chit-chat or small talk. Between these professionals, the two relatives exchanged an innocent gesture. Both women knew they would talk about the experience later, off site and away from the eyes of the Agency. Woman's intuition was at work.

Ms. Klein had just printed the personal email from her niece confirming this appointment. As both women were in the military, although their communications were monitored, they were allowed to access their personal email accounts through the interbranch communications, the military network MILNET. In a brief lapse in protocol, the Lt. Colonel's familial loyalties and prior bond with the candidate overrode her better judgment. She hand-wrote "Good luck!" on the paper, placing it on top of the candidate's file. Lt. Colonel Klein stood and looked the candidate with a dead pan face and spoke. "We were expecting you."

Gina replied, "I'll just take a seat," and then she turned and walked to the waiting area. Sitting down, she faced Klein and placed her attaché next to her, but away from the entrance door. There were magazines neatly displayed on the table. A variety of tabloids were purposely selected and made available. Gina fought her urge to open a magazine to distract her from the upcoming interview. Her nerves were starting to fray. She had done all of her necessary grooming outside and made a point of going to the restroom in the hotel prior to departing for the interview. Her goal was to stand ready and attentive throughout the entire interview process. She sat rigid and poised and began to wait.

Klein opened her examination worksheet and went into surveillance mode. Forgetting that this woman was a relative, Klein began scrutinizing the woman's every move. She was happy to see that the woman avoided the distracting publications. Her attire was impeccable. She even had the presence of mind to place her attaché away from the entrance, protecting it from potential incomers. The candidate was sitting at attention, waiting for the interview.

The candidate showed confidence in selecting a seat facing the front toward Klein. Although twenty other seats were available in the room, Gina had selected one of the two seats facing Klein. The candidate didn't fidget with her clothes or make any adjustment in her appearance. Her low-heeled black leather shoes were shined, and her suit was pressed. The cut was not too low, but it wasn't uptight either.

At exactly five minutes before the scheduled interview, the standard call was placed from the interview panel to Klein.

"This is the front desk. May I help you?" replied Klein as she picked up the soft muted black phone.

"Normal drill. Offer her a drink and bathroom break after you let her know we're running late. Given she was early, we'll pull her in at 10 after instead of 15. How is she doing so far?"

"Just fine. I'll let her know right away."

"Great. Thanks. Don't forget the new questionnaire for the handwriting analysis."

The candidate stood, expecting to go into the interview, but did not leave the waiting area. She was waiting for Klein to confirm the interview.

"I'm sorry, but the committee is running behind schedule. It looks like it won't begin until twenty minutes after the hour.

Would you care for a drink, or do you need the restroom?" inquired Klein.

"No, thank you. I'm just fine." With no sign of apprehension or disappointment, the candidate sat back down and continued to wait.

"During your wait, please complete this questionnaire and give it to the panel as you enter the interview." Klein had placed her personal note on top of the questionnaire, knowing that her niece would appreciate this gesture of support and encouragement. The candidate had read the note. Placing the personal note at the bottom of the questionnaire, the candidate began answering the questions.

As her niece completed the questionnaire, Klein began scoring the candidate. Gina was doing very well. Her early arrival, attire, seat placement, and responses were outstanding. The candidate did not appear frustrated in any way regarding the delay in the interview. Klein always exaggerated the revised interview time by 10 minutes. It allowed the Agency the opportunity to analyze two different responses. First, they could analyze how the candidate responded to a delay in the interview process. Second, they could analyze how the candidate responded to advancing the rescheduled interview by 10 minutes. Furthermore, declining both the drink and the bathroom break were pluses—so far, so good. In fact, Gina was doing better than all other recruits this month in terms of the lobby scenario.

The interview panel watched the candidate's every move. As with all such interviews, the entire event was being recorded for later viewing and analysis. They agreed that this one looked very good on paper and in person. But the face-to-face interview was always the clincher.

When Gina was invited to enter the interview room, the lead interviewer took the documents and passed them to a case agent. The agent was to grade the questionnaire and then prepare his evaluation for the committee. The agent noticed the personal note from the Lt. Colonel to her niece. He made a mental note to deliver it back to Lt. Colonel Klein. It was a breach in protocol, but he understood. Unfortunately, that simple little piece of paper became lost in the pile of papers.

* * * * *

As fate would have it, a copy of that note later made its way to Curt, and that eventually led him back to Lt. Colonel Klein. Without that piece of paper containing Klein's personal email address, Curt would never have been able to continue his pursuit of the truth. That handwritten note changed Klein's destiny, and her perspective on the Agency would never be the same. Klein's efforts to advance her niece's career would come with lethal consequences, and it all started from this innocent breach in protocol. She had made the personal decision to ignore the rules, rules created to protect everyone involved.

* * * * *

Curt kept thinking how Dane Phillips had been under constant watch by strange men for the weeks leading up to his unusual death. Immediately following his death, the men had disappeared, never to return. There had to be a connection. They knew Dane had died. In someway, these men had something to do with his death. What was the connection?

Curt's curiosity burned with intensity. He continued to watch the building. It had only been two weeks since Dane's death. The routine was the same, suited men coming and going. The Copy Cats van came twice a week. Still reeling from Dane's death, Curt watched the Copy Cats driver leave the building and drive across the street to a Subway shop. He seemed to be preoccupied with a cell phone conversation and stayed in the bright yellow van to finish his call.

Curt's stomach growled with a loud rumble. Eating sounded like a good idea. He exited the van and walked across the street. He was starved.

* * * * *

"I'm sick of carrying the load," the Copy Cats technician argued with someone on the phone. "We need a backup sooner than later. Let's get a local college student while we can train them during the summer months. We have to do something. That government building is increasing their maintenance schedule for monthly tear-downs. They burn through more copies than most law firms. They're real anal about the counters and encoders."

Curt stopped outside the deli and eavesdropped on the conversation. He acted as if he was enjoying a smoke before entering. As Curt finished his cigarette, the technician ended the call and approached the front door. Curt held the door open and followed behind him. The man appeared dazed, staring at the neon menu. He seemed preoccupied and shook his car keys as if agitated. After hearing the conversation, Curt had an idea and approached the man.

"I couldn't help but over hear your conversation. Are you looking to hire someone?"

The man seemed surprised but skeptical that this unkempt man would be qualified. Most people didn't appreciate the skills needed to maintain these machines.

"Well, in fact we are. It's hard finding someone who's qualified enough to understand the digital and computer systems, but still willing to get dirty." The man surveyed Curt and surmised that the getting-dirty part wouldn't be a problem, but the technical aspect? That was the issue. The man raised his eyebrows, scrunching his forehead into wrinkles as he gazed at Curt. He seemed to organize his thoughts before responding.

In a skeptical tone, the man asked, "Are you a college graduate? Believe it or not, we prefer Computer Science majors."

With confidence, Curt replied, "Right up my alley. I graduated from Cal with a BS in Computer Science. I'm not quite a computer geek, but I can hold my own."

The man's interest began to pique. Figures, Cal graduate. You never know, with those guys. The technician began to scrutinize Curt more thoroughly. The technician's white button-down collar and black wing-tip shoes were in direct contrast with Curt's shorts, t-shirt, and sandals. Knowing exactly what the technician was thinking, Curt continued, "I guarantee you that I clean up nicely. I had a contract job that I just completed. I have been seriously considering opening a copy firm as a franchise owner," Curt improvised. "I've concluded that there's no better place to learn the ins and outs of the business than getting hands-on experience."

"Are you serious?" asked the technician.

"As a heart attack," Curt replied.

As the technician nodded his head in agreement, a slight smile began to replace the contorted face.

"We're kind of in a tight pinch. We had made a job offer to this one guy who needed to delay his start date until mid summer. I liked the guy, so asked the boss to give him a chance. The guy ended up going with another firm. By the time we learned of his change of heart, all our other prospects had already accepted positions elsewhere. Given that I asked for this guy, it's kind of falling in my lap." The technician looked down at his feet and slowly rocked back and forth as he explained this to Curt. It was obvious that the technician felt some responsibility and blame for their company's staffing situation.

"I assure you, I will check out with your Human Resource guys. My GPA is very good, and my references are strong. I'm ready to go tomorrow." Curt stood straight up, rigid and tall, as he responded. The technician looked at his watch and said, "Let's eat, and you can follow me back to the shop. The technician broke into a large smile and began ordering his meal. Curt smiled, believing he might just be that much closer to getting into the building.

* * * * *

Curt sat with the technician and discussed how to best expedite the hiring process. With the urging of Melody, Curt was in the habit of keeping his most current résumé and college transcripts saved on his wireless laptop. As for finances, Curt had a received life insurance settlements from both of his parents' deaths. The military benefits, as well as the private insurance that his parents had purchased, translated into large sums of money coming to him tax free. As such, Curt lacked the normal pursuit of wealth that most people possess. Most adults spent their waking hours devoted to the pursuit of a career and the desire to accumulate wealth and status. But with Curt, his parents' premature deaths, while tragic, did have one positive benefit—financial security. His wealth had grown into multi-millions of dollars.

Within minutes of that meal, Copy Cats had his résumé, references, and grades for their review. By the end of their late lunch, the technician had coaxed his supervisor into squeezing in a morning interview with Curt. If all went well, he could schedule the visit to the doctor for the mandatory physical and drug test. If the boss felt good and gave his approval, Curt could start riding along with his new best friend, Alex Moeller—the Copy Cats technician. He had to get inside that building, and this job was Curt's best chance at accomplishing exactly that. It came sooner than he had expected—just two days later.

* * * * *

Curt's sudden career change came as a surprise to Melody. She felt he was overqualified for the position. But it was better than sitting at home, he told her. She thought that talking about opening a franchise had potential, but why a copy franchise business? Still, she kept her doubts to herself and outwardly supported Curt's decision.

Curt's interview went smoothly. He learned that Alex's father was the owner. They had acquired the Agency contract through yet another nepotistic relationship—Alex's uncle worked inside the Agency. The Copy Cats company was doing well, given its limited exposure and advertising. The lion's share of its revenue came from the Agency maintenance contract; consequently, it took priority over every other client they had. Copy Cats received payments from the Agency like clockwork. The Agency had never been late, not once in over twenty years.

It was this long-standing relationship that allowed such open access to the Agency. Even though the office was secure and heavily guarded, maintaining the copy machines, as in the private sector, was deemed more cost effective if outsourced. The private materials and personal and confidential data were simply not an issue with a copy machine. The data could be compromised only with the insertion of a separate data system, in which case the data would need to be pulled out manually via tape, disc, or some form of transmission.

The Agency had already thought through that potential breach in security. For years, they maintained strict surveillance of any potential outbound frequency transmission along all known and potentially viable wavelengths. The Agency also maintained constant visual surveillance of all technicians coming into the building. Copy Cats had been on the money, without any suspicions for the last twenty years. When it came to security, the fact that the owner was a relative of the director had no influence on protocol. They checked out. However, as with any human tendency, the long-standing relationship and consistent reliability and trustworthiness had created a relaxed protocol with Copy Cats. It was as if they were part of the Agency. This misguided tendency was the only weak link in security. It was the area Curt would exploit.

* * * * *

Curt's crash course in photocopy machine maintenance was intense. With a sense of urgency, Alex's goal was to get him up to speed on the Agency machines. Alex was surprised how professional Curt looked when he arrived wearing black wing-tipped shoes and a freshly pressed, white, button-down long-sleeve shirt and a red power tie.

"So, how do you like it? There's more to tearing into these things than you would think." Alex tossed Curt a probing question. In the back of his mind, Alex was concerned that his new best friend would change his mind. The process was rote and mundane, but very precise and computer based, especially with the newest imaging on the Canons. Alex waited for Curt to stand up before pressing him further.

"So what do you think?"

Curt genuinely enjoyed the challenge of learning a new skill. He had almost forgotten why he had pursued this job in the first place. Curt felt like a surgeon as he pulled off his latex gloves. Remembering Alex's explanation that without the gloves the toner would turn his hands a dark grey by the end of his first day, he placed the spent gloves on the carpet.

"I like it. I can't wait to start my own shop," replied Curt.

"I'm glad to hear that. I've got you slotted for your fingerprinting next Wednesday. The Agency requires it with a full background check. Your credit report came back fine. I need you to come this way."

Curt was led to the HR Department to sign his employment forms. Curt declined all of the group insurance benefits and had his picture taken. As they exited the room, he was handed a laminated ID badge, which Alex snapped onto Curt's breast pocket.

"It's ride-along time," smiled Alex. One could almost sense the tension drain from Alex as the responsibility of his work-load began to shift toward Curt. He was very pleased with Curt and felt that he was a perfect addition to their team. Alex had no idea how short lived it would be, though. The two of them gathered their equipment and loaded it into the same bright yellow van. A sense of wonderment crept into Curt's mind. He had been following it just days before.

As they climbed into the van, something began to bother Alex. He still had questions about Curt. Why didn't Curt ask how much he was to be paid? And he couldn't help but notice that he had declined all the insurance benefits. Alex scrutinized Curt as he adjusted his seatbelt. Alex pushed the thoughts from his mind. Who cares? Alex was getting some needed assistance. He was getting the help he had been asking of his father for over a year.

The initial fifteen-minute drive was unexpectedly peaceful—the calm before the storm. As the van approached the Agency, Curt's heart pounded. He was sure Alex could see his shirt move with each shattering beat. With Curt's heightened senses, everything became crystal clear. Alex exhaled, and cigarette smoke drifted out of the opened window, creating a foggy haze.

As they rounded the corner, Curt saw the familiar windowless two-story building. His anxiety level began to peak, and he almost started hyperventilating. What was he doing? Curt glanced over at the intense red heat coming off the end of Alex's cigarette. Curt's neck began to flush from the body heat steaming out from under his business attire.

Alex parked the van in the empty parking lot and slammed the door shut. Dragging matching maintenance rolling suitcases, Alex led Curt to the lobby doors. As the buzzer sounded, releasing the security settings on the front doors, they entered the building.

* * * * *

Lt. Colonel Klein buzzed the Copy Cats guys inside. She knew Alex and noticed his brisk walk. She guessed he was in a good mood.

"So who's your friend?"

"Hi, Diane." Alex was on a first name basis with Lt. Colonel Klein. "This gentleman is our newest technician, Curt."

Curt stepped forward and was surprised at the firm handshake Diane gave him. "Nice to meet you," he said.

"Likewise, Curt. Could I please see your ID?" Lt. Colonel Klein scanned in Curt's badge and emailed it to security. The two agents in the security room opened the email message with the scanned ID. Curt's face appeared on their screen. The guards focused their attention back to the live monitors and continued to watch the Copy Cats guys in the lobby.

"Go ahead gentlemen," said Klein as she motioned them into the main area. Curt followed Alex, relaxing as he gained a newfound confidence. *I've done it. I'm inside. Now what?*

Alex led Curt to the first machine. It was like the first machine he had been training on. These would be the only model of machines Alex would allow Curt to work on today. Alex wanted Curt to master them so he could handle the current two days a week the Agency needed. Alex would still handle the major maintenance scheduling, but Curt could handle the counter mechanisms, calibration checks, and toner adjustments.

"You take this one, Curt. I'm going to the Big Bertha down the hall. It'll take me at least an hour. The bathroom is right there," he said, pointing down the hall. The squeaking of the suitcase rollers faded as Alex disappeared around a cubicle. Curt's anxiety returned as he stood alone in front of the machine. Crouching down to gather his tool kit, he started to sweat as his body temperature escalated. It was as if his head had gained fifty pounds. He found it difficult to move his head and was grateful for the dark Ray-Ban sunglasses protecting his eyes. His eyes darted back and forth, scanning the entire area for anything, anyone. What was he doing?

The office was a field of cubicles. All the wall dividers were the same blue cloth with matching swivel-back rollaway chairs. The desks held large HP flat-screen monitors with matching scanners. The systems were all networked to the Agency mainframe. The desks were locked down with numeric pad code security attachments for each and every opening. It was beyond secure. There was an eerie silence. Only five of the fifty-five cubicles had any occupants. Other than that, the area was empty.

Curt opened the copier. He had the basic tune-up ritual down pat and started in. Pulling on his latex gloves, Curt took a knee on the carpet and reached into his tool kit. At that same moment, he noticed a pair of black wing-tipped shoes appear in his field of vision. It took all of his willpower to avoid looking up at the person's face. Curt ignored the man and continued to empty the toner trap.

The man stood over Curt, holding a worn legal-sized manila folder while sipping a cup of coffee. The man began to read the contents of his folder.

"How much longer will you be?"

Nonchalantly, Curt glanced up and replied, "Almost done, about five minutes."

The man appeared only briefly distracted and turned his attention back to the contents in the folder. At that moment, the man's cell phone began ringing. He reached for his phone and continued to drink his coffee. As the conversation progressed, the man slid the folder under his arm and pressed it firmly against his ribs, sandwiching it between his arm and body.

Curt continued working on the copier and muscled the toner trap back into place. After the trap was in place, Curt was surprised to hear the man's footsteps padding away on the carpeting, leaving him alone to his work on the copy machine. As the man's voice trailed off into the distance, echoing down the corridor, Curt released a deep sigh of relief. His shoulders seemed to relax as he exhaled. Turning his head away from the copy machine, his breathing stopped from the shock. On the table, next to the copy machine, sat the manila folder and its contents.

Curt's brain went into overdrive. What should he do? He had to be under surveillance this very moment. Without thinking, or considering how much time he had, he reached out and grabbed the folder. Looking inside the folder, he discovered that the contents were not fastened in any way.

In a brilliant stroke of genius, Curt slid the folder off of the table and placed it on the carpeting with one hand. He peered into the open copy machine, hoping that anyone watching him would think he was inspecting the toner compartment. He quickly disabled the counter mechanism. With his glasses shading his eyes, Curt looked down and opened the folder. All the paperwork was loose. Nothing was stapled or fastened in any way. The paperwork was divided into separate stacks. Each group of documents contained print screens from PDF files. There were newspaper articles and email messages.

In the monitor room, the men had long since lost interest in watching the copy guys. They were discussing last night's football games and arguing who was going to win the Super Bowl. But the surveillance camera caught everything. In the middle monitor, Curt's image was center screen. The angle was such that the location of the folder could not be seen. But the image of him making copies was unmistakable. Later, the tapes would be manually viewed then burned into a CD and archived for life. In a twist of fate, those images, although designed to capture and document a breach in security, would help him prove his case.

With a swift motion, he grabbed the entire file and placed its contents into the self feeding tray. He toggled the button to copy both sides. When he depressed the large green button, the copier hummed to life and Curt began copying the entire set of documents. Curt watched the speed feeder pull the documents into the machine. The noise of the machine and the papers being fed through the machine echoed throughout the room. He imagined that guards were running that very moment to arrest him. Beads of perspiration appeared on his forehead as he waited. Holding his breath, he waited for the last page to enter the machine. Internally, he was screaming at the machine to hurry up, hurry up!

The machine plodded on, doing its work. The last document was fed into the tray and was spit out floating onto the stack of the originals. In a controlled panic, Curt gathered the originals, placing them back into the folder and replaced the folder back onto the table. He reached back into the machine and re-engaged the counter mechanism. Trying to relax, Curt stood and removed his copies from the tray and stuffed them into his wheeled tool case. The entire process seemed like an eternity, but in reality it had taken less than two minutes. *What am I doing?*

The security team glanced back into the monitors and could see the new guy closing the machine door. They had watched this same routine now for the last six years without any incident. The senior guard had to go to the bathroom. The other guard had received a personal call on his cell phone. Even though the cameras recorded everything that Curt had done, no one had noticed. There would be no reason to suspect that their security was compromised. Consequently, another boring security tape of a day at the Agency would be sent to the archives. It was available if anyone was interested, but for the time being, nobody noticed and no one cared. When it finally was viewed, it would be too late.

Alex and Curt serviced all of the copiers before calling it quits. As Alex dropped Curt off at the Copy Cats parking lot, he couldn't help but feel sorry for Alex. The smile of relief and accomplishment at getting Curt up to speed so quickly would be short lived. This would be Curt's first and last day to work with Alex. Alex would continue to call to see what happened to his new best friend. Curt would ignore the calls and messages. He had achieved what he wanted. It would take a full month of messages to Curt before Alex gave up.

Curt drove home, eyeballing the copied file that sat in the passenger seat of his van. He wondered what was in those notes. What would he learn? He couldn't wait to get home and start reading. At the first stop light, Curt reached over and opened the manila folder that held the photocopies. Careful not to touch the paper, he tried to read some of the pages, but he was too distracted driving, so he tilted the folder at an angle, allowing the pages to slide back inside, and continued to drive home.

* * * * *

Curt sat motionless, perched in his secret room, the sliding door ajar. In front of him, sitting squarely in the middle of the wooden table, sat the copies. The skin of his fingers had never touched the papers directly. It is customary for copy machine techs to wear latex gloves to prevent deep staining of their palms from constant daily exposure to inks and toners. When Curt made the impulsive decision to copy that entire folder, he left no fingerprints on the machine.

The doors were locked and the window blinds drawn. He pulled out another fresh pair of latex gloves. With gloved hands, he sat motionless, holding his breath. Had he gone too far? He had to know what was in that folder. Curt held the papers and began to read.

The File

As Curt opened the manila folder, he noticed that the information on the photocopies detailed the biographies of seven individuals. There were numerous newspaper articles and emails. Each set of documents had a bio highlighting that person's accomplishments and relevant facts. It was organized in brief bullet points. Curt had not altered the order in which the file had been copied. As such, the organization of the documents was identical to that of the agent's original set.

The first document for each individual was a single piece of paper indicating a meeting date, time, and location. There were also handwritten notes in the margins of each document. The notes were undoubtedly scribbled in by the agent—the man at the copy machine. Several references were made to the individual's appearance, as if to verify whether that person's physical description had changed. Other details focused on other aspects of the individual's appearance. There was one mention of a particular individual who was balder, heavier, and whose face had slightly aged from the most recent photo. Curt paper-clipped the documents into seven groups based on each individual. He then chronicled them based on the meeting dates.

The first meeting had already taken place earlier that morning. It was with a prominent telecommunications mogul, Jim G. Robertson. A newspaper clipping out of the *San Francisco Chronicle* showed a photograph of the man shaking hands with Ted Turner regarding a potential cooperation with the mega media conglomerate Turner Broadcasting System. The notes suggested that some meeting was taking place in Sacramento at the Downtown Hyatt. Based on the meeting cover sheet, the Agency had met with this same individual on two prior occasions, once in Atlanta and the other time in Chicago. The agent had scribbled a dark number *3* in the margin beside the Sacramento meeting, and the number had been circled. Neither of the two previous meetings had any other notations.

As Curt moved the documents onto his desktop table, the local six o'clock news started on his plasma flat-screen. The anchor man Dennis Richmond was welcoming viewers and highlighting that evening's headline stories.

Curt's attention focused on the individual scheduled for a meeting the following Sunday at the *Bonaventure Hotel* in Los Angeles. Having completed his contract with Brunanski Construction, Curt's occupational responsibilities had all but evaporated. It would be easy for him to go to the meeting. The only question was whether he should drive or fly. Contemplating his options, Curt sat in his secret closet with the sliding door open so he could hear the television. He realized that he had literally nothing planned. His calendar was blank. His girlfriend was at a teachers' conference for the next two days, and he was simply bored. Why not? He thought. The newscast blared in Dolby surround sound, echoing throughout the house.

As Curt sipped his Dr Pepper, he heard something from the television newscast that caught his attention. He grabbed his glass and glanced out of the closet through the open sliding door.

A reporter was detailing the events live from the scene. "Late this afternoon, there was a multi-car accident on the westbound Interstate 80. The accident involved several semi-truck trailers and a limousine carrying a passenger to the Sacramento International Airport. One of the drivers pulling a trailer failed to see the limousine as he changed lanes and forced the limousine off the interstate. The vehicles were traveling over a large bridge that crosses the Sacramento River. The limousine broke the guardrail and plunged into the murky water below. There are rescue vehicles on the scene now. We have a crew on the scene. Once we learn more we'll go to them for a live broadcast. Other developments today involve...."

As the news continued with a grocery union strike, Curt turned his attention back to the documents. He was somewhat distracted by the accident on the Sacramento River. Leafing through the file, he noticed one document that seemed to be misfiled. It was a single piece of paper, a personal email to Ginastuff@yahoo.com. It looked like a quick message of encouragement for an upcoming interview. It was signed Aunt DK. The email contained a string of different conversations between a Gina and Aunt DK. The last email was sent by Gina and included a still webcam photo. Curt studied the photo and was certain he knew the location.

Peering at the background of the photo, he saw a large windowless brick building. Then it hit him. It was the Internet café across from the Agency. He made a note of the email addresses and dates of the emails into his laptop and left himself a reminder to visit the café. If he accessed the same computer that Gina sent the email from, he would be able to acquire her user name and password. The sender's address was Diane.Klein.ma07@mil.net/wc/agency.

Trying to place the document with the other individuals in the copies, he couldn't locate any females. He studied the note and dismissed it as something that was randomly placed in the agent's file. He placed it at the bottom of the folder. It would take another month before Curt remembered its existence. The value and impact that the sheet of paper would have on Diane's perspective on life and her loyalty to the Agency would be forever changed. It would also lead Curt into another adventure of his own.

Curt continued to review the documents. He focused on Peter Hong, a successful businessman. He had become a U.S. Citizen after the Korean War. His bio detailed his many accomplishments. He was the principle trade negotiator for the sprawling South Korean nation. The documents confirmed Hong's success at numerous western businesses. His western education and his ability to speak English, Korean, Chinese, and Japanese catapulted Hong. His language skills increased his involvement, elevating his importance to becoming a key person within his company and his government. His participation in Korea's initial trade negotiations with the industrial powerhouses of the west solidified his future.

Peter was his Americanized name. As an American foreign exchange student, he had attended UCLA. However, because of his traditional Korean customs, he didn't allow himself to marry his college love. Arranged marriages were politically based.

Unlike the western perspective on marriage, the Korean belief system as it relates to marriage is based on the union of families, not simply the bride and groom. A marriage was a political maneuver that had the common goal of enhancing each family in terms of status and economic prosperity. Marriage was an agreement between two families, not two individuals. Parents spent many thoughtful hours meeting and negotiating with prospective suitors. Love and emotions were not part of the equation. As expected, Peter accepted the bride his parents had selected. He returned to Seoul, married, and merged the families. As the eldest son, many expectations and demands were placed upon him.

Unlike the other bio photographs, Mr. Hong's photographs consisted of newspaper articles from Korea. Some were taken out of the *Korean Times*, a version of the *LA Times* with an Asian focus. Hong was a key figure in most of South Korea's international deals. Mr. Hong's educational background and language skills had paid off: From his involvement with the powerhouse Samsung and Hyundai corporations to his involvement with the 1988 Olympic Games, his résumé was impressive.

The newscast broke his attention away from reviewing Hong's information.

"We have breaking news. The limousine that plunged into the Sacramento River has been recovered and its two occupants have been identified. The driver, Kenneth Silvera, was a second-year college student attending *American River College*. The passenger was prominent businessman Jim G. Robertson."

The live telecast flashed footage of the black stretch limousine being pulled out of the river. The reporter continued to detail the events leading up to the accident, and a photograph of Mr. Robertson flashed up on the screen. Numerous publicity photographs began to fill the television screen as Mr. Robertson's life was detailed. One particular photo sent a chill through Curt, shaking him to his bones. It was the same photo he had just looked at in the folder. It was Jim G. Robertson with Ted Turner.

Curt sat up and walked out of the closet. His eyes never blinked as he approached the wide flat-screen TV. All his senses were heightened as never before in his life. His entire being, his entire mental energies focused on the screen. He couldn't hear anything but the words being spoken. He couldn't see anything but the images on the screen. He couldn't feel the cold chill of his iced drink numbing his fingers. What was happening? What had he uncovered? This was no accident. The probability of random events and the law of large numbers had nothing to do with the death of Dane Phillips and now Jim G. Robertson. There was no doubt in Curt's mind. These men had been murdered.

Curt turned back to the closet and saw the folder and its contents spread out on his computer desk. He knew with absolute certainty that the individuals detailed in the folder were in danger. He hurried back to the closet and studied Hong's information. Of the individuals detailed in the folder, Peter Hong would be the next victim. Should he warn Peter Hong? He had until next Sunday to figure out what he was going to do.

* * * * *

Sleep would be hard to come by. Curt's thoughts kept looping through seemingly infinite possibilities, in rationalizing and analyzing the circumstances. Yet he kept arriving at the same conclusion: The deaths of Phillips and Robertson were connected. The fact that the agent had a physical proximity to Phillips and specific information on Robertson regarding a meeting the day he was accidentally killed was beyond coincidence. That agent, that Agency, some organization of some sort had some part in the deaths of Phillips and Robertson. Curt concluded that every person described in the file was in harm's way. Phillips and Robertson had done something so wrong that it warranted their deaths. From the looks of it, the United States government had something to do with it. The building and its personnel said it all.

What have I done? That night, he repeatedly chastised himself. *I should never have gotten involved.* The only good news was that no one knew about him. Other than working for Copy Cats, he had no affiliation with the Agency. Well, he did live next door to one of its targets, but that was it. He could simply forget that this entire event ever took place. It wasn't his problem that these people were being killed.

The fact that he worked for Copy Cats was logical and legal. Copying the documents wasn't, but it appeared that no one knew what he had done. He was sure that his body had hidden his movements. He relived that event over and over, step by step, action by action. It took no longer than seventy seconds from the time he touched the file to the time he returned it to its place on the table. He had disabled the counter. He had worn gloves. No one had arrested him as he and Alex left the building. There were no call-backs from that incident at all. Only Alex from the Copy Cats had called to find out what had happened to him.

Other than that, there was nothing. Curt reasoned that if someone suspected what he had done, he would have already been arrested for no less than treason. He was certain that no one knew what had happened, and Curt wanted to keep it that way. Yet his thoughts kept returning to Peter Hong. *Shouldn't I do something?*

As the week passed, Curt read each case. He began to access the Internet to obtain all the information he could on the individuals from the file. But paranoia began to set in. He took his research to the library. He didn't want the Agency to learn that someone was searching for every single person on one of their hit lists. He went so far as to research only one person per session. He never accessed more than one of the individuals per day. And each successive day, he used a different computer on a different floor. He wasn't taking any chances.

Curt had created his own dossier. On the third day, he went to Walmart and purchased a rolling file suitcase so that he could better organize his notes. He lugged the suitcase like a law student studying for the bar exam. After six straight days of constant research, Curt had returned to Peter Hong's file. *What am I going to do?*

While driving home, as if drawn by destiny, he turned off the main boulevard and next found himself in the travel agency paying cash for a round trip ticket to LAX. The paranoia had taken over every decision he made. He abandoned the use of his home computer. He would not purchase anything related to the file from his house or online. He did his best to remain below the Agency's radar, and it was a good thing, too. His archived surveillance tape from the Agency Building was set for compression for permanent storage. As protocol dictated, it would require a manual review before it was compressed and stored. One thing about protocol and procedures, they were designed to prevent missing the little things. It was only a matter of time.

* * * * *

Curt's flight was uneventful. He had parked his car in short-term parking. The meeting was set for 12:00 noon. As such, Curt took the morning flight, arriving at LAX at 9:30 a.m. He took a cab to the Bonaventure Hotel and walked across the street. He found a coffee shop, ordered a tall coffee and bought a copy of the *LA Times*, then walked outside. He found the table that gave him the best vantage point to the entrance to the hotel and began his wait.

* * * * *

Curt's back began to ache from sitting in the steel-framed dinette chair. The paper-thin seat cushion had been of little comfort. His tall coffee had long since cooled as he waited. His stomach was still queasy from taking the reverse jump seat. His ears had finally readjusted to sea level. The last hour had seemed like only a few minutes had passed.

Curt had brought only Hong's folder with him on the trip. Its contents covered the table. Curt wouldn't have to wait much longer. Within minutes, Curt saw a long black stretch limo pull up to the hotel entrance. He waited to see who exited. It had pulled up to the valet, and the first person out was one of the men from the house across the street. Peering out from under his cap, Curt saw Mr. Hong exit next, followed by another Asian who appeared to be his assistant, and then an American in a black suit. They all entered the hotel, and the limo pulled forward away from the entrance and parked. The driver remained seated and turned off the ignition. The driver adjusted the sun visor and reached for a cigarette from his breast pocket. Curt ordered another coffee and continued his wait.

* * * * *

The small party was led to a private room within the restaurant where lunch had already been arranged. Outside of

Korea, Los Angeles possessed the largest Korean population. As such, authentic dishes were the order of the day. A multitude of kimchi dishes, assorted meats, hot broth, steamed rice, water and chopsticks stood ready for the guests. American style Caesar salads, fruits, and beverages were also available. Just in case, full menus were also displayed, should something else be desired.

Mr. Hong approached his seat, and the two waiters began pulling out the chairs. True small talk commenced surrounding a Korean pitcher now playing for the *Dodgers*. A brief but spirited male bonding took place as they exchanged sports stories. Each person shared his favorite sport and team.

As the subject remained on baseball, Mr. Hong adjusted his chopsticks in one hand to accommodate his spoon. He couldn't help but be surprised at the quality of the food. He could have been dining at a fine restaurant in downtown Seoul. The flavor and presentation were perfect. The kimchi were outstanding, and the cabbage kimchi possessed that unique sour, yet spicy combination that only a Korean would appreciate.

With a slight smile, Mr. Hong admired the American negotiation tactics. They always did their homework and paid close attention to the details—even the so-called waiters; they were most certainly government agents but were superb waiters in their own right. The only tell was their physical conditioning, which seemed somewhat out of place for waiters. But then again, they were in Southern California, the fitness-crazed capital of America. Mr. Hong resolved himself to simply enjoy the moment. The true business would be completed in the limousine. It would require a simple but direct verbal exchange. He was almost certain that the U.S. powers would hear every word spoken in the limousine. It wouldn't surprise him if they would be watching in real time, from some dark secret room.

Hong had a feeling that the Americans had discovered his uncle's separate little business dealings with North Korea. If they were going to shut that operation down, he already had a backup plan to use the fish market that his wife's father had already established along the Busan Coast.

Mr. Hong never openly discussed his relatives' secret dealings. He was purposely kept out of the day-to-day operations. His family never shared any of the sordid details, but he knew about those details, nonetheless. Family was family, and he helped them when he could. However, because his uncle's business had caught unwanted attention from the west, Hong had no choice. His business partners did not know anything about his family business and were caught somewhat off guard as to why they were being asked to back off a project in Seoul.

Hong's business partners did not need to be affected by his family's affairs. Regardless of how profitable his uncle's black-market business of shoes, purses, and name-brand clothing items had become, his loyalties required that he maintain his position and standing with his primary business associates. Hong would make sure that his uncle's little enterprise landed on its feet, but now, for the sake of his legitimate business associates, he was being forced to distance himself from his family and their goals.

Going through World War II, the Korean Conflict, and Vietnam gave most Koreans a unique insight into the American government and its psyche. It was common knowledge within the international community that scaring the Americans should be avoided. Korea had learned that you never push the American government into a corner. America was predictable—it would overreact. If the U.S. became frightened, it would make it crystal clear to the other country that they could face a serious and full-scale military first strike. The U.S. had already proven to the world time and time again that it would initiate a pre-emptive strike to avoid being caught off guard.

After the Americans' vulnerability was exposed by the Japanese at Pearl Harbor, Hawaii, on December 7, 1942, the world would forever feel America's wrath and paranoia for this deception. The United States of America remains to this day the only nation ever to have unleashed a nuclear attack on another country. Even its great Democratic King John F. Kennedy had showed his resolve during the Cuban Missile Crisis. The one consistent theme regarding the U.S. policy on such matters was simple—don't mess with the U.S.

Hong continued with his meal. He knew what had to be done. He was prepared to discontinue, for now, his family business. Patience was an Asian virtue.

* * * * *

The bartender continued drying the glasses, glancing up at the man sitting in the corner table. For years, the bartender had watched him come into the bar and sit for hours in silence. The owner had warned him long ago to leave the man alone, and never to complain about his dog's being indoors with him. Like before, the man had ordered a Samuel Adams lager beer and asked that the back television be switched to *CNN Headline News*. On this particular day, the man had pulled out a small black book and set his cellular phone on the table top. He appeared to be waiting for something on the news.

The man tilted his head and glanced back at the bar. The bartender could feel the man's eyes pierce through the air as if to chastise him for eavesdropping on his space. The man's stare was so intense that the bartender turned his head to avoid looking at him. In a brief awkward moment, the bartender succumbed and slithered to the other side of the bar. He would work on another project just to avoid the man's attention. The bartender hated the man and his dog. The feeling was mutual.

* * * * *

It had been well over an hour since the limo had dropped them off. Curt was growing anxious and walked across the street for a closer look. His imagination was running wild. He was sure Mr. Hong was in grave danger. He had to do something.

Finally, Curt decided to cross the boulevard. At that moment, he heard a siren blaring. As the emergency vehicle drove closer, its distinctive whine became louder and louder. He was sure it was coming for Mr. Hong. *Am I too late?* Curt hurried into the lobby and sat on the nearest upholstered chair. The ambulance passed in front of the hotel and continued on its journey. The siren slowly diminished until silence returned. Curt's hands continued to sweat and his temples pulsed as he thought through his situation. *What am I doing in L.A.? Now what am I going to do?*

Curt's mind raced. The notes from the folder indicated that there was a meeting at the *Blazing Wok* restaurant on the second floor. He decided to enter the restaurant and continue his surveillance there. The concierge directed Curt to the elevator. As he walked over, he saw the light blinking above the door while the elevator descended to the lobby floor. Standing in front of the door, Curt fidgeted with his backpack and clutched the strap as he flung it over his shoulder. White knuckles showed in his grip. The elevator bell rang and the doors opened.

* * * * *

The meal was almost complete. Mr. Hong excused himself from the group. He had promised his children a souvenir. His son wanted an L.A. Dodger cap, and his daughter wanted a set of Mickey Mouse ears. He had seen these items on his prior visits and knew that the lobby had countless knickknacks for the onslaught of tourists.

Hong entered the nearest elevator and depressed the button. The door slid shut, and he wondered how his uncle would handle a sudden change in the family business. He would be heading back on a twelve-hour flight to Seoul by mid afternoon. Mr. Hong was tiring of the constant negotiations and overseas flights, but business was business. The elevator bell tone snapped him out of his trance. As the doors opened, he was surprised to see a man holding a backpack rush through the doors.

* * * * *

The man continued to stare at the television. He reached into his breast pocket and pulled out a black book, opening the frayed pages to locate the last entry. There were numerous names that had a single line drawn through each letter from one side of the entry to the last letter in the person's name. In the background, the man could hear the *CNN Headline News* announcer read the most current national events. Another toddler had fallen down a hole, this time with a friend who was driving an ATV.

The man pulled out his pen and laid it on the table next to his book. If it was to happen, it wouldn't be long. He looked down at his dog as it slept at his feet. Glancing at the empty bowl next to his pet, he signaled the bartender to fill his dog's dish. He sipped his Samuel Adams lager and continued to watch the television.

* * * * *

As Curt entered the elevator, he was taken by surprise. He was standing face to face with Mr. Hong. Curt never expected to make direct contact. His goal was to watch and learn. With the excitement of the situation, the blaring of the ambulance, and his imagination in full speed, he felt compelled to tell Mr. Hong something. It was as if destiny had brought them to this point. Given the finality of the prior meetings, Curt believed he had no choice.

Without thinking, Curt approached Peter Hong and stared at him intensely, and their eyes remained locked for what seemed like an eternity. Neither man spoke. Hong could hear air rushing into the man's nostrils as he inhaled. The soft elevator music evaporated during that instant. They stood motionless. A sense of urgency, like an alarm, ringing at full volume began to invade each man's senses even though neither man had uttered a single word.

Curt stepped back so that his foot held the elevator door ajar, preventing it from closing. Curt broke the silence and spoke.

"Mr. Hong. Your life is in grave danger."

Mr. Hong watched this American in disbelief. After all of his years of negotiations, during the countless meetings, reading their body language, their facial expressions, in that instant, he knew this man was truly afraid. How did the man know his name? Who was he? He had to be working for the Agency. What could the Americans be up to now?

"I know you don't know me, but I am afraid that something bad will happen to you." Curt's courage began to fade. His need to warn Peter Hong was suddenly replaced by a sudden and intense sense of fear for his personal safety. *What am I doing? This is crazy.* Curt stepped back out of the elevator and both men stared without speaking. As the elevator doors began to close, Curt looked away and began running out the front lobby doors. As the fresh outside air hit his lungs, Curt slowed to a quick walk and turned away from the awaiting limo. Ducking around the corner, he hailed the first Yellow Cab he saw. His nerves would have to wait two weeks before returning to normal.

Curt had chosen a path that had dire consequences. *What have I done? What'll I do now?*

Mr. Hong watched the man back out of the elevator. They kept eye contact until the doors closed. For the first time, Mr. Hong had a true sense of fear. *Why had the Americans felt it necessary to threaten me with physical harm, and to do so in such a direct manner? This is only our second meeting. Is there something else more sinister, more serious that I do not understand? Has my uncle intensified his black-marketing beyond luxury consumption goods? Has he crossed some invisible line of which I have no knowledge? Has my uncle stepped up his business to include the unthinkable—drugs or counterfeiting money? What just happened?*

In the past, the Americans had never personally warned him or any member of their negotiation team. With a calm exterior and with a professional intensity, Hong prepared himself to step out of protocol and resolve the matter once and for all. The Americans intended to make it very clear that his company needed to comply.

He depressed the lobby level button. As the door slid open, he saw no sign of the mysterious man. Exiting the elevator, Mr. Hong decided he would resolve this issue as soon as they entered the limousine. A strange tactic, an unusual method, but the message was clear. Hong's response would be equally clear. There would be no doubt in anyone's mind that his business partners would back out of the contract negotiations for the packing plant.

Entering the gift shop, Mr. Hong exchanged a polite smile with the young clerk. Looking at Mr. Hong, no one could have guessed that he carried any concern or worry. He was always the professional. Business was business. Looking out of the large plate glass windows and seeing the endless stream of business opportunities that America offered, it still bothered him that his colleagues couldn't participate more fully in these enter-prises. But the issue of perceived biases against Korean business development in America was yet another matter.

As promised, Hong purchased a Dodger cap and Mickey Mouse ears. He carried his gifts back with him to the elevator and headed back to the luncheon.

* * * * *

Curt kept looking over his shoulder out the back window. The driver continued to watch the man. His eyes narrowed as he studied Curt fidgeting in his seat, unable to remain still.

"Could you please circle the block?" Curt yelled from the back seat. Nodding his head, the driver did as he was told. As he turned the corner, he noticed the passenger craning his head as if trying to see if he had been followed. The driver looked over his shoulder, thankful the taxi he was assigned for the day had the thick plastic see-through barrier. He didn't trust this young man.

As they completed their tour around the block, Curt instructed the taxi driver to park just behind the valet area.

"Let's wait here a few minutes. My friend told me he may need a lift to LAX too. It'll only be a few moments." Curt returned the driver's stare in the rearview mirror.

"It's your call," replied the driver. "The meter will continue to run, sir."

Curt pursed his lips and nodded his head. "No problem. Thanks." They didn't have to wait long. Five minutes later, Hong exited the building and approached the awaiting limousine.

* * * * *

As Hong returned, everyone stood. The meal was completed and they headed back to the limousine. Once they entered the vehicle, they each took their same positions as when they had arrived. The vehicle's air conditioning was on full blast while the vehicle remained idling at the hotel curb. Before the driver was instructed to pull forward, the agent began to speak. The limo remained parked until the conversation had been completed. This would be Hong's last chance. All the listening and recording devices were in full gear. The equipment had been checked during the meal. Everything was ready.

"Mr. Hong, we've explained our position on numerous occasions. We appreciate the fact that this issue has no direct conflicts with the U.S. Military. However, our sources believe that your pursuit of the Seoul packaging plant could unbalance certain dealings that we have, let's say, nurtured. As I've indicated, we would never insist that your company abandon these negotiations if it were not of the utmost importance to our country." The agent sat patiently as his words were translated into Korean. He knew Hong spoke perfect English but was always impressed at how he could feign an inability to speak English. He never spoke it or acknowledged this ability on any dealings with the U.S.

Mr. Hong arched his back as if to sink into the comfortable seats of the black stretch limo. Sitting to Hong's right, his assistant acted as his interpreter. Sticking to the company protocol, he spoke only Korean, using the interpreter exclusively. This tactic allowed Mr. Hong a built-in time delay while the discussion was translated, allowing him vital time to digest and work through the true message, hints really, of these conversations. Hong's response would, as always, be concise, on point, and thoughtful. What really was being conveyed?

Peering through their dark sunglasses, the agents sat opposite Mr. Hong and the interpreter. The Agency driver monitored the recording equipment and video transmission signals as he was prepared, if necessary, to initiate the staged accident in the stretch limo. As protocol dictated, a lead car and follow car, each occupied by three agency team members, were in tow. The limo was bugged with high-tech digital feeds. The entire operation was recorded in encryption. The West Coast division was online, analyzing the entire meeting. Normally, Mr. Hong would have one final opportunity to comply. Someone back home had different ideas, though: This was his last chance. Normally, second-chance meetings were used to stage a dress rehearsal for a final run. This process allowed the A-Team an opportunity to understand and predict how the target would react in a given situation. These dress rehearsals were vital to successful final chances. In this business, "third time's a charm" had a very definitive outcome—compliance or elimination. Given the finality of the situation, if Mr. Hong did not comply, the agents would exit the vehicle at the hotel and the A-Team would handle the rest en route to LAX on the 405.

As the interpreter translated the most recent dialogue, Mr. Hong's eyes analyzed the American's body language and style of speaking. Unlike the first meeting, the words used were more indirect. Today, the agents spoke of the U.S. Military and the packing plant in Seoul. Until now, vague discussions surrounding certain new pursuits by his company had never been mentioned. And there had never been any direct mention of Seoul.

The unique aspect of the situation was that Mr. Hong had a family member working in the particular packing plant being discussed. Hong also knew that some of the materials were shipped to North Korean companies. He also knew that some of the shipments were kept completely separate from the remaining order. They were uniquely packaged. Hong had even learned that the boxes holding these special orders possessed minute amounts of radioactive elements that allowed easy detection for tracking purposes. Sophisticated electronic devices had been considered, but the attention such devices would attract was the issue.

The nuclear idea was an affordable solution. Hong himself had ordered the rescheduling of certain satellites to pass over from their French allies. He had also asked the programmers to track these particular shipments under the cover story that they were monitoring any nuclear shipments going north.

The cover story was nearly true, but the basis had nothing to do with making South Korea more secure from a nuclear threat. It boiled down to basic human greed. The north was starving for the comforts of the west. This form of tracking allowed an accurate means of detecting any misdirected or hidden shipments. Even illegal smugglers had quality-control issues. Hong didn't view black marketing of comfort goods as anything other than taking advantage of a business opportunity. It hurt no one, and it benefited all parties. There was no vital compromise to either country's security. It was simply capitalism at work.

Hong speculated that the ever-vigilant U.S. intelligence had also detected these special shipments. Hong was certain that these illegal shipments to communist North Korea involved luxury items and nothing truly nuclear. The minute trace amounts of radiation would prove that point. However, he also appreciated that the U.S. was very interested in preventing anything positive from being delivered to their neighbors to the north. The last thing he wanted was for this personal family matter to become a national issue. Saving face was of the utmost important issue for Hong, as it was with any Korean.

Hong had been briefed by his superiors and his government. As expected, South Korea had taken this meeting, as with any meeting with the U.S., with absolute seriousness. Such consideration required that the Koreans contemplate a worst-case scenario. After endless discussion, it was unanimous that whatever the U.S. was concerned about, the Koreans would resolve it. There was no need to disrupt the economic prosperity that South Korea had experienced. Hyundai, Samsung, and now their movie entertainment companies KBS and MBC had all expanded their market shares tenfold. They had no desire to jeopardize their continued prosperity.

While the interpreter completed the translation, Mr. Hong contemplated his best response. Then he broke his silence. "We understand your concerns. We have never intended to step on the toes of the United States government or its business partners. We are appreciative of your continued involvement with South Korea's internal issues and your support for our business pursuits within the U.S. That being said, is it safe to say that your government would look kindly if we were to withdraw our pursuit of the contract for Seoul Packing Enterprises?"

Everyone present had a look of complete surprise, even the interpreter. Hong had spoken in perfect English. With a gaping mouth, the agent simply nodded his head with an expressionless face and remained speechless. Hong pursed his lips and tilted his chin in a downward gesture. "Then, we'll consider this issue resolved."

Hundreds of miles away, tucked into a dark Agency surveillance room, the monitoring team was silent. The issue was now resolved. Without any steering committee or legislative involvement, a decision was made that would save countless hours of preparation and prevent potential bloodshed for Hong and Seoul Packing Enterprises. The Koreans believed that if they obtained that contract, it would ultimately result in some form of retaliation, probably an industrial accident. They were right. The Agency had narrowed the scenarios down to a chemical contamination or a natural gas leak. In either case, the agency was instructed to incorporate a deterrent message to South Korea to avoid such future happenings. To make the point, they were instructed to include scenarios that caused a large number of casualties. If it went this far, the powers in Washington wanted to emphasize their dissatisfaction regarding non-compliance.

As the agents absorbed what had just taken place, the limo pulled out of the hotel. The Agency sent out the proper messages. The A-Team was released from this assignment. The Field Agents remained in the limousine to properly escort their guest to the airport.

Hong looked out of the dark, smoke-colored windows of the stretch limo. He could see a small coffee house with outdoor seating. Hong saw only one customer seated outside. He contemplated how that establishment, with its location near the hotel, and in such a large city as Los Angeles with a population well over three million, could be servicing only a single customer. He recalled the fact that many of his business partners had been unjustly prevented from purchasing a Starbucks franchise. The Asian perspective was that there was a conspiracy that prevented Asian ownership of such establishments in America. Turning his attention away from the window, Hong smiled as he noticed the neon sign. The coffee house was not a franchise, but privately owned—probably by an American. It was no wonder there weren't more customers.

* * * * *

As Curt saw the limo pull away from the curb, he instructed the driver to follow.

"I guess my friend will be taking the limo." The driver pulled into traffic and followed the vehicle. As they merged onto the 405 freeway, the taxi continued to follow the limo. Curt's mind went into overdrive. He was certain that something was going to happen to Hong, just like Robertson. Each time they passed an eighteen wheeler pulling a trailer, Curt's arms tensed and his hands clenched tighter. His breathing become rapid and his exhalations became more pronounced as he pushed the air out of his nostrils. Soft snorts from his breathing sounded like a bull breathing.

Curt felt certain that there would be some kind of staged accident concentrating on the limo. He leaned forward, peering through the taxi's barrier. As the driver glanced back at Curt, he tugged on his collar. His passenger's agitation was making him nervous. They exited the freeway, following the signs to LAX. The driver figured they must be going to the airport.

* * * * *

The man's cell phone began to vibrate on the wooden table. His dog awoke from his nap and sat up at attention. It was a Pavlovian reflex that the dog exhibited, based on his countless other visits to the bar. Soon after his owner received a call, they would leave.

The man picked up his phone and read the text message. It simply read "H compliant. Aborted."

The man lifted his pen and scratched out Peter Hong's name. In the margin he wrote the letters *C* and *A*. It was his personal acronym for compliant and mission aborted. The two entries prior to Peter Hong were Dane Phillips and Jim G. Robertson. Each entry was scratched out but no letters were scribbled in the margin. Their names were lined out with a single dark straight line.

The man stood and exited the bar, holding his dog's leash. As the bartender watched the door close, he breathed a sigh of relief.

* * * * *

113

The taxi followed the limo as it stopped at the Korean Airlines terminal. Curt waited for the doors to open and was relieved to see Hong exit. He waited for the men to depart before he paid his fare and walked past the entry that Hong had used. As he approached the next entrance, he could see Hong through the windows. He was standing at the ticket counter as his assistant handed their passports to the airline employee. Curt walked toward a bank of telephone booths and entered the booth closest to the ticket counter. Sitting on the cold metal stool, he peered around the corner.

Curt's forehead had wrinkled as he studied Hong. He looked fine. No accident, no one rushing through the terminal brandishing a pistol, nothing. After Hong and his assistant backed away from the counter, they walked toward their departure gate. Curt rose. Making sure he kept a safe distance back, he followed. Turning the corner, he watched Hong and the other man continue through the metal detectors and collect their belongings at the end of the x-ray conveyor belt. Pushing away from the wall, Curt shuffled back toward the entrance to catch the bus back to the domestic departure terminal. Curt's head dropped toward his chest. He felt a huge emotional letdown. Hong was fine. Nothing had happened. *What a waste of time.*

* * * * *

The flight back to San Jose International was uneventful. Time had passed in a foggy haze. Sitting on his sofa, Curt held the universal remote control without turning the television on. His thoughts relived all of the events. The strange men spying on his neighbors; his neighbor's sudden murder; the men disappearing; his decision to infiltrate the Agency where he actually met one of the agents; photocopying the file; learning that Jim Robertson, one of the persons detailed in the file, had been killed in an unusual automobile accident. Then, his decision to travel to L.A. to warn Peter Hong, meeting him in the elevator and following him to the airport, only to find out that nothing bad had happened? After all his work, after all his planning, planes, and taxis, Hong was fine, unharmed.

Laughing out loud, Curt flung his arms upward and let them fall down, bouncing off the soft throw pillows. With a huge smile, Curt depressed the remote control, turning the TV on, and began surfing the channels. Stopping on *ESPN*, he caught up on the baseball highlights. During a commercial break, he flipped the channel to *CNN* and walked into the kitchen to start a fresh kettle of boiling water for a cup of hot tea. Tea always brought him peace, a sense of comfort. As he turned off the water and placed the full kettle onto the cook top, something he heard caught his attention. He started the flame and jogged back into the living room. There, displayed on the television screen, was a full-face picture of Frank Marconi with a news ticker scrolling across the bottom of the screen. Marconi was one of the seven individuals whose paperwork had been included in the agent's file. Curt froze in his tracks and listened with a laser focus. In an instant, his emotions swung back from embarrassment for feeling stupid for his actions in following Hong, followed now by fear. The television newscast continued.

"Early this morning, an icon in the newsprint industry died suddenly in an electrical fire in his vacation home located in South Lake Tahoe. The investigators are focusing on the attic area, where they believe a junction box was the source of the blaze. Fire cause-and-origin experts are digging through the debris. His wife and three children were also killed in the fire. Due to the recent drought, combined with extremely hot summers, authorities expressed initial concerns that the fire could have sparked a forest fire. The California Department of Forestry has reported that the blaze hadn't spread beyond the property boundaries because the 4,000-square-foot vacation home was surrounded by a large grassy lawn, which acted as a fire break."

As the announcer began to recount the man's professional accomplishments, Curt ran to the closet and dragged his portable hanging file folder into the living room. Pulling out Marconi's file, he began to read the notes. It was almost a verbatim repeat of the highlights listed in the Agency's notes. As Curt reviewed the scheduled meeting dates, he hadn't focused on Marconi because the meeting wasn't scheduled to take place for another two weeks. As he read further down the page, he saw a note scribbled in the margin. Someone had noted that a potential reschedule may be required. It all depended on when Marconi took his vacation to Lake Tahoe.

Curt raised his head to face the television as he listened to the broadcast. As the announcer concluded the report, Curt felt a chill race through his veins. "The accident might have been avoided had Frank Marconi not changed his plans. He had originally planned to attend the Summer Classic All-Star game in Arlington's Texas Ranger Stadium until his son had qualified for a regional wrestling tournament."

Curt sank back into his sofa. He felt a sudden urge to talk to his girlfriend. As he formulated his thoughts, the tea kettle started its high pitched whistle. He needed someone else to hear his theory. He was certain she wouldn't be pleased to hear how he'd been spending the last few weeks, or the real reason he had taken up the job with Copy Cats. Regardless, Curt needed some fresh eyes from a different perspective.

He wanted to be present at the next meeting the Agency had scheduled with Jeff Drakeson. The Agency was scheduled to meet him in the San Francisco Bay Area. No elaborate planning was required. They could drive over and observe. More than ever, Curt was certain that these events were not coincidental occurrences. Something was wrong. He knew it. The kettle began screaming, like a fire alarm demanding his attention. The constant noise finally broke Curt's trance.

* * * * *

That afternoon, Curt picked up Melody at her house. He lugged his portable hanging file folder and told her the entire story. She hadn't interrupted him. As he recounted the tale, she sat wide eyed, leaning forward more and more. She burst into laughter when he admitted nothing had happened to Peter Hong. She tried to speak, but Curt wouldn't be interrupted. He continued on, explaining how Marconi's entire family had died in Lake Tahoe. No longer concerned about leaving fingerprints, he raised the meeting notes from the file, handed her the paper, and replayed the broadcast he had recorded on his TiVo.

Melody looked down at the hanging folder briefcase, the television, and the note in her hands. She finally spoke.

"You're one crazy son of a bitch! I still can't believe you snuck into their building."

Curt studied Melody's reactions.

"At first, I thought you were going to tell me how stupid you were when that guy in L.A. turned out fine. But, wow!" Melody turned and walked over to the kitchen table. "Something has to be going on." After a brief pause, she looked up and continued. "What next?" Looking at Curt's solemn face, she couldn't believe his next words.

"There's another meeting tomorrow. I want you to come with me."

* * * * *

The man struggled with a key as he opened his private office. Then he unlocked his large wooden desk and placed his black book in the top sliding drawer. As he shut the drawer, he glanced down, smiling at his dog. The dog was panting, exhausted from his walk. The office security had long since ceased their annoying dirty looks as he escorted his dog through the metal detector. He was happy that his years of service had earned him the respect he felt he deserved. It was something he had always wanted as a lawyer. Still, he appreciated that working for the government had its own privileges.

The man opened his laptop computer and accessed his secure email. All transmissions were encrypted. He typed in a brief note reading "Where are we with Drakeson?" and hit Send. Within minutes he had a reply: "Tomorrow. New Bay Meadows. Third Chance."

The Race Track

Holding the paper, Melody stepped toward the television, listening to the newscast once again and concentrating on the announcer's words as he explained that the vacation to Lake Tahoe had been rescheduled. After hearing those words, she jerked her head away from the television and nodded her agreement. It was worth at least checking out. In the file detailing Jeff Drakeson was a newspaper article indicating an event was to take place the very next day. There was also a photograph and email printout with his bio. The email noted that Drakeson would be attending the New Bay Meadows Race Track. His horse would be in the third race of the morning.

The Agency bio was the same as the others—sparse and direct, with no speculative notes or narratives. The reports, paragraphs really, listed brief facts. Curt guessed that most of the briefings must have been done verbally and then organized in bullet points. Given the apparent murderous outcomes, it didn't surprise him. In order to be better prepared about why the Agency wanted to meet Drakeson, he turned to the Internet.

* * * * *

During his research, Curt learned that the horse Pent100 had been owned by cyber-millionaire Kurt Mantan. Soon thereafter, it was sold to Drakeson. Although Pent100 hadn't won any of its races, it was showing promise. Drakeson retained a young new jockey by the name of Michael Paul. Paul had trained with the legendary Willy Shoemaker. A new unorthodox training program was being tried. Paul was using a juice supplement, Tahitian Noni Juice, as well as magnetic therapy from an Asian firm, Nikken.

These products had just entered the U.S. Drakeson had also hired the services of an animal therapist. Although it sounded strange, certain authorities in the horse culture were giving their nod of approval. The skeptical U.S. medical community found that the juice and magnets had begun to show real progress. In fact, many professional golfers swore by them. As for the animal therapy, there were several documented cases suggesting that some people had a way of somehow communicating with animals. Hollywood had caught on to the idea and created a movie, *The Horse Whisperer*, based on that premise and starring none other than Robert Redford.

Drakeson always wanted to be on the cutting edge. As long as it brought results, nothing was unconventional. Results were the bottom line.

Curt began to piece together a more detailed bio on this Mr. Jeff Drakeson, the multi-millionaire. Some basic facts were available on the Internet. Surprisingly, his background was actually quite public. Although going to another meeting seemed risky, Curt was certain that the very public meeting at Bay Meadows provided him and Melody the best opportunity to witness firsthand one of these secret meetings. What connection did these men have with the men in the dark suits? Did they have Drakeson's home under surveillance as well? With so many people around, they certainly wouldn't attempt to kill him at the New Bay Meadows Race Track. Curt and Melody agreed that the setting provided the safest and most discreet way for them to check things out. This go-round would be much safer than Curt's earlier stunt as the copy guy. Curt had no way of knowing that the Agency had no such limitations. The Agency would simply adjust to one of their many preplanned contingencies.

Curt learned that Drakeson was married and had two children, Suzanne, age twenty, and Anthony, age eighteen. He had been married to the same woman, Sandy, for over 23 years. He was born in the small farming community of Red Bluff in Northern California. It was here that Drakeson had acquired his love for animals.

His father was one of the prominent ranchers within the community. The family business involved supplying a significant percentage of cattle toward the western U.S. beef production for The Burger King Corporation. The Drakesons also competed nationally in terms of supplying one of the strongest gene pools for the famous Brahma Bulls, specifically for the Professional Bull Riders Association. His father's passion was well known within the livestock community. This notoriety and respect allowed the perfect platform to catapult the ambitious young Drakeson to the next level within the industry.

Jeff had dreams of modernizing the Drakeson Corporation by modifying the marketing and rearing facilities to not only enhance the quality of the livestock but also increase its distribution to other markets. With this dream, Jeff began attending the local community college in Redding, located near Shasta, the dormant volcano to the north. After receiving his AA degree in Animal Husbandry, he transferred to UC Davis. It was appropriate that the Davis mascot was the Aggies. After three more years, Jeff obtained a BS in Animal Husbandry and a Minor in Computer Science.

While attending UC Davis, Drakeson developed a love for computers. In the early '80s, computers were just starting to come into their own. But in the '90s, a true cyber explosion took place, with a huge leap in technological advancement. With this new wave of technology, Jeff's entrepreneurial spirit rose up and demanded attention. With inner foresight and drive, he engrossed himself in all the opportunities that the field of computer science had to offer. In an attempt to break into this field, he took an internship at the Hewlett Packard plant in nearby Roseville. It was during those few short years that Drakeson's vision of the cyber explosion was nurtured.

Drakeson was first introduced to basic PC applications at HP. There he dreamed of creating his own software program using the strength of microchip technology to enhance the genetic sequences to match and maximize the variety of gene pools available in the livestock production of his family's business. With this original intent, he began working toward his Master's degree in Computer Science at CSU Sacramento. This school change not only offered a shorter commute but also gave Jeff access to Sac State's new computer department that challenged some of the renowned technical institutions.

Through Jeff's attempt to keep up with the ever-changing personal computer craze, he found himself with three different computer systems: an IBM-compatible Hewlett Packard, an Apple Macintosh, and a Commodore Amiga. During the early years of the personal computer era, although IBM-compatible models were the most popular, the Apple Mac and Commodore were true contenders. The Apple Mac was considered the most user friendly. Equally impressive was the Commodore Amiga's strong video card system that provided topnotch capabilities without the need to change out video cards and different motherboards. In fact, during these early years, many cable television program scheduling systems were organized and displayed using Amiga, not IBM compatibles.

Ultimately, it was the public's need and desire for user-friendly systems that finally coaxed IBM-compatible computers to change the way they dealt with their customers. The increasing demand for PCs was no longer limited to professors, architects, and statisticians.

The initial industry focus catered to the electronic gaming community. The general public began demanding more sophistication and, of course, more variety. The public wanted more challenging games. As a result, new systems were developed and grew into household names.

The marketing giants were amazed at how quickly new branding was taking place. What took Coca Cola and Q-Tip decades to accomplish, in terms of being household names, was accomplished almost overnight by such start-up companies as Nintendo and Atari. It didn't take Wall Street and its investors long to recognize where the money was. Those early entrepreneurs first recognized that this next generation of children would have an insatiable appetite for the new form of interactive and computing entertainment, and they were betting that these same families also had the financial ability to constantly purchase and upgrade the systems. Wall Street was hoping that the Baby Boomers were ready to spoil their kids.

It was this constant and widespread ability of mainstream American families that first proved to Wall Street investors that the public was indeed willing to spend large sums of money on gaming systems. Ultimately, the games and systems became a large-scale marketing plot to exploit this opportunity by strategically marketing these games based on scheduled obsolescence. It became a constant orchestration by the personal home game industry. As consumers continued to pay top dollar for the systems and individual games, both the systems and games became more and more expensive.

This realization absolutely changed the way in which the once mainframe-based company IBM awakened from its isolated fat-cat dream world. The computer consumers of the world no longer demanded large 2,000-pound monsters used to crunch large amounts of data. The general public, with its introduction of these high-tech games, combined with IBM's lack of interest in that segment of the market, allowed the competition to accumulate the financial backing to crack the virtual monopoly IBM had on the cyber world.

IBM ultimately conceded victory to its competitor, Apple, by abandoning its clumsy and complicated DOS operating system within its PC machines and introduced Windows 95. This software package basically imitated the Macintosh operating system with its point, drag, and click functions.

IBM almost waited too long and barely survived. It had missed the boat by not recognizing early enough that the public was willing to spend so much on a personal computer—primarily for entertainment. During these turmoil years, Drakeson was in the right place at the right time. Although his original dreams of designing a genetics software program to help with his family's business never materialized, something just as lucrative did. As the general public began purchasing their PCs, the Internet started to develop. Initially, only a few Internet providers succeeded.

The initial Internet Service Providers (ISPs) were very expensive. They offered costly hook-up fees where the users were charged by the minute while online. During those infancy years, much information was created offline to save airtime. When the document was completed, the user logged-on and transmitted or received the data and then immediately logged off. Surfing the Internet was an expensive luxury.

Drakeson was one of the early pioneers. He religiously upgraded his PC every three months. He had to have the latest, fastest, and quickest-thinking PC around. The early model modems were slow, and the transmission lines were poor. Consequently, interruptions and garbled data were common occurrences. To the cyber community, though, it was just one of the inconveniences of staying on the cutting edge. But the ISP issue could be fixed. It was here that Drakeson made his move and ultimately his millions.

As technology in the speed of modems and size of hard drives and their peripherals became available, Drakeson and four of his college buddies all invested in the idea of creating an affordable ISP on the local level. With their Master's degrees in hand, they decided to venture to the biggest Cyberville of them all, the Silicon Valley, and moved to Santa Clara. They set up shop out of their home garage after punching a hole between their duplex garages to create a four-car-garage office space. They didn't know they were creating the Bay Area's first ISP that was readily available to the general consumer.

They began advertising in all of the Bay Area Universities and later in publications, radio, and cable television. But most of their publicity came from grassroots word of mouth. And having some of the brightest minds available in the local neighborhoods of UC Berkeley and Stanford didn't hurt, either.

When they first started, their most difficult challenge was to keep their lines open. The initial solution was to constantly upgrade the number of modems they had available. However, as their subscriptions increased, and as technology contributed, the ultimate solution was to upgrade their phone line to a T-series. This allowed for faster speeds and more phone-line capabilities with different phone numbers to access. This idea was the precursor to the large national ISPs such as America Online—AOL.

From those humble beginnings in the garage, Drakeson's final cyber-kingdom involved a four-story building in San Jose, which housed 124 employees. Later, he was bought out by a startup company that after many name changes settled on calling itself Netscape. At thirty years old, he was a multimillionaire. Even with his money, Drakeson couldn't stay away from the computer industry for long.

After a brief hiatus, Drakeson started another computer company. But the mission statement for this company was an attempt to duplicate the PC fantasy warfare games and bring it into the real world. He started another company named Cyber Fire. With the increased attraction during the Reagan era for Star Wars type technology, Drakeson was attempting to bring some form of missile defense system into reality.

It wasn't the hardware that was the problem. Modern warfare had perfected the explosive technology and that form of delivery system. The problem was tracking multiple inbound missiles traveling at over twice the speed of sound, with the ultimate goal of knocking out the target, but doing so at great distances. His first customer turned out to be the big fish of all fish: The U.S. Department of Defense was shopping to perfect its guidance system for the defense of inbound intercontinental ballistic missiles, or ICBMs.

The project was called Patriots, and Curt and Melody speculated that this was the project that interested the Agency. If something was going to happen, it was going to be done at the New Bay Meadows Race Track. They were right.

* * * * *

"I'm so sick of the government always scrutinizing our results!" groaned Jeff Drakeson.

The large conference room was quiet. Although there were 23 engineers, project managers, and computer programmers, you could hear a pin drop. It had been the fifth straight testing of the Patriot's pre-contact detection sequences that were causing the problems, and the problems had to be fixed.

It was in the Nevada desert at Fallon Naval Air Station's bomb fields where the problem was first detected. From the on-sight visuals, it appeared that each interception was successful. However, after a closer examination, large pieces of the inbound missiles were discovered. Not only their size, but also the proximity to the target in which they were found was very disappointing. Although the missiles were being diverted and missing their targets, the incoming debris was unacceptable. Total destruction was the goal. Anything short of this left a real possibility that the incoming missile would remain operational. Such a result had an unacceptable outcome: nuclear annihilation.

The company's proposal and government contracts called for destroying the missile to prevent damage and injuries to the anticipated metropolitan populated targets. Diverting the targets and destroying most of the inbound projectiles was unacceptable. Further enhancing the need to resolve this problem was the cost, at three million dollars a pop, not including the sophisticated mobile staging center and guaranteed training and support contracts during the employment of this defensive weapon.

The project had been ahead of schedule. Unfortunately, the time surplus was wiped away as the company tried to fix what had become an ongoing five-month problem. Their surplus evaporated, leaving a deficit, and they were far behind schedule.

Drakeson's company was only one of many subcontractors working on the job. With this recent development, the New England–based customer who had the direct contract with the government wasn't interested in the problem. If Drakeson's company couldn't get it right, one of the eighteen other sub-contractors that had bid the job could make it right. Being the lowest bidder was an art.

Winning the bid on military projects was a double-edged sword. The pocket was definitely deep, with enough financial resources to finance a list of change orders and supplements a mile long. But without results, improvements, and a strong likelihood of reaching success, such projects could be a company's last. As Boeing and Lockheed Martin had found out time and time again, becoming dependent on such jobs came with a big price tag: security during the project and potential devastation if the project failed or became obsolete. If the products didn't work as proposed, Uncle Sam didn't have to buy them.

With all of the R&D, human capital, and physical resources dedicated to such projects, even these huge companies couldn't afford to keep multiple lines of operation going at the same time. Consequently, companies that specialized in high-risk military projects typically had all of their eggs in one very fragile and demanding basket.

Of course the upside was that most military projects came with great financial rewards. The downside was that the cyclical nature of such projects was hell on a workforce. There was never really true job security. In the back of everyone's mind was the question, *Who is next?* No layer of the team was immune from such rough times. Everyone eventually got laid off. In fact, not a single person on Drakeson's cooperative military contingent had ever avoided being laid off.

When Drakeson's portion of the program was ready to be tested, it was delivered to their military counterpart. This team's authorization allowed them alone to integrate and work with the entire system and actually hook up to the weapon. Due to these security issues, any subsystem contracts had to be self-contained, with schematics and written procedure installations. This eyes-only mentality, even in the development of these projects, was where the term *plug and play* had been created.

Subcontractors never saw their project in its entirety from a nuts-and-bolts perspective. And only when different subsystems became incompatible with other subsystems were the groups ever allowed to interact with the other teams. Only the general contractor and sponsoring agency had that luxury. The coordination of these subsystems was the responsibility of the primary general contractor and the overseeing military sponsor. The subsystems each had a private and military contingency. The military contingents were all classified with the suffix of *E*.

Each project was divided into separate teams. Each team was divided by its function. Drakeson's team was Team 4, which was in charge of the missile guidance software and inbound detection programs. Their military partners were from Team 4-E, which was in charge of the directive blast sequencers designed to destroy the inbound missile. Both teams' collective goal was twofold: to prevent inbound missiles from hitting the intended target and to disintegrate the inbound weapon in its entirety. These two subsystems had joined their efforts in an attempt to resolve the current performance issues. Something was going wrong.

Simply put, the problem involved Patriot's inability to completely destroy inbound missiles with velocities greater than Mach 2.41. At reduced speeds, it performed very well. The question was how to increase its ability to destroy missiles with greater approaching speeds. Unfortunately, inbound ICBMs were the Patriot's primary intended target, and they had a standard approach speed of approximately Mach 4.7.

The entire project began speculating that it was Team 4-E's problem. The initial plans of 4-E called for a larger payload of explosives to achieve the necessary blast force to destroy the missiles in their entirety. The physics of speed, mass, and time synchronization weren't so simple. The configuration and demand for high aerodynamics to achieve the needed high intercepting speeds was tasking. Team 4-E's plans were under constant modification.

* * * * *

Curt and Melody agreed to have an early lunch in the dining room, as indicated in the folder. The odds were remote that they would be close enough to see or hear anything, but given the recent developments, Melody had to agree that it was worth investigating. The more she analyzed the situation, the more confident she grew that something was going on. It was just too coincidental to be a random event. The Agency was somehow involved.

* * * * *

The project managers were trying to hammer things out. "Why are Team 4 and 4-E still working the bugs out on the contact report? We've told them three times that we're satisfied with the results," said the general contractor.

"The only thing we can deduce is that the project managers are taking it upon themselves to meet the final specifications. We have expressed our belief that although the guidance and blast sequencers are currently below final specifications, we have confirmed our optimism that it will meet final approval."

Kirkland, listening to this discussion, frankly didn't care if the weapon ever did obtain final approval from the military. A lot of speculation on the street was that such a weapon was redundant. The ultimate weapon was one to be installed in the outer atmosphere to be housed in strategically fixed orbits.

Kirkland believed that the project was a premeditated goal aimed at creating a weapon outside of all current treaties with both the former USSR and China. Deep down, he knew the design called for nuclear enhancements. His mind wandered back to the meeting and its discussion.

"Once they're installed, then we should be ready to go to Phase Seven."

"We know, we know," responded the superintendent of production. "But it appears that one of the CEOs for the sub is trying to reach final specs in an attempt to shorten final production. I've personally met with him and assured him everything is fine. We don't need to hammer down the timetable for final specifications until next July. But he just isn't listening. I'm beginning to get the impression that they've got so much riding on this contract that they're afraid we won't accept the prototype subsystem into production and are trying to come under budget and finish early by working out their final bugs during our interim testing."

"Well, get him on the same page as the rest of the team. He needs to sign off on his internal tests before we can begin production on the prototypes. We've got an interim staging scheduled in the Middle East next month. We've got too much riding on that dog-and-pony show to miss the deadline. If we cancel that show, the Saudis and Israelis will most certainly back off on their order."

Charles Kirkland was the President and CEO of CK Enterprises, and he had been absorbing the project managers' discussion on the problems with the Patriot Project. He carried a lot of weight and had the final say on all aspects of this project. Even the military grunts avoided eye contact with this guy. For a crusty seventy-five-year-old with no prior military experience, he had the grimace of any four-star general.

It was becoming quite clear that this Drakeson wasn't getting the message. Although the R&D for the project was being funded by the good old U.S. of A., the big bucks were in the intermediate uses for the subsystems in other outdated equipment. This was one of the major reasons ninety percent of all defense systems were created on a plug-and-play philosophy. Although the popular rationale was easier reparability and quick upgrading without gutting entire systems, the ulterior motive was to pirate the technology to other obsolete weapons abroad. And holding up a perfectly good system that was meeting the tolerances for a popular AAA defense system was unacceptable.

The superintendent felt the heat from Kirkland's glassy eyes burning a hole into his forehead. At that same moment, five other men in the room stopped shuffling their papers and raised their eyes. Kirkland's temples were pulsing. His facial muscles were tight, and his mouth was clamped shut. The room became very quiet. The general contractor finally found the courage to make eye contact with Kirkland.

"Is it time to arrange a special meeting?" he asked Kirkland.

With a confident nod, Kirkland sealed Drakeson's fate. A final meeting would be called. There would never be any direct acknowledgment by the U.S. government regarding the intended refitting of certain Allied weapons through the R&D and costs of the bottomless-pit funds available on this project. Although corporations pirated privileged research to other projects all the time, because this cooperative development was sponsored solely and directly by the U.S. government, such luxuries were not an option. In fact, it was technically treason.

Such a scheme couldn't be compared to corporations' taking advantage of developments and new technologies that they created on their own. It wasn't a product that they had the freedom or right to bring to market. No patent pending or ownership rights could be alleged. The bottom line was that the efforts were for and solely on behalf of the United States government. Lacking the government's express permission, all facets of the project were the property of the USA.

Kirkland didn't see it that way and never did. The simple truth was that the project was guaranteed to yield numerous technological improvements for desperately needed AAA defenses around the world. Kirkland had been banking on these interim projects from the very start. Drakeson just didn't understand. He had no clue.

* * * * *

The morning started off in typical San Francisco Bay Area fashion, somewhat chilly with the morning fog—a marine layer, the locals called it. For Curt and Melody, everything was about to change. Today would be their last normal day.

Curt hadn't shared the existence of his monitoring closet with Melody. For some reason, he just didn't feel comfortable revealing the fact that he was a certified high-tech "Peeping Tom." He embellished that his initial concern was raised when he saw the two men sitting in the vacant home watching the young cop from across the street. Why wasn't there any furniture? From Curt's limited vantage point, looking between the slats of the wood fence, he saw only aluminum folding chairs.

After the second day of their surveillance, Curt had decided to follow them after they retired from their daily spying. It was very exciting for Curt to spy on the spies. However, after the sudden death of the young officer, combined with the disappearance of the spies, Curt was certain that the two events were related. It was that curiosity that drove him to continue to follow up and track the spies.

That same adrenaline rush he had during those initial days was returning, except this time he had a plan. He also knew who and where they would be. The other twist was that he no longer had the luxury of hiding behind his monitors. He was going to be out in the open, watching. Curt rationalized that there was nothing to worry about. No one was expecting anyone to be watching their moves.

Curt's research, combined with the Agency's file, provided him with the mental advantage. There would be hundreds of people in attendance. They could easily blend in. Drakeson was most certainly safe in such a public place. Curt hoped that they could get close enough to hear some of the conversation. They planned on staying all day if they had to. The file unfortunately gave no indication as to when the meeting was to take place. But as with the other victims, no specific details were given. The only information provided was who and where. Curt and Melody would have to wait and see.

* * * * *

Drakeson was excited. Pent100 had been training with a new therapist. The upstart jockey Michael Paul had noticed a vast improvement in not only Pent100's motivation during training, but also in a willingness to approach other horses during tight turns. In prior races, the tight bunching, combined with the frequent whip strikes from other riders, had spooked Pent100. The horse had been in the habit of holding back to avoid such situations.

The therapist had explained to Mr. Paul that she would try to communicate with the horse. Paul thought that the therapist was another crazy Californian trend, but it was the owner's money. He would go along with whatever it took. Besides, even if this horse never won, he was gaining valuable riding time in one of California's premier tracks. If he could log more real race time, he'd be able to position himself for another horse.

Mr. Paul had initially believed that Pent100's problem was conditioning. But after training with him for a week, he knew that wasn't it. This horse had lungs. Paul and the other resident riders noticed that Pent100 was skittish running all-out with other animals. That was typical with young thoroughbreds. It usually took some time before they became accustomed to running in such an artificial and demanding environment. How did the therapist narrow it down so quickly? Without watching any of the films or watching Pent100 running with other horses, she had come to a similar conclusion.

No one was allowed to enter the indoor arena with the therapist. Everyone crowded into the upper viewing room.

They had dark tinted the windows—just for Pent100's special therapy lessons. At $500 an hour, the owner's manager wanted to watch the show. Everything was about results. Paul was asked to view the first few sessions for his input. It was obvious that everyone watching the initial session was more than a little skeptical.

The woman brought only a wooden folding chair. Pent100 was brought in without a saddle or bridle. The woman's chair was placed away from the center of the arena to give Pent100 most of the oval arena to himself. As the animal entered the arena, he seemed to be somewhat startled at the stranger's presence. He began to snort and jerk his head as if warning her away.

The woman kept her head down, and she appeared to be communicating with the horse with similar verbal grunts and snorts of her own. After several minutes of exchanging sounds, the woman stood and slowly walked toward the animal. Pent100 had been around people all of his life and was accustomed to being approached by humans. The woman continued to gesture with her head by bobbing it upward in quick thrusts combined with snorts and grunts. She raised her right hand while keeping her head and eyes lowered to the ground. The woman reached for the animal's neck with both hands and allowed the pads of her fingertips to brush his throat and mane.

The horse remained still but leaned forward toward the woman, allowing her better access to his neck. The woman stepped forward while moving her hand down the animal's large neck. At the base of his mane, she began to massage the neck and shoulder area just outside of the long frocks of hair. During that brief time, the horse seemed to relax in front of everyone's eyes. With great interest, Mike and the manager watched. The other trainers and riders in the viewing office remained quiet.

Each of the men present understood the body language of the animal. They each recognized the importance of what they were witnessing. It was as if the therapist and the animal were communicating at a basic non-verbal level. There was something very different about what was taking place. She was doing more than just standing next to and touching Pent100. Hers and the animal's movements and facial expressions were something all together different. It was as if she was reaching into the animal's very essence, his very existence, interacting with his soul, his being. They were talking.

After twenty minutes, the animal was at ease with the therapist. He appeared confident and in control. He was not fidgety or restless. The therapist looked up at the viewing room and smiled. Mike thought at that very moment that she knew what the problem was. He couldn't wait to hear what she had to say.

The woman left her chair in the arena and opened a side gate and left the arena floor. As she walked through the tunnel, the men met her at the door leading down from the viewing room. She smiled and led the men into the lower office. After the last man entered the room, Mike shut the door.

"That was some piece of work down there, ma'am," he said.

"Pent100 is very sensitive," she replied. "Not that you're not aware of that," she interjected. "Mr. Drakeson explained to me on the phone that Pent has been having some problems of late. Not really finishing his races at his potential. And after our little session, I have to agree."

"What do you mean exactly?" asked the manager.

"Well, many times performance is a physical issue. But from what I can tell, Pent is in excellent shape. He strode into the arena without any apparent physical discomfort. From his appearance, he's in excellent physical conditioning. But appearances can be deceiving. So I had Mr. Drakeson overnight me a report detailing his day-to-day training. From what I can tell, Pent is receiving a superb workout regimen in terms of developing his physical aptitude," she explained. "His problem is purely mental."

"So what do you recommend?" asked Mike.

"First, let me tell you that I don't know how it works really, but I have this gift. I've always had it. Animals and I have been drawn together ever since I can remember. It's as if I can see simple pictures. Almost cartoon like images. I piece the images together and interpret their meanings. I truly believe that these images are being conveyed to me by the animals. Sounds like a bunch of crap, but so far it works."

The room became very quiet. Even though they were all initially impressed by what they had witnessed, the explanation she had offered seemed too farfetched. The therapist could sense the incredulous atmosphere. Her experience told her just to go forward with her impressions and let them be the judge.

"Well, anyway," she continued, "the impression I'm getting is that Pent doesn't understand the importance of the races. To him, it's just a game. And he also has a fear of being hit in the face by the other jockeys during the tight cornering. I've tried to convey to Pent that holding back is the wrong thing to do. If he would simply pull in front of the other riders and horses, he could avoid both fears. I also emphasized that his relationship with you would become better."

Everyone listened to what she said, but avoided eye contact. It still sounded just too farfetched.

"So, he told you all that, did he?" asked the manager, a bit sarcastically.

"I know, I know. Sounds like a bunch of shit, but... that's what I'm getting."

"So now what?" Mike asked.

"Keep doing what you're doing, but increase the number of other riders during your morning sprints. Not as many horses as a regular race, but enough to give him the feeling of it. Say about half the number of a real race. I'll stay the rest of the week and meet with Pent every afternoon. We'll see if I got it right. There is usually a noticeable difference even the first time out. But after a week or so, I usually get good results," she explained.

The other men stood silent. They waited for the manager and Mike.

"Well, shit. Pent cost so damn much in the first place, it'd figure he needed therapy," joked one of the other riders.

"I've heard of stranger things before," said the manager. "Drakeson knows his shit. He didn't become a millionaire by accident. Weirder things have happened."

With that, the therapist stood and prepared to leave. "I'm at the Hyatt downtown. I'll be here tomorrow morning to watch the sprints. I want to meet with him after his cool down, but before he's placed back in his stable. Then I'll meet him again in the afternoon, as planned."

As she reached for the door, Mike called out to her. "How many of these horse sessions you done, anyway?"

"Well, technically, this is my first. I usually work on dogs and cats."

"Oh," replied Mike, less optimistically and a little deflated. "We'll see you tomorrow, then."

As the door shut, the men looked at each other. Not a single one of them thought it was going to work.

* * * * *

"So how is Pent100 doing these days?" inquired Drakeson.

The trainer seemed annoyed as he untangled the twisted telephone cord. "I would never have believed it, Jeff. That damned horse is getting better. Go figure. I would never have guessed."

"What specific improvements have you noticed?" asked Drakeson, as the beginnings of a smile began to break through. That horse was his saving grace. His life had been absorbed in his biggest project yet—Patriot. For the last six months, he had been pushing his team to narrow the specifications and results. Although the general contractor was comfortable with what they had achieved, Drakeson felt that increasing the productivity was the answer. At this stage of production, he felt confident that increasing the speed tolerance of the software and destruction sequences now was time well spent. He rationalized that it was better to resolve things now rather than two years from now. His entrepreneurial mind would never understand a decision to move forward when it was easier to resolve problems now. Putting it off for a later date seemed costly and unnecessary.

"Will Pent be ready by this weekend? And I mean more than just ready to show up for a routine race. Is he ready to actually compete?"

"I've always said this good ol' Pent has potential. Let's put it this way. The way he is taking the third and fourth turns in training, combined with his renewed confidence in tight, he just might place.... Nah, shit. Pent, he'll do better than just show. Me and the boys will be laying some real money on 'im this weekend at Bay Meadows," responded the trainer.

Drakeson's grin grew wider, into a full-on smile. He had been hoping that something in his life would get done on time and with results. "Then I'll see you there! I need a break from these desert meetings. I'm tired of hanging out with the local pilot jockeys and playing the local craps tables as my nighttime entertainment. And thank George for taking care of Pent100 for me while I've been gone."

"Jeff, you know I love this job. I wouldn't be anywhere else. I keep telling my wife that she needs to pinch me and remind me that I'm actually getting paid for what I do. I'll see you in a couple of days, boss."

As Drakeson hung up the phone, he felt a distinct sense of accomplishment. He always felt a sense of pride when working toward a goal. Many people on the outside would look at him as someone after the almighty buck. But the truth was, he was a perfectionist in terms of being a doer. His motivation and personal drive were the factors that steamed him ahead of others and allowed him to be successful. Although his wealth allowed him to enjoy life to its fullest, it was never the thing that pushed his button. It was his uncontrollable desire and need to do things right, on time, and better than anyone else.

"Excuse me, Mr. Drakeson," called Duane. He was the assistant superintendent in charge of the military and civilian cooperation team that worked directly with the U.S. military attaché in charge of the entire project.

"Please come in," replied Drakeson, as the young man entered. Duane was about thirty-five years old, with a short haircut, not quite as severe as the Marine Corp crop cut, but shorter than the average civilian suits on Wall Street.

"I was asked again by the general contractor and my superiors if you couldn't see it our way in terms of signing off on this round of tests. Your efforts are outstanding, and we're all very pleased at the preliminary results. My superiors acknowledge your concerns that spending our time now makes economic sense in the long run. And they also acknowledge that your contract doesn't call for a completed product until twelve months after our counterparts address multi-utilization of air, sea, and ground testing. But the fact remains, we had planned to utilize this technology in other tests during the interim phases."

Mr. Drakeson could tell that this man was only the messenger. And he had been over this issue several times already. Proceeding now and ignoring our known problems was unacceptable. "Young man, I know you don't understand my position. But this project means too much to me to miss this opportunity. At most, we could make so much progress by steaming ahead now, while the issue is at hand. We're already in the desert accumulating tons of data to narrow down the problem. At most, it will only put us four months away from getting to Mach-3 tolerances."

Lt. Colonel Duane J. Coleman looked sternly at Drakeson. "Are you sure that's your final position, Mr. Drakeson?"

"I'm sorry, son, but it is. It's my style: Do it right the first time. It's my way and my right under our contract with the general contractor. I'm obligated to have a completed project on a certain date. It's my prerogative to get there my own way."

"Understood. I'll see you Thursday afternoon, then, at the test bunker?"

"Not this week. I'm heading back to the Bay Area. I've got some other business to attend to."

"Is that wise? I mean, leaving now, given your desire to finalize the guidance and tracking system data collection?"

"No problem at all. My right-hand man and team could crunch this without me. I'm just a control freak. That's my nature. This team is the best at what they do, probably, in the entire western world. They can handle it without me. But being a nosey boss, I get to the luxury of playing hands-on. No, Colonel, we've got it covered."

As the Colonel left Drakeson's temporary office, he slid into his sky blue Taurus, depressed his car cell phone keypad, and speed dialed number two. The XO at Fallon had lent Coleman the vehicle during his brief stay. He had been flown in from Colorado Springs the prior evening.

"Hello."

"Yes, this is Colonel Coleman. I guess my stay is a brief one at that. Could you have my pilot draw up a flight plan to *Alameda NAS* for this afternoon? I need to make a quick jump there for the next few days. Tell him I'll let him hop to Lemoore and see some of his West PAC buddies over the weekend before we head back for that cross-country run."

"Yes sir. I'm sure the L.T. wouldn't object too much to that one."

"I'll be checking in at 1800, ready to fly at 1815. Is his Hornet ready to fire?"

"Roger that, sir. I'll have the practice white tips unstrapped. It's too bad, though. I know the lieutenant was looking forward to dropping some bombs. He'll just have to show those Air Force bums that his skills could still outdo the rooks. He's still got braggin' rights about hitting a moving runway. You know sir, the rivalry between Navy and Air Force will never end," joked the XO.

"That's true. But the fact is, XO, we've got gold bars and they've got lead ones," laughed Coleman.

As Coleman hung up the cell phone receiver, he knew he had to relay the information about the Patriot program. He had specific instructions to relay his information via the MILNET at Alameda NAS. Strict communications protocol was required; no written documents, letters, or memos. He had assisted on such defense contracts in the past. Ever since he had landed in the San Diego NAS team at Miramar and then been recommended to the Monterey Language Military School, he had been getting some pretty cushy assignments. The word on the street was he had excellent opportunities to go into the private sector before his twentieth year.

But after fourteen years in, he couldn't see wasting his military pension by going out early. If he did, he knew he'd do some reservist stuff to get his last years in. He was too close to get out now. As he paused at the stop sign and then headed for the driving range, he wondered what was so important to send him out to interview Drakeson. Oh well, just do what you're told, and what goes around comes around.

* * * * *

En route to the race track, Curt pulled into a small strip mall, where a tiny coffee shop was nestled between a dry cleaner and a Subway sandwich shop. Across the street stood a plain, two-story, windowless brick building. As he parked his van, Melody crinkled her eyebrows and looked confused.

"I need a caffeine boost before we hit the race track." Curt did not want to add more stress by telling Melody that the Agency building he had snuck into was 500 feet behind her. He also wanted to access the computer Gina had used when she had sent the email. Safely inside, Curt pulled the email print and looked at the photograph as it related to the panel of computers facing away from the window. Using the photograph Gina had taken, he was able to pinpoint which computer she had used to send the email. Glancing at the choices, he was certain that he had found it.

Curt strolled up to the counter and ordered two specialty drinks. Knowing that it would take several moments to prepare, he sauntered over to the computer and sat down. Not wanting Melody to see what he was doing, he reached into his jacket pocket and pulled out a small portable flash drive. As if in a deep exaggerated yawn, Curt pretended to stretch and slid the stick like device into the computer. He shook the mouse and began importing a program designed to obtain protected storage passwords.

As the program opened, the computer flashed a warning that someone was about to access a protected storage of memory. With a click of the mouse, Curt was scrolling through the last 30 days. He found the date of the email. There with all of the other users, was Gina's username and password to her *Yahoo* account. Curt wrote the information on the email printout, just as his coffee order was called out. He stood, took the drinks and exited the building. He would later drop the email back into his other file documents, where it was almost forgotten. That email would prove to be the most important thing he had. It would save his life.

* * * * *

The Bay Meadows Race Track was just opening its front gate as Curt and Melody entered. Four men were milling around the entrance area. They all were engrossed in the *Race Track Weekly*, studying the odds for today's races. They looked to be serious thoroughbred enthusiasts.

Curt and Melody stopped at the souvenir area and purchased the same type of paper the men had been reading. They also grabbed some loose flyers available at the kiosk beside the exit doors. The expansive view from the top stairway grandstand was awe-inspiring. A soft mist from the mid-morning marine layer hovered in the air. It floated within the track and muffled sounds. The effect was a crisp dampness with an eerie quietness. A door to the restaurant swung open, pushing the air toward both Curt and Melody. The wet air splashed into their faces with enough force to lift their hair away.

Two men wearing dark government-issued sunglasses strode through the doorway. The two groups stood face to face for a brief moment. Curt's face went blank and turned pale. Melody had no way of knowing that these were the men Curt had been talking about.

"Are they still serving breakfast?" asked Melody.

"Yes, ma'am," replied one of the agents.

Both agents stepped aside to make room and held the doors open. As Melody walked in, she felt a slight resistance in Curt's hand. She gently tugged Curt's hand to start him into motion. Before exiting the doorway, the other gentleman called back into the restaurant.

"Make sure we get that table by the window, Jose."

Curt and Melody glanced toward the countertop and saw the server nod in acknowledgment of the men's request; then the server walked over toward the oversized round table that was isolated from the others. The table was posed in front of a large, plate glass window overlooking the track. He began organizing the napkins, utensils, and floral centerpiece.

Curt tilted his head toward the table. Melody's eyes bulged, and in a knowing gesture she raised her eyebrows. The meeting would take place at that table.

The volume of typical soft clanks, dings, and background noises began to overshadow the soft background music. Preparing for the onslaught of race enthusiasts, the waiters and other attendants could be seen scurrying in and out of the kitchen. Curt and Melody were seated close enough to the meeting table to watch without being too obvious. The same waiter returned to place a reserved sign on the table. Sipping their iced tea, they continued to wait.

* * * * *

Drakeson walked through the doors with a confident stride. He was dressed in khaki shorts and a polo shirt. He wore high-top Nike shoes with a bold black swoosh. He removed his dark Ray-Ban sunglasses and hooked them on the front neckline of his shirt. The waiter greeted him and led him to the table. As if on cue, another server brought a tall Bloody Mary with a skewer of green olives stacked onto a plastic toothpick that peered above the rim of the glass. He took the glass and sat at the reserved table.

Curt leaned forward with his hands facing palms down on the tablecloth. Melody began reading the menu when the two suited agents joined Drakeson. Curt and Melody were far enough away that they couldn't hear the conversation. They wouldn't need to.

"I wish I could say that I'm surprised to see you boys," Drakeson mumbled as he sipped on his drink.

"We've got the check-off form right here. Are you sure on your position?"

"All we need is your John Hancock, and we'll be on our way," interjected the other agent. Both agents remained motionless, waiting for Drakeson's reply.

"Boys, I just don't understand. Our final completion deadline is months away. What difference does it make for us on this interim timeline, anyway?"

Both agents sat motionless, devoid of any expression. After a brief silence, one agent reached into his breast pocket and pulled out a silver ink pen. This same agent reached his right arm across the table and held out the pen for Drakeson, while the other agent slid the form out onto the table. Drakeson sat motionless, projecting a stone face. For a brief moment, he seemed to be reconsidering his position. What would it hurt? It was only an interim check-off.

* * * * *

Curt was peeking over his iced tea. Melody glanced at the trio in her peripheral vision. Then, it started. One of the agents reached across the table and handed Drakeson an object of some sort. Was he going to sign something? They had an angled vantage point obstructed by the agents' backs.

* * * * *

The agents looked at each other. They knew it was time—the moment of truth. This was Drakeson's final chance. Everything was ready. The gelatin capsule was loaded. As before, during this moment, when the target had made his decision, things began to move as if in slow motion.

Another patron burst through the doors, and a cool breeze drifted inside. Before the doors closed, the distant screech of a seagull echoed. Inside, the chatter of human conversation and the clanking of drinking glasses being arranged filled the background noise.

Drakeson looked at the form and the pen. He blinked his eyes and looked up at the agents. He had made his decision. "I'm sorry, boys. I just can't do it."

With the finality of those words, everything was set in motion. The agent nearest the window picked up his water glass and moved it to the other side of his napkin. This subtle gesture signaled the initiation of standard operating proc-edures. One of the agents working as a stand-in waiter for the man who called in sick this morning, and the other agent masquerading as a bus boy, were from the A-Team. They knew by that signal that they were going with one of the predesigned plans.

The agent holding the pen stood and depressed the base of the pen. A distinct clink sound caught Drakeson's attention. The agent tilted his head as if examining the pen. This designed distraction called Drakeson's attention to the pen. On cue, the agent dropped the pen as if it were an accident. He had practiced for well over an hour the night before to assure that it fell toward Drakeson. In a padded thud, it bounced off the table before landing at Drakeson's feet.

"I'll get that," offered Drakeson.

As Drakeson bent down to pick up the pen, the other agent tilted his own pen into Drakeson's drink, pushed the top depression mechanism, and released a gelatin capsule. The capsule slipped into the red liquid and vanished below the pooled surface. It was designed to quickly dissolve in liquid, including an acidic Bloody Mary. Both agents waited for Drakeson to take a drink. Everything was going according to plan.

* * * * *

"It looked like that guy dropped something," whispered Curt, as he tilted his head ever so slightly to get a better glimpse. The ceiling lights reflected off the pen. Curt caught a glimpse of light refracting off the metallic pen as it tumbled off the tabletop. Melody was watching the other man. It appeared that he had leaned forward and done something.

* * * * *

"Well, I understand your position. Let's toast to a rapid return to Fallon NAS and to signing off on the project," offered the agent. All three men raised their glasses. A muffled clink echoed out over the room as their glasses touched.

"To the first win for Pent100!" blurted Drakeson with an ear-to-ear smile.

The agents' body positions remained frozen with their hands upheld in toast as they watched Drakeson move his glass to his thin, mustache-covered lip. The ice cubes clanked and rattled against the sides of the glass as the Bloody Mary mixture disappeared into Drakeson's mouth. His Adam's apple protruded as he swallowed. He had no way of knowing that this was his final drink—ever. Drakeson set his glass down with a heavy thud and exhaled in a loud "Ahh." He stood and shook both of their hands and began walking. Drakeson could almost see the bright green grass through the front glass doors.

"Oh, my God, he's headed straight for us!" exclaimed Curt.

Melody's face was expressionless, trying to hide her terror. Only her eyes bulging gave any indication that she was conscious. Her eyes pulsed with each step Drakeson took toward their table. Her face was the epitome of the term, *deer caught in the headlights*.

The chemical began to take effect. The first thing Drakeson felt was a sudden loss of vision, followed by a quick loss of breath. His forward momentum kept him moving for one final step. It was as if a sudden burst of cold air had blasted against his face. Mid stride before the lead foot touched the ground, the chemical took complete control with its full lethal effect. Drakeson's brain shut down all voluntary muscle control, focusing all of its efforts to combat the invading chemical. All physical motor skills ceased to work. There was no flailing or convulsions. He collapsed, his body going limp, mid stride. Drakeson fell, moving forward and tilting downward to his right. His forward momentum pushed his two-hundred-fifty-pound frame toward the patrons at the next table. There, he fell into Curt's lap.

Curt pushed his iced tea glass forward and reached out to cradle Drakeson's head as the lifeless mass fell toward their table. Everything seemed to happen in slow motion. One agent stepped forward and watched Drakeson's lifeless body melt into the man at the table, but something caught his attention: The man cradling Drakeson's head wasn't looking at Drakeson;

147

he was looking into the agent's eyes. It was the way their eyes met and the position in which the man was crouched. This picture was something the agent had seen before. It was like an impression, a pose, something like *déjà vu*. He had a weird sense that he had experienced this before. The pose. The position of the man's body. The agent began questioning himself: Where had he seen this man before? The agent's mind wasn't playing tricks. His mind began to race. He was almost certain that somewhere, sometime before, he had seen this man. But where and when?

* * * * *

Curt's eyes locked onto the man's face. There was no doubt. This was the same man from the building. He was the man with the file folder. The file folder he had copied. It was the same man he had spied on from the safety of his closet. It was the man who had been watching the young CHP officer just before his death.

Unknown to Curt, his body was posed in almost the identical position to that event at the copy machine. One could have taken a photo snapshot of both of these events and superimposed one over the other. They were almost identical.

* * * * *

The agent's instincts took over. As his partner and the agent waiter moved into position to attend to Mr. Drakeson's body, he moved away from Curt's table, moved up beside the agent waiter, and quietly instructed him to pull the glasses off of Curt and Melody's table. "Get the prints," he whispered. Then he took over helping his partner with the body.

The agent squinted his eyes as if his mental concentration could force the waiter into action. No one missed a beat. It was standard operating procedure. The waiter walked over to their table and pulled the glasses. Neither Curt nor Melody noticed.

They were focused on the two muscular paramedics who had arrived more rapidly than one might expect and were frantically working on Drakeson.

The Agency would soon know if either Curt or Melody had ever been fingerprinted. It would take precisely twenty-two minutes from the moment they pulled the prints and began cross-referencing them through their entire database. Their high-speed computer and unique organizational subclassifications for prints made national searches much quicker. The team would scan in the prints and email them back to the Agency to initiate their search. However, researching the witnesses was a side issue.

The agents' primary concern was Drakeson's body. An IV and oxygen tube had already been inserted into Drakeson's limp body, but he was already dead. The official coroner's report would estimate his time of death to be thirty-eight minutes after the fact. After the chemical first entered Drakeson's bloodstream, it took only twenty seconds for the first trace elements to attack his heart tissue. After another sixty seconds of exposure, the heart had begun to fail.

It had taken the Agency several tries, but it had perfected the mixture. The chemical was unique in that it would be absorbed by the body tissues and remain off conventional toxicological radar. The off gassing and trace elements were designed to be similar to the synthetic adrenaline typically used to revive cardiac-arrest patients.

This job would be just like any other. Based on Drakeson's age, weight, and family history, the conclusion was obvious: He was a middle-aged executive, exposed to high degrees of stress, and someone who neglected his physical health. These facts pushed people to assume that Drakeson was ripe for a massive and fatal heart attack.

The Agency paramedics strapped Drakeson into a gurney and rolled him out of the restaurant, purportedly heading for Kaiser Hospital in Oakland, only minutes away. The waiters and patrons were stunned into silence at the turn of events.

The racing enthusiasts' day had changed from anticipating a casual relaxing afternoon at the track to seeing a live version of *ER*, up close and personal.

Curt and Melody were stunned. They sat frozen, staring at the debris from the medical supply packages and loose plastic surgical-end fittings strewn against the bright periwinkle blue carpeting. The disinformation protocol had been set into motion from the second Drakeson had fallen. The paramedics had said to each other that the man had a sudden cardiac arrest. Their voices were somewhat elevated so that the witnesses could overhear every word. But Curt and Melody had different opinions. The paramedics had used a defibrillator, feigning attempts at shocking Drakeson's heart back into rhythm. Curt and Melody watched as his body jerked with each jolt. There was no doubt in their minds that Drakeson would never be revived.

Other than the unknown agents participating in the charade, Curt and Melody were the only others present who had any idea that what they had just witnessed was a murder. Mr. Drakeson had been openly killed in broad daylight, with numerous witnesses, yet even the security tapes would document his heart attack. There was no reason for anyone to suspect otherwise.

Curt glanced at Melody and waited for her to make eye contact. Curt stood and walked toward the front door. Without any fanfare, Melody followed. Neither agent noticed. The agents were in their damage-control mode, placing the proper verbal spin on the situation. Staged conversations were performed to solidify and guide the witnesses to mold their recollection, almost creating their memories of the events for them. The bus boy was busy removing any trace of the Agency's presence. The medical wrappers that held the supplies would never stand up to scrutiny; they were government issued and had no private company insignias or trademarks. No possible trace of where they were produced was available.

150

Ironically, the attention to details that focused on creating a sterile and unidentifiable supply of equipment was in itself a red flag. The Agency had learned this lesson the hard way. In an earlier case, a family member of one of the targets attempted to pursue a medical malpractice lawsuit against the paramedic firm that responded to the scene. The fact that they couldn't locate the unit was blamed on the medical community's collusion to protect itself from lawsuits. No action ever came of that case.

But like a living organism, the Agency evolved and learned from its mistakes. Had the waste from the medical supplies been saved from the scene, and had the lawyers had the opportunity to examine the materials, questions would have been raised as to why a supposedly privately held company was using government-issued supplies. A further search would have been able to track the San Diego Naval Hospital and the United States government. Fortunately for the Agency, that never happened.

In Drakeson's case, no hospital would record an autopsy, and no ambulance would have a record of the call. It was all agency orchestrated. Any inquiries would be defused with the ineptitude of the coroner's office and underpaid paramedics. They simply misplaced another corpse. It was standard operating procedure. The additional request for the fingerprints wasn't the immediate priority. With everyone focused on the evidence removal and solidifying the rumors, no one noticed that the couple at the table had left. It was only after the waiter reported back to the agent, confirming that the glasses had been pulled, did he notice their empty table. Things were always busiest following a public elimination.

It was probably nothing—just the adrenaline of the moment. But protocol was protocol. If anything was found as far as the identity of that couple, the Agency would begin surveillance. They would also take a look at each person's residence. It almost always turned out to be a waste of time.

This standard operating procedure had been created for some reason, though. Once again, they were right.

* * * * *

A man sat at the back table, watching *CNN Headline News*. Out of habit, he waited for public confirmation. It seemed more real, even though he had already received his encrypted email. The vibration of the cell phone had stirred his dog, who was anticipating their departure. Annoyed at the delay, the dog stared at his owner and continued to wait.

Nothing was being reported. He waited until the next commercial break and decided to catch the headline later that evening. Pulling out his black book, he drew a straight line through Jeff Drakeson's name. A personal flash of guilt entered his consciousness. Although Drakeson had been on the radar of the NSA and FBI, no specific request had been made regarding adding his name to the knock list. The request had come from Anthony's other employer, Kerr, Neebling and Blair. Eliminating Drakeson opened the door for one of Kerr, Neebling and Blair's clients, Kirkland.

During a contract review, the firm learned that its client was working on a redundant defense contract. If they were given exclusive production rights, it was a foregone conclusion they would stand to gain untold riches based on an extended contract. These clients had a niche in the specialized market of warfare and could temporarily monopolize the technology. The partners had sought James Anthony's assistance with their dilemma. Once Drakeson was eliminated, they would make a huge purchase of their client's stock.

Anthony sent a text message to his partners. It read "let's buy the stock." The message signaled that the Drakeson matter was done. They would each make untold millions. Anthony realized the elimination of this obscure manufacturer of weapons was no great loss to society. Nor did Drakeson's death adversely affect the United States. One could argue, given his stubborn and inflexible personality, the removal of Drakeson helped the overall prospect of peace by allowing the other company to streamline the production process. In his own self-rationalization, Anthony had almost convinced himself that he should receive an award for eliminating Drakeson.

As he walked out the door, he felt a real sense of vulnerability. He had just abused his authority. He had used the assets of the government to arrange the hit of a lawful citizen of the United States, and no one in the Agency knew. The Agency had followed protocol and procedures. Drakeson was on their knock list. Anthony should know: He had placed him there. As far as the Agency knew, everything was as it should be.

* * * * *

The drive home was somber. Neither Curt nor Melody said a word. There was nothing to be said. With their own eyes, they had witnessed the meeting, the apparent heart attack, and the agents. Melody was doing a lot of mental catching up. It had been less than twenty-four hours earlier that she had first learned about any of this. She found it difficult enough to comprehend why Curt had gone so far in his little charade. His short stint as a photocopy guy, and stealing documents from a government agency was beyond her understanding. Just to rationalize his actions was difficult enough. Now, in a sudden realization, she believed Curt's fears were well founded.

She organized her thoughts and turned her head, studying Curt's face. She closed her eyes as she began to reflect on what had transpired. There was no doubt he had changed. When Curt had returned from his year studying abroad in Europe, he had returned a different man. In the past, he had been quiet, keeping his thoughts to himself. Upon his return, however, he possessed a subtle self-assuredness. The old Curt may have contemplated the circumstances surrounding his neighbor's suspicious death, but he would never have acted upon those feelings. Now, he had not only proved his suspicions but had become personally involved.

As Melody opened her eyes, she thought she detected a small smile form on Curt's lips. Turning away, she felt an intense need to make sense of what she had uncovered. Her thoughts turned to her good friend and past lover, James Anthony. He was a U.S. Senator. She wanted to return to the safety of her home.

The Senator

Sitting behind his oversized cherrywood desk had never felt so good. As a child growing up, weathering the cold winters on the North Platte, never in his wildest dreams would he have believed it possible. The oldest of four boys, Senator Anthony had always been the idol of the family. Like most Midwesterners, his family had a small corn farm. At the age of five, he possessed the skills to control the family's John Deere combine tractor and made serious contributions to the productivity of the family business. With the modernization of those steel oxen machines, even a child could keep the corn rows straight. The Senator's father made him wait until his tenth birthday before he could take the combine out solo, though.

Often, the Senator relived his memories of operating the tractor. The power, confidence, and independence were characteristics that a young person yearned to appreciate. Being allowed to operate those machines instilled, at an early age, the ability to dream, take control, and be responsible for his actions. His responsibilities resulted in a quantifiable contribution to the most noble of causes—the support of his family.

The inner confidence and drive that young James Anthony possessed grew. His life was a string of success stories, from his time at Scottsbluff High School to the University of Nebraska and into Law School at the University of Chicago. Being a Midwesterner, he couldn't bring himself to abandon the Midwest ideals for a prestigious East Coast education. The Midwest had its own culture.

The bragging rights for everyone in Nebraska stemmed from the knowledge that during each home football game, the Cornhuskers Stadium became the most populated spot in the state. Every Nebraskan knew this trivial fact by the age of two. If only for a brief four hours, the term "Go Big Red" had a religious quality to it. In Senator Anthony's case, the dogma of football, combined with his involvement on the family farm and being the firstborn in his family, created a set of circumstances that nurtured an inner drive to succeed that was beyond understanding.

After graduating from law school, James was wooed by recruiters from many of the top firms in the nation. After narrowing the list, he chose the Boston firm of Kerr, Neebling and Blair. The firm's heavy involvement in construction defects had interested young James Anthony, and the six-figure salary plus a nice signing bonus made his decision easy. At first, he believed he would leave Nebraska for only a few years. As long as the money kept coming, he would remain temporarily relocated to the godforsaken East Coast and suck it up.

During his second year at the firm, he was selected as part of the law team, although his activities were relegated to research. As luck would have it, he participated in the first big construction-defect case in New England. His involvement in this case, combined with his outstanding public speaking skills, soon caught the attention of the partners, who assigned him to the cash cow of the firm: Kerr, Neebling and Blair had represented every U.S. Senator from the State of Massachusetts since before JFK.

He was destined to have this opportunity and to shine. James's background in agriculture turned out to be pivotal in assisting the Massachusetts Senators in terms of support for important legislation that was meaningful to the bread-belt states, thus enabling the Senators from those states to find it

156

within their constituents' best interest to support bills important to New England voters.

James's thorough understanding of, and appreciation for, the plight of the farmers was sincere. Many times, James made special face-to-face visits to Senators, bringing that personal Midwestern style into the discussion. During those meetings, each participant knew where James's financial loyalties stood. But the sincere and full appreciation for their constituents was clear. He may live on the East Coast, and in Bean Town to boot, but he was also a true Midwesterner at heart. This reality resolved many miscommunications. It was almost always a win-win situation. The Midwest Senators began to see James Anthony as one of their own.

James began participating in the drafting of numerous bills relating to defense contracts involving the research and development of most of the missile defense contracts that had been proposed during the Reagan and first Bush terms. When it came to campaign contributions and fundraising, James became a natural at schmoozing. He became one of the go-to guys in the firm. James Anthony's twenty-year stint with the firm was climaxed not by a quick rise to partner, but through the decision to pursue a career in politics.

James's understanding of the bill-preparation process and fundraising, coupled with the national relationships he had created, made his rise to politics a natural progression. Ironically, his first opportunity in the political arena did not take place until well after he accepted the role as the managing partner of the new West Coast office of what was now Kerr, Neebling, Blair and Anthony, Attorneys at Law.

The firm's initial involvement in construction defects gave them an advantage in terms of process, discovery, and case resolution. Given the abundant litigation in California in the '80s and early '90s, it only made sense for the firm to expand westward. After considering the San Francisco Bay Area, the Greater Los Angeles region, and San Diego, and looking at the great number of condominiums built in Southern California, the firm finally located its office in Pasadena, just east of L.A. It placed them in the center of the battlefield, with James at the helm.

It was inevitable that James should be successful in construction-defect litigation. Over a three-year period, he successfully settled five outlandishly huge settlements. His team began pioneering the concept of collective plaintiff approaches that morphed into the class-action lawsuits of today.

The untimely death of a state legislator prompted Old Man Kerr, back in Boston, to suggest that James Anthony contemplate a new career—politics. The firm looked at James's background and took a long view: The firm could greatly benefit by having a state assemblyman position whose eyes aimed at the national spotlight. Having an ex-partner in this position would give their firm direct access to contract negotiations on an exponential basis. The goal was for James to become a true insider with specific loyalties to the firm.

After numerous closed-door discussions, the other partners unanimously encouraged and coaxed a surprised James Anthony in his decision to pursue politics as his new career. The consulting contracts, with guaranteed return provisions preserving James' financial situation for the next ten years, gave him the confidence and security to grudgingly accept this new set of circumstances. The firm's long-range goals now became James's real reason behind the reason to pursue this new venture.

After three two-year terms in the State Assembly, James Anthony moved into the national scene as a U.S. Senator. He maintained one home in Pasadena, California, and another in a prominent Chevy Chase, Maryland, subdivision for the political elite. During his eighteen years in politics, he remained on as a consultant for the firm. It still irritated Anthony every time he saw the firm's letterhead. His sacrifice when agreeing to go into politics for the firm never affected his paychecks. Yet, it surprised even him at the disappointment he felt the first time he saw the firm's name: His name had been removed.

His ego was bruised. Anthony had never failed at anything. Losing his name from the stationery was a serious sore spot. He kept a full box of the original letterhead to remind himself that he was a success. He simply worked for the firm behind the scenes. Besides, he still received a quarterly consulting fee from the firm. It wasn't like he had really left the firm. He was a key player. Still, he hated the new name. Then again, being a U.S. Senator wasn't all that bad either.

Decision Time

Curt and Melody had returned to his house. Melody remained speechless. She couldn't believe what had happened. The intense fear from witnessing the assassination and from having physical contact with the victim had drained their energy. At one point, Melody had cradled Drakeson's head in her hands while they waited for the paramedics to arrive.

In a continued silence, they each looked up at the ceiling. Their brains seemed to be stuck in infinite loops, dissecting their situation and contemplating their next move. When they did eventually break their silence, they recounted the entire event. They discussed every detail—their arrival, the table placement, their physical location, as well as their thoughts, feelings, and fears.

As they relived the experience, their bodies began to react to the adrenaline rush. Their heartbeats and voices began to increase in volume and intensity. The legitimate sense of fear began to set in. What they knew, witnessed, and could document, along with what Curt had done by infiltrating a government agency of some sort, had now placed their lives at risk.

"Do you think anybody suspects us? Could anyone at that agency know something about us?" asked Melody.

"How could they? Who are we anyway? Just some unknown spectators at the race track. Why would they even suspect that we would know anything about what they have done? I don't think so," explained Curt as he paced to the kitchen. In times of deep stress, he usually drank either Dr Pepper or hot tea. It was time for tea.

He began boiling the water in a classic tea kettle that his mother had given him years ago. When humans are afraid, it's human nature to pursue things of comfort. A recent study had uncovered that even murderers would contact their mothers after taking a life. Curt's reckless behavior, as well as his illegal infiltration into a government agency and witnessing the murder of a civilian, was far too much to process. The closest thing of comfort was his mother's tea kettle. He found that boiling the tea and hearing the steam whistle was distraction enough to forget the dilemma he had created, even if only for a moment. Sipping the tea gave him a mental vacation from his current predicament. Had they realized how close the Agency was to finding them, they would never have taken the break. They needed to run away, but they just didn't know it.

* * * * *

Now Curt and Melody were back at her place, and the murder was still on their minds. "Curt, I think we need help."

He rolled his eyes as he turned his head away. It was a subject they had both agreed not to discuss. When Curt was away in Europe studying abroad as a foreign exchange student, Melody had volunteered to help a local politician climb to the national spotlight. Her vast experience and contacts in New England, not to mention her good looks, created a temptation that the candidate couldn't ignore. As a volunteer, Melody found herself working directly with James Anthony.

As time passed, they crossed the line and had a brief affair. It had never become public knowledge, but the details in which she described her so called innocent involvement with his election efforts, the personal struggles he had endured, and the way she gazed off into the distance when she mentioned that summer, revealed the truth.

After returning from Europe, Curt and Melody had reunited and began to rebuild their relationship. She avoided discussing the specifics of her relationship with the newly elected Senator. Curt's inquires were deflected away. She avoided topics that could lead to further questions that, if answered, would reveal times when she and Anthony had been alone together, after everyone else had left. Such revelations would make it obvious that they were lovers. It would remain her secret. Melody's vague responses and avoidance affected Curt.

She saw the hurt look on Curt's face. Without discussing it, she knew he knew. From that point, they acted as if nothing had happened, focusing their energies instead to build upon the feelings they had created before their brief separation. After that day, whenever conversations took place in front of each other and the topic required discussing events from those days, there was an unspoken agreement to work through that awkward moment by not elaborating on any information revealed. They maintained an accord, an informal agreement to avoid the minefield that circled the subject of Senator James Anthony—until now.

Things were different this time. The issue at hand was beyond important. It was life threatening. Curt turned back, facing Melody. She watched his male ego melt away, making room for reason and logic. He pursed his lips and nodded his head in agreement before he spoke. "You're right. Can you call him?"

* * * * *

The Senator's personal cell phone rang. Looking down at the number, he saw the prefix 408 area code. The first person he thought of, he hadn't heard from in many years. Although he had changed his telephone countless times, he had kept the same number. It was one of those numbers that important people had been given. He wanted these people, if the occasion arose, to be able to contact him. This was one of those occasions.

James glanced at his appointment calendar, making a mental note that he had at least thirty minutes before his next meeting. He was hoping it would be her and answered the phone with confidence, then listening with great anticipation.

"This is James Anthony. May I help you?"

"James...." Melody paused. She hadn't spoken with him for several years. Back then, they had spent many hours together. Their backgrounds were very similar. Their passions and focus had complemented each other nicely. But she knew he would never divorce his wife, nor would he jeopardize losing the respect of his family. Regardless of their age difference, there were true deep emotions. "... It's Melody Bergmann."

Hearing her voice brought an instant smile to his face. He had missed everything about her; her smile, her mannerisms, her intellect, and her passion. He had always loved her. He had also known that they had no future.

"How have you been? It's been so long, too long. Where are you?"

"I'm still in California. I've got a big problem."

James couldn't help but think the worst. Had she gotten pregnant by him, given birth without telling him, and now was looking to ruin his career, his life? His smile vanished, replaced by strained eyes and a wrinkled forehead. Dreading her response, he dove right in. He wanted to hear the news and get it over with. Anticipating a bombshell, he responded.

"What happened?" Trying to disguise his discomfort of the situation, he tagged on a sympathetic diversion. "Are you hurt?" Holding his breath, he awaited her response.

"You won't believe this, but my boyfriend Curt Anderson and I uncovered a big problem. I don't want to go into it in too much detail now, but did you hear about Jeff Drakeson dying?"

James recoiled. It wasn't possible that anyone knew what had happened. He had just left the bar twenty minutes before. The hit had just taken place. It wasn't even public yet.

164

Gathering his energy, James composed his thoughts and responded. "What are you talking about? Who's Drakeson?"

"He's the CEO of a weapons manufacturer. He was killed at the New Bay Meadows Race Track today." Melody paused, organizing her thoughts before continuing. "We were there."

James broke into a cold sweat. His breathing quickened and his heart seemed to pound like a ceremonial drum as his pulse strength surged in an adrenaline rush. At first uncertain what to say or do, he then did what came naturally: He lied.

"Melody, I'm sorry, but I don't have the foggiest idea what you're talking about." Improvising, he decided he needed more time to formulate a response. He needed a plan. He needed time to think things through. "I'm just about to walk into a meeting. Can I get up to speed on this Drakeson character and then call you back? Is this a good number to reach you?"

"I'm sorry, James. Of course. Yes, this is my cell phone."

Gathering his composure, he concentrated on how he was projecting his voice. He didn't want to speak too fast or sound overly dramatic. He defaulted to his professional noncommittal tone and continued. "Does anyone else know about this?"

Melody's female intuition detected a subtle change in James's voice. She closed her eyes and dismissed her thoughts, attributing her feelings to the stress of the situation. Responding in a soft whisper, as if avoiding the ears of others, she responded.

"No. No one else knows." She had just sealed their fate.

* * * * *

It was only a matter of time. The Agency building had an elaborate surveillance system. Cameras were stationed throughout the entire building. Over fifty-six cameras, each with its own independent recording system, dotted the premises. An entire department had been created that oversaw the transfer of those recordings to CD. Part of the protocol was for a human to view the recordings before the CDs were labeled and stored. There was no expiration date. The tape that captured Curt's actions was sitting in the surveillance department, lined up with the hundreds of other tapes. Given the rate of viewing time, normally it would take at least one month before it was scheduled for transfer and then archived. This time, however, the zeal of a rookie, fresh on his new assignment, would increase the department's rate of viewing; human eyes would see it sooner than scheduled. The rookie assigned was detail oriented and eager to establish his worth to the Agency. He wouldn't miss it. It was just a matter of time.

* * * * *

In a soft, vulnerable voice, Curt asked Melody, "What did he say?"

Melody was still replaying the conversation in her mind. She knew James. He was hiding something. Hearing Curt's voice, she turned away, looking out the window before she responded. "He was about to go into a meeting. He wanted to research Drakeson and then call me back. We'll have to wait."

She sat on her sofa and nestled in for the wait. Curt strode into the kitchen, looking through Melody's kitchen for a tea kettle. He wanted to brew a fresh pot of boiling water for tea. He had to improvise and used a pan. Old habits die hard. He always turned to this ritual in times of stress. They waited in separate rooms for the return call, both lost in their own thoughts.

* * * * *

Senator Anthony's mind whirled. He was running through his options. He had made the decision to place Drakeson on the knock list. As the Chairman of the National Security Committee, he was the only person allowed direct communication with any of the Agencies. If questions began to be raised concerning the death of Drakeson, the committee would be unable to protect him. All killings were a collective and unanimous committee decision. Although the committee never became involved in the details of these matters, all persons who were placed on the list were documented.

These lists were top secret and required a periodic Presidential review. The cases would never become open to public scrutiny, but such an inquiry would take on a life of its own. Within the confines of this dirty part of politics and the government, retribution for the mishandling of this type of information, the abuse of this power and authority, had its own consequences. It was an unspoken understanding that choosing to become involved with these kinds of issues, regardless of one's position, required accepting a special set of consequences. This was a lesson that several past Presidents had to learn: No one was exempt.

Senator Anthony's ego hadn't expanded to the point of self-delusion. He knew that if the firm that had sponsored him throughout his entire professional life caught wind of this potential leak, he would pay the ultimate price. He appreciated his own self-worth and recognized his vulnerability. He was replaceable. He also knew that he was isolated; he had acted on his own.

James had already contemplated his options. He could attempt to support the truth by pointing out the recent stock transactions by his past partners, but he knew they had probably acquired the stock through one of their untold corporations. Trying to prove and link the partners to the transactions would take time.

Time worked both ways. It would give his past partners the opportunity to make the necessary arrangements to distance themselves from the purchases. But it went with out saying they would also be arranging his own demise. James knew that if he went down the path of government informant, he would be dead before the sun rose the next day. Turning informant wasn't an option. He picked up his secure telephone line and dialed the Southern West Coast Agency. He needed to speak to Director Gamboa.

* * * * *

The director was sitting in his spacious office, faced with a full day of reports to review. The NSA had asked him for his assistance in recruiting a female language specialist who could also turn heads. He had a few women in mind and was waiting for their responses. Recommending these candidates had its own pitfalls. Those select few had to be single without any form of significant other in the picture. They almost always had to be willing to go undercover. Doing so at this level required the agents to create new identities and to lose contact with all of their prior relationships. These agents would fall off the public sector's radar altogether. The Agency would erase their prior identities; for all intents and purposes, they would cease to exist.

Director Gamboa found these selections to be the most difficult. As he studied his most qualified candidates' personnel shields, his secure phone line rang, emitting a unique ringtone to alert him that it was the Chairman of the National Security Committee. His mind raced as he contemplated which unlucky person the powers had added to the knock list. As he answered the phone, he blinked his eyes, forcing back his personal disdain for this part of his job.

"This is Director Gamboa."

"Director, we have a situation." The director bit his tongue to prevent a sarcastic response from blurting out. It seemed that the Committee always had a situation. The Senator continued with his request. "We need to move two people to our Naval friends at Pearl. They are to be shuttled via civilian commercial airlines. We don't want them to be singled out or to raise any unnecessary attention by going through military channels. I want two separate Agency Divisions to handle the transfer. I want your guys for an airport departure confirmation only. We'll use the Northern West Coast Agency for protective shuttle from their current location to LAX."

The director listened without interrupting. The Chairman, James Anthony, had always been detailed and thorough in his prior assignments. This one must be important. Usually, a secure email would be sent. He couldn't remember the last time such a request had been called in. This must be important and urgent. The director pulled the receiver closer to his ear and concentrated on his orders.

"I will personally arrange the transportation. At no time is any of your team to make physical or direct eye-to-eye contact with these individuals. Only you will have their identity. Is that understood?" Taking a deep breath, he waited for the director's response.

"Yes. I understand."

"Are you logged onto the MILNET? I have the information available." The director shook his computer mouse and the screen came alive. He clicked on the icon and confirmed he was ready to receive. Prior to calling the director, he had called Melody and received their information. She was waiting for further instructions.

"I'm ready." The Senator had his message pre-drafted and it was ready to send. After hearing the director's verbal confirmation, he sent the encrypted message. Within seconds, the director received the email. Wasting no time, he opened it and began reading. The passengers would be a man and woman, Curt Anderson and Melody Bergmann. There were more instructions detailing their flight times. The man had a direct flight from LAX to Honolulu, Hawaii. The woman would take the same flight but was also to be taken the next day to Sydney, Australia. As the director read the message, Senator Anthony interrupted his thoughts.

"I need you to print that message now. It is for your eyes only. Then immediately delete the message and power-down your computer. When you've done that, let me know. I'll wait." The director did as he was instructed, staring into the telephone receiver as if he could look through it to see the Chairman. He knew something was up. After pulling the two pages of text off his printer, he powered-down his computer and pressed the phone close to his face pressing the telephone receiver against his ear, concentrating on what was to follow. He wanted to hear everything the Senator would say next.

"It's done. I've got the printout in my hand."

"Good. No more emails on this one. I'll call you back in thirty minutes." The Senator hung up. The director started reading the printout. His neck began to tense as he leaned down, concentrating on this new assignment. Something didn't feel right. He was correct.

* * * * *

The Agency fingerprint analyst had identified only one set of prints that were lifted at the race track. They belonged to a schoolteacher named Melody Bergmann; in California, every teacher is fingerprinted. Nothing matched the second set of prints. To prevent documenting the presence of their agents on assignment, only outside reference and resources were utilized in the fingerprint search. All Agency personnel and independent contractors were excluded. The last thing the Agency wanted was to document the exact identities of their agents. In a twist of fate, this procedure prevented them from locating information they already had internally from Curt's Copy Cat's security clearance. This process helped keep Curt's identity off the radar-for the time being anyway. To prevent these types of situations from happening, the DMV would later change their process by taking the thumb print on all future driver licenses.

The Analyst pulled Melody's public information—her driver's license data from the Department of Motor Vehicles and a full credit report from three bureaus—and began backtracking her past to uncover her personal life.

Within the first five hours of discovering her identity, he had tracked down her home town, located her parents' information, and had her current residence located with a satellite photo from *Zillow.com*. He had mapped out the address with directions from the Agency. As standard operating procedures dictated, this information was organized into a three-ring binder and shelved for later use.

There were so many potential leads created from public killings. It was rare for these peripheral issues to increase in importance to a point that would justify further research. However, as protocol dictated, getting the individual's personal details as soon as possible after the killing increased the Agency's ability to initiate a full, detailed investigation should the need ever arise. If a closer look was warranted, wire taps, physical surveillance, and interviewing of all known associates could be initiated with minimal down time. The Agency wanted to be prepared.

The Analyst labeled the binder and placed it on the shelf with a dozen others. Only after the case file was closed would these potential loose ends be boxed and stored with the entire case file. The Drakeson case was very involved and would eventually require two large case-storage boxes. The Analyst then sent an email to the senior agent assigned to the case to confirm that the follow-up research was complete. He looked back at his in tray. There were three new assignments from the prior evening. He exhaled a sigh of frustration and then reminded himself that he had to pay his dues; it was job security. Glancing at his watch, he opened the next assignment.

* * * * *

Senator Anthony reviewed his notes. He wanted to think through what he was going to say one last time before calling Melody back. He had their transportation resolved. He wanted to isolate Curt and Melody. As he ran through his mental checklist, he kept returning to the most curious part of this situation—how did they know that Drakeson had been killed? It was staged as a heart attack. By now, even the media were reporting it as such. Anthony didn't want to discuss Drakeson over the telephone, but he had to know everything that they knew. He also wanted to keep them from discussing the matter with anyone else. He had to instill a sense of fear in their minds. He had to act fast.

It had been several years since he had thought about her. Listening to her soft voice brought a rush of emotions. He knew he could trust her. He was going to have them both pack their belongings and he would meet them in San Jose. They would drive together by limousine to LAX. The ride would give him enough time to listen to their story and earn their trust. He would do everything he could to make them feel as safe and protected as possible. He had to persuade Curt and Melody that their safety required transporting them out of the jurisdiction of the Agency.

As Anthony had thought through his plan, he had a deep understanding of the Agency's overall structure. This knowledge allowed him to utilize all of the Agency resources, while keeping the activities he needed to take place separate and confidential. Neither division within the Agency would know what its counterpart was doing. He would also orchestrate the focus so that it would appear as if Curt and Melody were a new assignment. Senator Anthony had to prevent the Pacific Rim Division from linking its assignment to Drakeson in any way. Because of the chain of command and security issues, each Agency Division acted as a stand-alone entity. Anthony knew the workings of this bureaucratic system and could use it to his advantage.

As far as the Agency Divisions were concerned, it was a simple matter involving witness-protection detail. The Pacific Rim Division would assign its own senior agent. No communication between the Divisions would be required. Orchestrating this witness relocation was standard operating procedure. Most agents considered these as low-level assignments. They had given the derogatory title of "glorified babysitting" to such assignments that usually involved annoying air travel and brief layovers.

Anthony reasoned that the drive from San Jose to Los Angeles would give him the extra benefit of being able to hear the details straight from their mouths, and to watch their actions and body language. It would give him the best chance at deciding how to resolve the matter. Before he picked up his secure line, he was almost certain Curt had to be eliminated.

He wanted to save Melody, though. As he heard the dial tone and the telephone begin to ring, he couldn't be sure if delaying his decision on Melody was personal or professional. Hearing her voice, he closed his eyes and pursed his lips closed. He felt his spirits rise and almost forgot that the purpose of the call was to resolve the Drakeson issue and not to try to rekindle an old affair. At that moment, he knew that his decision to postpone her situation was motivated by self-interest. Taking a deep breath to clear his mind and regain his focus, Senator Anthony began to speak.

"Melody, I researched the matter and it appears this Drakeson died of a heart attack, from natural causes at a horse track, no less. Why do you believe it was something else?"

"I don't think we should go into too much detail over the phone," she replied. "Curt received some information from some sort of agency. It looks like a government agency." Melody cradled the phone with both hands and spoke slowly, thinking through what she told James. She didn't want to get Curt into trouble, but her primary concern was to assure their safety. She needed Senator James Anthony's help and guidance. The file Curt had copied was most certainly a kill list of some sort. If what these individuals had done cost them their lives, what would happen to someone who had obtained the list? Melody knew that except for Peter Hong, these individuals were U.S. citizens. It wasn't a time of war, and these people had rights.

Pausing, she inhaled to calm her nerves before continuing. "We think Jim Robertson and Frank Marconi were also targeted." Melody listened as James went silent. A cold chill washed over her face. She could sense that she'd hit a nerve of some sort. How could James also have knowledge of these other men, without the benefit of research? She needed to hear his response.

Senator Anthony almost dropped the phone when he heard her mention Robertson and Marconi. As his mind processed their names, he recalled that all of these men were assigned to the Southern West Coast Division's knock list. Closing his eyes and gathering his thoughts, he knew what needed to be done. He had thought through what he would say and redoubled his efforts to stay on point, with only a slight improvisation.

"I don't have any information on these two other people, but I will. As for this Drakeson, there was one thing that seems out of line." He paused for effect. He needed to convince her to meet him. He couldn't risk scaring them away. They needed to trust him, and he wanted to establish himself as their only safety boat for their situation. With this focus, he continued. "Drakeson's body never showed up at any of the local hospitals. The family is up in arms about it, threatening to sue the ambulance company."

"That's weird, isn't it?" interjected Melody.

"It gets even weirder. None of the local hospitals or ambulance services has any record of anyone being transported from the New Bay Meadows Race Track. His body has vanished." Senator Anthony had hoped that revealing these truths would do the trick. He continued to listen for her response. He wanted to gauge what she might be thinking. Unwilling to wait any longer, he pushed a little more. "Drakeson's company is also involved in current weapons defense systems. I think we need to meet."

She looked at Curt. He had listened to every word. She shrugged her shoulders, gesturing to Curt. Taking her cell phone, Curt broke his silence and spoke.

"Senator, this is Curt. I've been listening to everything. I have one question."

"What is it?"

"Do you think we're in danger?" Curt looked up at Melody. They both needed to hear his answer. After a short pause, the Senator replied, "I think you might be."

Looking at the ceiling, Curt continued. "That's what I think. What can you do?" As they both sat on her sofa, Curt reached out and squeezed Melody's hand.

"I'm flying out to the West Coast tomorrow for a meeting in Los Angeles. I'll arrange a flight to you in the Bay Area, and I'll pick you both up at Melody's house. Get packed for a brief trip. Do not discuss this matter with anyone. In fact, don't speak to anyone about anything, at least not until I have a chance to look into this matter further. Don't email anyone. Don't even use your cell phones. We'll drive down to L.A. in the privacy of a limousine. We'll have six hours together. We'll be uninterrupted and alone. We'll be in a safe, controlled environment for you to tell me everything."

Melody and Curt had the phone cradled between their heads. They both struggled to listen to the phone. Curt lifted his head away from the phone and nodded his head in agreement. Melody stood with renewed confidence. "What time will you get here?"

"My flight arrives at 7:28 a.m. your time. I should be to you by 8:30."

"We'll be waiting." With no exchange of pleasantries or endearing good-byes, Melody spoke in a strong voice. "Thanks, James."

"No problem," replied Senator James Anthony. As the line disconnected, he thought through the conversation. He had decided to release as much of the truth as possible. He selected only the information that would, in time, become public knowledge. His goal was to gain their trust and instill enough fear in their minds to warrant his assistance. Anthony felt that he had accomplished his goal.

As he placed the airline tickets for Curt and Melody into his briefcase, he slid them into separate plain envelopes. The last part of his charade was to convince Melody to conceal the fact that her itinerary was different than Curt's for a good reason. He would not explain the last bit of the puzzle until the last moment before they arrived at the airport. They would each be issued their own tickets. Neither would require the assistance of the ticketing agents. The two of them would be hand-delivered to the gate and would be among the first to board.

Glancing up onto his desk, he was distracted by his family portrait. It was taken the year before, just before Christmas. He pushed back the anxiety that was building inside him over this unforeseen development. He reminded himself that he was doing all of this for his family. He almost believed it until he thought about Melody. Well, mostly for his family.

Hawaii

The Senator's limo pulled into Melody's driveway. They had followed his advice and hadn't left her home, accessed their computers, or answered their cell phones. They had dropped out of contact. Curt had a small supply of clothes at Melody's, and they packed only their essential toiletries and casual clothes. If they needed anything else, they could buy it in Los Angeles.

The driver came to their door and instructed them to bring their items to the limo. He informed them that the Senator was waiting in the vehicle. As they entered the large limousine, they saw James Anthony sitting at the far upper section of the passenger area. Smiling, he reached out to shake Curt's hand and then gave Melody a brief hug. He leaned forward and directed the driver to close the separation window. After the deep-tinted dividing window had locked in its upright closed position, the vehicle backed out of the driveway and sped away toward the freeway. Clearing his throat, the Senator spoke.

"We use this limo service for all of our Bay Area meetings. It has been searched for listening devices, and it's clean. The divider prevents the driver from hearing anything we say. I also have a scrambling device." He opened his hand to reveal a small electronic device similar to a compact, hand-held recorder. He depressed a button and a red fluorescent sensor began to flicker as a beam began streaming into the air. "If there is any form of recording device within twenty feet of our location, this device will emit a distinct warning alarm. It also emits a low frequency sound that scrambles any form of recording device. If anything gets by the warning alarm, only an unrecognizable garble of noise will be recorded."

Looking at Curt, the Senator asked him to try to tape a voice message on his cell phone recorder. Curt turned on his cell phone. After a brief delay as it booted up, he tried to tape his voice on his phone.

"Testing, one, two, three. Testing—." At that very moment, an annoying high screech began to fill the limo. Curt stopped to replay his recording. An unrecognizable garble, just as the Senator had predicted, resonated from his phone.

"As you can see, you are free to speak. We are alone, just you two and me. We have a five-hour drive ahead. Curt, please tell me exactly what happened."

Sitting back, the Senator looked at Melody and then at Curt. Curt began to speak. He retold the same story he had relayed to Melody. As before, he omitted any mention of his secret room hidden behind his master closet wall. He focused on how he infiltrated the building, being hired on at Copy Cats, and ran through the list of names inside the file.

He kept speaking non-stop. They had reached Bakersfield on Interstate 5 before he stopped. The Senator had not interrupted, allowing Curt this entire time to speak. As he listened, he watched how Melody reacted to what Curt recited. After a brief moment of silence, he reached into his jacket pocket and pulled out his personal cell phone and began making calls. He had three more hours to get everything ready.

* * * * *

As a United wide-body 747 took off from Los Angeles International Airport, Curt and Melody awoke from their trance-like stupor. The vibration from the jet blast shook their seats, which were bolted to a large plate glass window in the terminal. They made eye contact and exchanged anticipative looks. They couldn't wait to leave California and make their escape. Since the two of them had left the hotel, Melody clutched her carry-on luggage tightly against her chest. The boarding announcement to Honolulu, Hawaii, couldn't come soon enough. It was a nightmare that seemed to have no end.

Curt couldn't believe it had only been two days ago that he had shared with Melody what he knew about the Agency. From that day, their lives had forever changed. The Senator provided his personal escort from the hotel and a promise of constant protection until the final arrests were confirmed. The Senator convinced them that the overt sign of force while delivering them to the airplane was a necessary precaution.

The Senator had explained that they would stay out of the mainland and be under the protection of the Naval Secret Service division and witness protection security team. Since it was unknown how long all the arrests would take, Curt was issued a ticket with an open return date.

The Senator also explained that civilian travel was the safest way to courier them away from danger. Arranging a special military flight on such a short notice would bring unwanted attention. They needed time to investigate and verify that all of this rogue agency's operations were identified and stopped. Until such time, there was no way of knowing if the internal contracts on both Curt and Melody's lives had been halted. Given the direct involvement with the Agency and military intelligence, civilian travel was considered the safest mode. Using non-governmental means to escort the couple to safety, combined with itineraries under false names and using only the Naval Secret Service, was their best option.

As additional precautions, the agents selected to protect them to their safe house had been hand picked. Each agent's personnel records were thoroughly examined. The Senator's personal security team ruled out any candidates who had any potential connection to the Agency. There was no doubt in Curt and Melody's minds, therefore, that the personnel assigned as their escorts were trustworthy. It was clear that until the entire Agency issue was resolved, Curt and Melody's lives were in jeopardy, so they needed all the protection they could get. So far, the Senator's involvement had been a Godsend. He had been true to his word, and all aspects of their departure had gone as explained—until now.

Curt's bloodshot eyes ached. As his tired eyelids closed, they scraped across his weary pupils. He could see two agents sitting at the end of the row of chairs like two formidable rooks on a chessboard. Two different agents were stationed at the corners of the gate terminal areas. Curt was certain that numerous other agents were in the airport area as backup. He felt more comfortable having these four agents on his side. They made no attempt to be discreet. In the center of the aisle, Curt and Melody waited for their flight.

After the Senator heard Curt's story in the limo, he had arranged for them to be shuttled to a government safe house offshore. He had taken them to a discreet office building, where Curt gave a formal statement detailing everything he knew about the Agency murders. It had been documented by a court reporter and transcribed, reviewed, and formally signed as authorized by the Senator himself. While that took place, the U.S. Protective Custody Division finalized Curt and Melody's travel arrangements. If it hadn't been for Melody's contact with the Senator, they would have most certainly been killed. While Curt gave his statement, Melody was meeting with the Senator. It was the first time they had been apart in forty-eight hours.

As Curt's bodyweight settled into the stiff airport chair, he began caressing Melody's hand. In his mind, he replayed the Senator's description of what he believed would be a realistic time frame for the Agency arrests to be concluded. It was during that part of their meeting with the Senator that Curt had made the decision to propose to Melody. It was long overdue. Fear of commitment was no longer an issue. Curt wasn't going to delay the advancement of their relationship any longer. He needed to regain control over his life. This experience had forever changed their lives and strengthened their relationship.

Curt intended to purchase an engagement ring in Hawaii and propose as soon as possible.

"Curt! You're squeezing my hand sooo hard!" moaned Melody.

"I'm sorry. I was just thinking of something." He released his grip, and Melody stretched her fingers, massaging them to regain circulation. The silence of the moment was broken as a little girl and her mother shuffled toward the row of chairs opposite Curt and Melody. The mother looked to be in her late twenties. She wore loose-fitting faded blue jeans and struggled with a duffel bag bulging at the seams. A bright neon orange sweater poked out of a side pocket and displayed crisp new fresh creases. It was in deep contrast to the worn haggard clothes that hung off of the woman.

The young girl looked to be about four years old. She had on faded denim Oshkosh By Gosh coveralls. Her long blond hair was bunched into one large pony tail that swung below her Green Bay Packers knit hat.

"Aren't you hot with the hat on, honey?" The mother's face beamed with the deep love she felt for her daughter.

Smiling, the girl said, "No, Mommy. I like grandpa's present!"

The little girl's cheeks and bright white teeth lit up the waiting area. Since their arrival, an elderly couple had been mesmerized by the little girl's every move. With wide smiles of enjoyment on their faces, they gazed with affection at the mother and daughter. The elderly woman began leaning forward as if to interact with the little girl. The little girl was excited about her flight to Hawaii. She didn't even notice the attention she was receiving. It was their first trip outside of Wisconsin.

Even Melody couldn't resist talking to the new arrivals. "Have you two been to Hawaii before?" The little girl was a pleasant distraction from their current situation.

"No," interjected the mother. "My husband is coming into Pearl Harbor. We decided to meet his ship there as a surprise. He's in the Navy, and we have been planning this for a long time. We thought about taking a military hop, but there's never a guarantee on those flights."

The mother appeared eager to make adult conversation. "The Pacific Fleet will be holed up at Pearl Harbor for two weeks before coming back to San Diego. He's been gone for six months! We're both so excited." the woman explained. "My parents took care of our airfare, and we made arrangements with some friends based out of Pearl for temporary housing. We'll all stay there until he has to head back to the States with the rest of the fleet."

As Curt listened to the conversation, he thought back to similar adventures he had taken with his mother. He was still sensitive to military life. Curt wondered if she realized how the government had altered her vocabulary. She had incorporated the military jargon in her civilian speak and was probably unaware that she even did it. As he looked at this young family going to meet the husband—the father—many unexpected feelings and emotions began to stir in Curt.

The loudspeaker clicked alive as an attractive female attendant stepped forward at the small reception desk in front of the boarding gate to begin her announcement. "We will begin boarding United Airlines flight number 7128. This flight is direct service to Honolulu, Hawaii." As the announcement was read, both of the seated secret service agents bolted to an upright standing position in unison. Making eye contact with each other, they exchanged hand signals to their counterparts who waited in the corner gate areas. It was at that point that Curt noticed a flesh-toned hearing aid device resting in the right ear of each agent.

Curt and Melody stood and shuffled toward the gateway door. The Senator had arranged for them to travel in first class. Being part of that elite class provided not only the luxuries of the in-flight accommodations but also the privilege of being first to board. Curt helped Melody stand. He clenched his tickets in his free left hand.

"Melody, let me get your ticket for you," he offered.

"That's okay. I've got it right in my pocket. It's all ready to go." She smiled at Curt, averting her eyes toward the ticket taker. Curt was somewhat taken back but then realized that she must feel the same way he did. They both needed to regain some control over their lives, even if it meant only holding onto their own airline tickets. Reflecting on what they had just experienced, Curt appreciated the comfort he felt from clutching his tickets. She was probably experiencing the same sense of control and comfort. Those pieces of paper represented more than just airline tickets—they represented freedom.

Curt and Melody remained standing at the gate. The little girl began hugging her mother with an almost exaggerated stranglehold on her neck. She flashed a huge smile. For a brief moment, the little girl's excitement was directed at Melody and Curt. As they began walking toward the gate, Curt looked back and exchanged a warm smile with the little girl. The young mother was urging little Katie to leave her new sweater in the bag. It would be much too hot to wear in Hawaii.

Melody filed in behind Curt, who boarded first. Even though their tickets were already taken and torn by the attendant, they both held their boarding passes and itinerary sheets with a tight-fisted grip. They continued into the tunnel, hand in hand. As they walked, a sense of relief washed over their faces. With each step they took, they were marching closer and closer to safety and freedom. Walking down the stuffy expandable walkway tunnel toward the awaiting jet, they began to relax. The weight and stress of the last seventy-two hours was setting in. The adrenaline rush that had been keeping their minds focused began to wear off. Curt's body began to throb, begging him to sleep.

In the boarding area, one agent watched Curt and Melody walk through the tunnel. He confirmed that their tickets had been scanned and that they had completed their journey through the doorway. The closest agent moved toward the large windows. His eyes peered through the tinted glass, staring at the narrow gap where the plane and the walkway meet, giving the agent a clear view of each person who entered the plane. His responsibility was to report visual confirmation once they had both boarded. After witnessing the subjects enter the plane, he raised his arm and spoke into the receiver mounted inside his cuff, "We have touchdown."

This same agent then turned and nodded toward another agent cradling a receiver from a pay phone booth. On the land line, he confirmed that the passengers had boarded the plane. The man did not wait for any reply and returned the receiver to the telephone holster. Without fanfare, he exited the terminal, walking toward an unmarked van waiting in the loading zone.

* * * * *

Two more agents waited until the plane reached cruising altitude. Limitations were always found in any operation. In airborne situations, there were always brief periods when no communication from the airplane could be obtained. It was like communicating with the first lunar ships as they traveled to the dark side of the moon. They couldn't maintain constant communications. Nothing could be done about the situation, but, given that this was a simple case of transporting some snitches in the witness protection program, there was little concern over the details. It was just another case of glorified babysitting. They had done this type of detail countless times.

One agent would ride in coach and one would ride in first class. All of the background checks of every passenger aboard the United flight checked out. Aside from two DUIs, eleven moving violations, and three late taxpayers, there were no apparent Agency infiltrators onboard. Prior to boarding, another agent was disguised as a male flight attendant in the first class section. This would give the Agency the best surveillance and mobility within the cabin area. Neither Curt nor Melody knew who were working as the onboard protection detail, but they were told that there would be three agents on board.

184

Although onboard security was provided, the agents were doubtful that any hit would be initiated. Taking Curt and Melody out now would be an unnecessary risk, from an Agency operational perspective. Any orders of lethal force would most likely have been placed internally and not from the street. Paybacks at that level were only in the movies. The additional security was merely precautionary.

* * * * *

Curt and Melody entered the plane and were pleased to see that the first class section of the plane was large and spacious. As they walked down the plush first class aisle toward their seats, Curt began to relax even more. Given the popularity of Hawaii, combined with Honolulu's being the gateway to the Pacific, the amount of travel through this island paradise was tremendous. Curt offered Melody the window seat, but she declined. She knew that during the five-hour non-stop flight she would need to make several restroom visits.

Curt glanced back at the spacious restroom and softly smiled at Melody. He pondered that, only hours before, they had been running for their lives. Now, their biggest concern was who had the shortest distance to the restroom. But Curt had never been so wrong.

As they made their way to their seats, they began organizing their personal items and stuffed their boarding tickets into their bags. Curt grabbed both his and Melody's carry-on bags and threw them in the overhead compartment. Watching Curt stow them away, Melody seemed concerned over how roughly he handled her bag.

Curt could tell Melody was concerned and apologetically smiled down toward her. He then reached back up into the overhead compartment and pulled out a book from his back-pack. Then he slid down into his overstuffed seat. Melody glanced up at the overhead compartment before she slumped into her aisle seat.

Dazed and unfocused, Curt and Melody numbly stared forward vacantly at the back of the chairs before them. They were exhausted. As the other coach passengers began filing onto the plane, neither Curt nor Melody said a word.

The male flight attendant approached Curt and Melody. "Would either of you care for anything to drink?"

In unison, Melody and Curt blurted out, "Bloody Marys!" They broke into laughter as they both rarely drank. They not only deserved to celebrate life, but also were in desperate need of alcohol to relax.

As Melody snuggled into the oversized leather chair, the little girl Katie and her mother strolled past the first class seats. It would be a full flight, and boarding would take at least twenty minutes.

The drinks arrived, and the attendant placed them on their awaiting trays. Curt peered into Melody's eyes. In a mock ceremony, they touched their glasses together. There was no need for words. The fact that they were almost in the air, together and alive, was unbelievable. They drank in silence.

* * * * *

The two agents who had been sitting closest to Curt and Melody strolled out of the terminal and headed toward the parking area. The agent assigned with the task of visually verifying Curt and Melody's entrance onto the plane again walked over to the tinted glass and continued to watch the final boarding of the coach passengers. He also watched as the baggage was being loaded in the underbelly of the plane. Another agent went into the snack bar and ordered a drink and hot dog. He would have to remain there until the plane was actually airborne.

As the rest of the passengers handed their tickets to the attendant, another announcement was broadcast over the loudspeaker. "This is the final boarding call for United flight number 7128 to Honolulu, Hawaii. This is the final call for Honolulu. Thank you for flying with United Airlines."

The agent peering through the window watched as the heavy motorized loading ramp pulled away from the plane's underside. The agent stepped back from the window and walked over to the same telephone. The agent in the snack bar casually loaded his hot dog with onions, relish, and ketchup. He was in no hurry.

* * * * *

Curt and Melody had polished off their second drink before the final call was announced. Melody smiled at Curt and explained that she wanted to go to the bathroom before takeoff. They both agreed that they would pass on the in-flight movie and catch up on some much-needed sleep. As Melody walked up toward the lavatory, Curt rose to his feet to return the book to the overhead compartment. Who was he kidding? What he needed was to kick back and get some sleep, too.

Curt rose and opened the compartment. He wanted to find pillows and blankets so he could cuddle up close to Melody during their trip to freedom. As Curt pulled his backpack aside to get to the pillows, Melody's purse fell open. Its contents, along with her airline ticket, spilled onto the bottom of the overhead compartment. Curt grabbed the ticket and began to return it back to her purse when something written on the ticket caught his attention.

He had read his own ticket at least twenty times since their arrival at the airport. He had to keep reminding himself that everything was all right and it was really true. During their wait in the terminal area, he opened and read his itinerary many times to reassure himself that they were escaping to paradise.

It was no mistake. Melody's return flight information was different. Curt folded the ticket jacket and read the itinerary. His heart skipped a beat. Melody's ticketing showed a departure from Honolulu the day following their arrival—a one-way, non-stop flight to Sydney, Australia. *This can't be right.* He read it three times. *What does this all mean?*

* * * * *

As Curt thought back, he realized that Melody had been possessive about her tickets. She wanted to give it to the attendant herself. In fact, at the hotel, she declined his offer to hold the tickets. He had misread her intentions. Curt concluded that Melody wasn't clinging to her ticket to freedom. She was hiding the fact that she was leaving to Australia the next day.

Curt's face flushed a deep red in confusion. He stuffed her ticket and other contents back into her purse and shut the overhead compartment. He slid back to his seat and covered his face with both of his hands. *What is this all about? What am I going to do?* He couldn't ask Melody about the ticket. She had to be involved in this entire affair in some way. He had to think of a way to change the apparent outcome. He had to get off the plane. Curt began to weigh his options. *What am I going to do?*

* * * * *

The onboard escort team was, in reality, more covert in its protection than originally explained to Curt and Melody. This decision was an attempt to draw any loose Agency members out into the open. Although a hit may not be in the works, a tail could be; there was a chance that Curt and Melody may be followed. Neither Curt nor Melody knew the details of why the Agency would still want them dead. But nonetheless, they appreciated the protection provided.

The last agents assigned to board the plane entered the boarding area. They noticed the remaining two agents, one at the concession stand and the other one watching through the tinted plate glass window. Each agent nodded to the others in recognition and respect for their counterparts. The only common characteristic among the agents was their dark sunglasses. Everything was going as planned.

Handing their tickets to the attendant and walking down the tunnel, they were the last passengers to enter the plane. The small, stocky, more senior agent was assigned to the first class section, while the rookie female agent went in coach.

Each agent established eye contact with the male flight attendant and located Curt and Melody before taking a seat.

Everyone was in place. Once in Honolulu, Curt and Melody would be transferred to the land team. The agents settled into their chairs and buckled their safety belts.

* * * * *

Melody came out of the lavatory. Zombie-like, she shuffled over to the nearest attendant and asked, "When can I use the onboard telephone?"

"Due to the potential interference during takeoff and landings, the phones can only be used after the flight is at its cruising altitude," replied the attendant.

Melody forced a smile on her face and returned to her seat. She was too scared for her own life to think about anything but her own situation. She loved Curt, but it was his actions that had set the circumstances in motion. The Senator had made it clear: There was no way to save Curt. She knew that other agents would be on the airplane during their trip.

For all she knew, the seats were bugged. She had no way of speaking to Curt about what she knew. Even if it was safe, she was in survival mode and felt too scared to do anything about it. All she knew was that she would be separated from Curt upon arriving in Hawaii. She would continue on to Australia on a separately flight and await further instructions. If she didn't agree, the Senator's comment made it clear when he said that traveling by air was safer than driving on any highway. This subtle remark needed no clarification. She understood she could do what she was told and take her chances, or face certain death with Curt. It was her choice.

Melody believed her prior relationship with the Senator had saved her life. Of course it had crossed her mind that the Senator was involved. But if he wanted her dead, why go through the theatrics of taking them to Hawaii at all? They could simply dispose of them both stateside. She focused on the fact that she was given a different ticket. She also was not imagining that she was traveling to Hawaii. These facts were the only evidence she had. She had to believe that she would be spared for some unknown purpose.

As she walked down the aisle, she saw Curt leaning over her seat, staring out the opposite porthole window toward the front of the plane. He looked confused and scared. She misunderstood and had no idea that Curt knew something was up. As she sat down, Curt stood.

"I need to use the restroom too," replied Curt. With a forced, thin-lipped smile, he joked that the drinks had gone straight through him.

Curt sidestepped Melody and entered the aisle. While walking toward the restroom, he glanced back. "I've ordered us another round of Bloody Marys."

Melody laughed and settled into her seat. They exchanged brief eye contact before he proceeded toward the lavatory in the front section of the plane. That was the last time he ever saw Melody.

Curt's nerves were a wreck. As he entered the first class lavatory, he couldn't control his hands. They began shaking as he began to hyperventilate. He couldn't understand why his hands were ice cold when he was sweating. He locked the door behind him and splashed water on his face. Leaning over the small stainless steel sink, he contemplated his options. *What am I going to do?*

* * * * *

The flight attendant was preparing two Bloody Marys when he noticed the young woman speaking to his co-worker. After Melody left for her seat, he approached his associate and inquired as to what Melody had been asking. The attendant explained that the young woman wanted to know when she could use the onboard telephone.

This seemed strange to the agent, given that both Curt and Melody had been given specific instructions not to divulge their whereabouts to anyone until the entire Agency issue was concluded. They were warned that it could take up to six months. The male flight attendant started to watch Melody closely. *What is she up to?*

* * * * *

As Curt came out of the lavatory, he glanced down the aisle. The flight attendant was just delivering the drinks. Curt could see his back. As the man bent down to place the drinks on the outstretched trays, Curt could just see the top of Melody's head. Curt quickly shut the door to the lavatory and sidestepped through the hallway toward the front entry door, making sure his face was turned away from the passengers. A different flight attendant was about to seal the front door when Curt approached. She looked surprised and somewhat annoyed at the unexpected intrusion. Curt was gambling that she was not part of the protective team.

"I'm sorry, but my friend just informed me of an issue that needs to be resolved before I can go. I will catch the next flight and meet up with her and my luggage in Honolulu." Curt looked into the flight attendant's eyes and held his breath.

The attendant paused, processing what she had been told. With a polite smile, she reached down, grabbed the latch, and pulled it open. The pressurized seal released with a rush of air as she retracted the heavy door. Curt stopped at the threshold, frozen between where the doorstep of the jet and the boarding gate met. She held the door open, staring back at him with a forced smile. The hot outside air washed over his face, snapping him back into the present.

Curt entered the long walkway ramp leading back to the terminal. With each step he took, he cringed, as if fearing someone would grab him from behind and stop him. He glanced back at the young woman.

"Thanks again," Curt mumbled as he began to enter the expandable walkway.

Walking back the opposite way through the expandable walkway, Curt looked over his shoulder toward the shiny white 747 as its door shut. He noticed the heat of Southern California had already warmed the tunnel. Curt maneuvered around the bend in the tunnel. As he approached the last bend before the long walk back to the terminal, he stopped and peered around the corner. He had no idea what his next move would be. It was only a matter of time before someone would notice his unexpected departure. If the plane could begin taxing toward the runway, he would have more time to figure out what to do next.

Glancing around the walkway corner, he could see the door leading back to the gate and lounge area. Only moments before, he had entered this same door believing that he was on his way to freedom. Now he felt trapped like a cornered mouse. Curt crouched down and sat on the rough commercial carpet. The only light that entered the walkway came from the four-inch door window. No one other than the flight attendant knew he had exited the plane. And no one else knew he was there. Curt decided to wait in the tube until the jet had long since taxied away.

* * * * *

As the 747 began taxing away from the gate, Melody began to wonder what was taking Curt so long. She kept looking at his drink. The glass began to collect droplets of moisture from the condensation. She debated whether to drink his and order him another one when a flight attendant came back from the front of the plane and began explaining the emergency procedures, as required by the FAA. The plane continued rolling to the runway as she explained how to use the seat cushion as a floatation device. At the conclusion of her speech, Melody motioned her over.

"Excuse me, ma'am. Could you please check on my friend in the restroom? He's been in there an awful long time."

"I'm sorry Miss, but he de-planed just before we pushed away from the gate. He said he had an emergency and would catch the next flight. I thought you knew."

Melody's face went white. She didn't know what to do. She stared expressionless back at the attendant. Finally, she broke her silence and blurted out, "Is there any way I can use the phone any sooner?" and grabbed at the headrest in front of her where a telephone was embedded.

"I'm sorry, Miss. We're only seconds away from takeoff. I'll contact the crew and verify the absolute soonest time you can use the phone. I'm sorry." The woman left Melody's side and moved toward her own jump seat near the flight deck and began buckling up. The attendant was confused as to why the man would surprise his girlfriend by deplaning without telling her. She was thinking that it must be a rocky relationship.

The male attendant had collected the first-class beverage glasses just minutes before and was busy with the other passengers in first class. He hadn't noticed Curt's absence. He had seen him enter the restroom and believed that he was just slow in returning. But after he saw Melody's expression, he knew something was wrong.

* * * * *

Curt could hear the roar of the jet as it echoed in the background. He glanced back up the ramp toward the door and could see some activity by the flight attendants. From the small window, it looked as if someone was changing the door sign.

193

Curt waited until the figure had long since walked away from the doorway before he made his move. Curt walked up the ramp and stopped just outside the doorway.

He peered out of the little door window where he saw that only one of the four secret service men remained. He was sitting on a chair finishing his drink. There was a bright yellow mustard stain on his green polo shirt. Curt would have to wait for this agent to leave before venturing from the safety of the walkway.

* * * * *

It seemed like an eternity, but only five minutes had passed. Melody knew that Curt must have found out. She knew that she had to report what had happened to the Senator as soon as possible. She didn't realize that the male attendant had also noticed Curt's departure and was thinking that Curt wouldn't make it too far. He, too, had to wait to reach cruising altitude before he could notify the ground team that Curt was on the run. By the time he had recognized there was a problem, it was too late. Flight 7128 was next in line to take off, and he was already strapped down in the side jump seat. As soon as he could, he would pass through the first class section and notify the other agents of the situation. They had no clue anything was wrong.

* * * * *

Curt's back was starting to bother him as he crouched to look through the glass window. The secret agent was standing in the middle of the main walkway that leads to other gates. He had both his hands stuffed in his pockets, looking into the large airport windows. He must be waiting for the plane to take off before he could go. Curt continued to wait.

Then Curt decided it would be safer for him to go back down the walkway and wait behind the last bend. Just as he began to move away from the door, he noticed the agent turn around and walk down the terminal. The plane had taken off.

* * * * *

The huge jet turned onto the runway. The distinctive engine whine began to vibrate through the entire cabin. An expected but eerie silence settled over the passengers. As in every take off and landing, those few seconds just before the wheels separate from the earth's surface are when fear creeps in and changes the mood and aura of an aircraft.

Melody tightened her grip on the hand rests as the jet began rolling down the runway. As the speed increased, the jet craned upward, the normal forces of gravity pulled down on each passenger as the jet began to move upward to take flight. The forward thrust and increasing speed reached a high constant whine; the nose of the jet tilted upward and then bolted into the hazy Southern California smog.

As the jet engines of the aircraft propelled tons of metal and the weight of the passengers and their belongings into the atmosphere, the recognizable airborne sounds of flight engulfed the cabin space. Although the passengers heard the muted roar of the jet engines, a new, different hissing sound, combined with the changing air pressure, now dominated the senses. As Melody realized that she had survived another take-off, she began to relax and contemplate her changing situation. It wouldn't be long before she could make that call. She had no idea how Curt found out.

The wide-body 747 began to turn westward. She could hear the landing gear retract and was adjusting to the steady hiss of the pressurized air conditioning. She was looking forward to not only cruising altitude but another Bloody Mary. She glanced out of the porthole window and watched the beaches and shoreline disappear to a uniform blue hue. The small whitecaps from the steady breeze were the only thing that disrupted the flat expansive Pacific Ocean. It wouldn't be long now.

* * * * *

Curt waited a few more seconds before opening the door. Luckily, the next flight wasn't scheduled to arrive at that gate for another 2 hours. There were only two people in the entire gate area. There was no attendant at the desk either. Closing the door, he noticed the terminal side of the door was restricted and required a code entry. No such security device existed on the other side of the door. There was no need to secure people exiting a plane, only those attempting to board it.

Curt walked through the gate and entered the nearest bar. He sat at a small table in a dark section of an alcove. He ordered a Coke. He needed to think this through. He knew he had only a short time before Melody and the onboard agents would alert whoever of his change in plans. As he nursed his drink, he watched the *CNN* sports edition update the world on the latest scores. Unfortunately, Cal was losing to Stanford. But it was only the third quarter.

* * * * *

As the 747 began to level off, the flight attendants began to unbuckle and rise up from their jump seats. They then went to their stations to begin preparing the serving carts with peanuts and drinks. Melody was waiting to see the flight attendant she had spoken to during takeoff so she could make the call and order another drink.

The jet engines eased back as it reached cruising altitude of 33,000 feet above the Pacific Ocean. Melody anxiously looked up the aisle awaiting the flight attendant. The safety-belt signs blinked off, and a mechanical bell sounded to let everyone know that it was now safe to unbuckle their safety belts and move about the cabin. Finally, she noticed the attendant she had spoken to; the woman came around the corner and reached for the public address microphone.

"The captain has turned off the seat belt sign. It is now safe to move about the cabin. However, we recommend that you keep your belts securely fastened while you remain seated in the event of unexpected turbulence. Also, we have reached cruising altitude. You may use the onboard telephones." The attendant looked directly at Melody to make sure she had heard the announcement. Wasting no time, Melody picked up the lightweight cordless phone, pulled out her credit card, and slid its magnetic coding along the strip reader. After the green light confirmed that the telephone was active, she started to dial.

* * * * *

As Curt waited for the *CNNSI* edition to come back from commercial break, he had already decided he had to get out of the airport without being seen. He decided to go to one of the gift shops and buy anything that would allow him to blend in with the rest of the tourists. He was contemplating a Disneyland shirt and an LA Dodgers cap when a Nike commercial was interrupted for a special bulletin.

"We have just received word of an explosion off the coast of California. It appears that at least one jet leaving from Los Angeles International Airport has just exploded.

"At this time, we are unable to confirm which airlines or flight or flights were involved. Nor do we have any reports on any survivors. We go live now to Los Angeles."

Curt's face went ghost white. Deep inside his heart, he knew that it was his flight to Honolulu, Hawaii. People began to crowd around the bar, and an eerie silence fell throughout the airport as the *CNN* news reporter made his announcement from a helicopter somewhere off the coast of California.

"We are reporting to you live off the coast of Santa Barbara, California. We were in the process of filming a report on the recent oil spill problems allegedly caused by offshore oil tankers when we heard a deafening explosion. We were en route from the outer drilling platforms when our pilot reported seeing a bright explosion. Thinking it could be another oil platform accident, we broke our flight plan and flew toward the blast area.

"We are flying over the apparent down area. As you can see from the live feed, there are no large pieces with which to identify the plane. However, given the large area of debris, we are assuming that it is a commercial passenger jet. So far we have not seen any bodies or survivors."

During the report, the camera continued rolling live footage of the scene. Large amounts of luggage and pieces of fabric and general debris filled the bar's thirty-one-inch television screen. The bar was still as everyone took in the finality of the situation. It was obvious that there would be no survivors. As the crowd observed the destruction and horror of the screen, the realization began to set in. Everyone in the airport bar was either returning from a flight or was about to board a plane; every one of them, except for the bartender, had just experienced a brush with death. It was as if everyone reached the same conclusion at the same instant. It was a somber moment.

In frustration, people began yelling out to no one in general, just to be heard. "Oh, great!" shouted a businessman sitting at the corner table. "And I'm about to take a flight. That's just what I want to see. If it's a United flight, I'm grounded. I'm not going." His tattered rolling carry-on luggage, tucked under the table and his crumpled suit were a dead giveaway that this man was one of the countless frequent flyers. Other general groans erupted, followed by "Shhh...!"

The *CNN* announcer continued his report. "As we fly around the wreckage, we have a confirmation from the *CNN* studio that a Coast Guard crew is en route as we speak. We are approximately twenty miles southwest of the City of Santa Barbara. We see no other boats on the horizon at this point.

"Wait,... wait.... The cameraman has spotted a large piece of the wreckage. We are flying in for a closer look. Again, this is *CNN* live off the coast of Santa Barbara to report the downing of what appears to be a large commercial passenger jet. As we come closer to the object, it appears to be the remains of the jet's tail fin."

As the Sony TV screen held the onlookers' attention, the *CNN* camera routed live footage across the U.S. and the rest of the world. As the camera shot zoomed in, something caught Curt's attention. He held his breath.

As everyone's attention focused on the damaged tail fin, Curt's attention was drawn to a single piece of debris that floated lifeless in the bottom right corner of the screen. At that precise moment in time, not a single other living human being understood the significance of that footage. Curt didn't need to look at the tail fin. He immediately knew everything about the plane's identity. He knew the airline and flight number. He knew its destination and many of the passengers. Next to the tail fin floated a bright red-orange object. Its fluorescent colors stood in deep contrast to the white tail fin and the blue ocean. It was little Katie's sweater.

"We are getting a distinct marking off of the tailfin," continued the announcer. "It is definitely bluish color. The design is round with a blue and red design...." The announcer's voice changed tone, as if he were asking someone else for confirmation of the insignia. There was now no doubt. As the news media would later confirm, it was indeed United Flight 7128 to Honolulu, Hawaii.

Curt's stomach sank. He was supposed to be on that plane. He was supposed to be one of the statistics of that flight. He rose and began walking to exit the bar before the speculation and commentary on the crash began. As Curt entered the main hallway of the United terminal, he could faintly hear the news reporter's voice.

"It appears to be uh, a United Airlines insignia. We are unable to confirm it at this point, but based on the photo, it appears to be a United Airlines tailfin." the announcer yelled over the sound of the helicopter's rotor blades.

"You're damned right, it's United," shouted the same business man in the crumpled suit. "It's United; I'm not flying today," he grumbled. Everyone in the bar and within the United terminal let out a collective gasp. There was no doubt: The close-up of the crashed tail fin was a perfect match to the huge United insignia displayed outside the wall of the bar. The crowd began looking at their tickets, baggage claim tickets, and disposable ID tags. All of them wore the same, unmistakable United Airlines insignia shown on the television.

"We have received confirmation from the *CNN* studios," the announcer continued. "Based on these live photos, we can confirm that it is a United Airlines jet. We are still awaiting the flight number and its destination. In addition, we are unable to report whether there are any survivors at this time. We can also report that we now have the Coast Guard vessel in view on the horizon. Again, this is *CNN* reporting. We are live off the coast of Santa Barbara."

Shouts of disbelief and anger began erupting throughout the airport terminal. Given the awesome live coverage of the explosion, most of the people waiting to board their planes were visibly shaken over the wreck. The crowd continued to stare at the television in disbelief, and soft whimpers could be heard.

Curt's stomach was turning over and his head was about to split from a sudden headache. He felt nauseated and ran to the nearest restroom. As he entered the room, he threw himself into the first available stall and vomited.

Through the daze and confusion, Curt knew that he had to get out of the airport. He also knew that Melody was dead. He also wondered if anyone alive knew that he had left the jet.

Curt stumbled to the sink and splashed water on his face. Then he scooped a mouthful of water, rinsed out the bile, and spit into the porcelain sink. As he looked up and focused on his reflection in the wall mirror, he had an overwhelming urge to hide. Curt started for the gift shop.

As he exited the restroom, a gift shop was on his immediate right. He quickly dodged into the shop and made a beeline to the novelty area. He picked out a Los Angeles Dodgers snap-on hat, a Disneyland t-shirt, and a pair of sunglasses. He paid with cash and left. He entered the same restroom as before and made a point of avoiding the same stall. He tore off the price tags and pulled the new t-shirt over his head. He shoved his old shirt into the plastic bag and adjusted the cap over his hair. Then he donned his new sunglasses.

As he exited the restroom stall, he studied all the people present. He didn't recognize any of the five men. He avoided eye contact with everyone. Before exiting, he glanced at his reflection on the wall mirror. He paused momentarily as he entered the large expanse of the terminal area, studying each face as he hurried past other travelers. He only wanted to escape somewhere else—anywhere else.

As he rushed through each security checkpoint, he examined the attendants' faces. Again, he did not recognize any of them. He was glad to see that the attendants were concerned with examining people exiting the gate areas. Curt didn't notice any additional security, either. The news of the accident had only just moments before been announced. It was still too soon for the word to begin to spread, but it would. For the time being, it looked like a normal day at one of the busiest airports in the world—a mass of humanity shuttling, waiting, and hurrying to their next destination.

Curt walked for the nearest exit and felt the warmth of the sun on his face. As he walked across the busy frontage loading area, he headed for the nearest curb and hailed the first taxi he saw. As he climbed inside the cab, he barked out directions. He had decided to go home and see if he could get inside without being detected. He wanted to get the file on the Agency and pick up his car, and he needed a place to cool down and think. There was no doubt that it had been his United flight that was downed. He couldn't be seen ever again, at least not as Curt Anderson.

* * * * *

The St. Andrews Bar was quiet. The lunch crowd had already cleared out. Charlie was there as usual, getting the most popular mixes ready for the inevitable rush of the cocktail hour. In the "Capitol City," the first Friday after the summer legislative break was always a busy day. During this early afternoon wait, the only sounds in the bar were the television and his movements. One could hear the tattered rag as Charlie cleaned the bar and the clinking of the bottles as he readied the mixes. There were no patrons.

The front door opened. It was the same quiet figure shrouded in a light brown trench coat. The man's face was tilted downward toward the ground, but Charlie already knew who he was. This time, the man held his dog on a leash and shuffled over to his favorite table. By now, Charlie had come to expect an arrogant attitude from this man. On previous visits, Charlie had told him that only service dogs were allowed inside. But this man of power and privilege simply smiled and ignored him. He did whatever he wanted, wherever and whenever he wanted. Without being asked, he prepared the man a Bloody Mary with two green olives. He also poured a bowl of milk and placed both drinks on a tray. As he rounded the bar, he grabbed the remote control and carried the drinks over to the man.

Delivering the drinks, he said, "It's nice to see you again."

Charlie forced a polite smile and nodded in return. He set the drink on the table and handed the man the remote control. Placing the milk in front of the dog, he was careful not to startle the dog. The dog accepted Charlie's drink, but remained motionless and kept his position of protection next to the man's chair. Charlie backed away from the dog, returning to the opposite end of the bar.

The man reached deep into his jacket pocket, withdrew a black book, and placed it next to the remote control. Removing his leather gloves, he changed the channel to *CNN*. He then pulled a black felt pen out of the breast pocket and uncapped it. He opened the diary to the last entry of names. Only two names remained. He placed the uncapped pen down next to the diary and looked up at the television. *CNN* was showing a live broadcast from a helicopter just off of the Santa Barbara coast. The flight number had yet to be confirmed. The man waited.

* * * * *

Curt instructed the cab driver to let him off at the train station. From there, he took the AMTRAK up the coast as far as it went. It was a beautiful ride along the coast. It traveled from Ventura to Santa Barbara, concluding at San Luis Obispo. The spectacular views of the central coast of California allowed Curt time to relax and think things through. Unfortunately, San Luis Obispo was the end of the northerly route. Curt was overly cautious as he exited the train. He walked into the small college town before him. As Curt shuffled across an asphalt parking lot, he paused for a moment and contemplated whether he should stop for a meal at Café Roma.

Curt made his way to the bus station and paid cash for his one-way ticket to San Jose. As the bus drove to Highway 101, it meandered through the quaint college town environment of the California Polytechnic State University campus traffic. The main one-way streets of Marsh and Higuera reminded Curt of his days at Berkeley. Things were so simple then.

Once Curt's bus left San Luis Obispo, it took another two hours to drive up Highway 101 before entering the southern end of San Jose. As Curt entered the bus depot, the televisions were reporting on the unfortunate downing of the United flight. It took the authorities some time after the takeoff to positively identify the jet and make the public announcement.

By the time Curt's taxi entered his subdivision, it was dark. As he neared the main entrance, a white tow truck with AAA signs on the doors rounded the corner. It was carrying his white VW van. There was no doubt it was his, based on the bright yellow bumper sticker in back and his graduation tassel swaying from the rear view mirror. Curt controlled his emotions and instructed the driver to turn the corner. Curt wanted to avoid a direct frontal view with the tow truck. The tow truck went down Swallow Street and exited the subdivision. The driver appeared to be taking the car toward the center of the city.

Curt instructed the cab to circle the entire subdivision three times before approaching his street. There were no other unusual vehicles parked or pedestrians around. There was no reason for him to believe that the Agency knew he had left the plane and was still alive. The fact that they had removed his vehicle as soon as it got dark encouraged Curt. The Agency must have believed he died in the crash. With no apparent surveillance within the neighborhood, the cab approached his home. A FOR SALE sign was planted in middle of his lawn.

* * * * *

The man reached into his pocket and pulled out a doggie treat, placing it on the edge of the ceramic dish. The dog remained in a sitting position looking into the man's eyes. Only after the man looked at the dog and nodded his head did the dog lean down and take the food. As the dog leaned down, his gold license and tags chimed together. The dog's dark coat was in deep contrast with the shiny metallic collar and tags.

The man had just seen confirmation of the flight number. With the great precision, he crossed out the only two names that had yet to be lined through—Curt Anderson and Melody Bergmann.

As the man stood to leave, another story about the plane crash led the local KCRA 3 News broadcast and began blaring as the man stood to leave. The man nodded to the bartender and reached for the dog's leash.

"Just put it on my tab," the man said, as he dropped a crisp twenty-dollar tip on the table. "I'll probably see you next week," he added.

The bartender smiled and continued to clear the countertop. As he looked up at the elevated television, he called out to the man, "It's a shame about that plane crash, huh, Senator?" After a brief uncomfortable pause, he continued, "I'll see you and Theodore next week, then."

As he walked to the front door, the Senator replaced his notebook into his pocket and replied. "It's tragedies like that one that keep me from flying. There are just too many unexpected accidents that happen these days. We take the train or drive. You can never be too safe."

"Yeah, I know what you mean. Have a good evening, Senator Anthony."

The Senator held Theodore's leash and pushed the heavy bar door. The evening lights broke through the Sacramento fog as he stepped onto the cold concrete sidewalk. He cut across an alleyway that ran behind the Convention Center and up to the Hyatt. As he waited for the crosswalk light to turn green, a white Sacramento County Sheriff's vehicle cruised by. The man looked out at the Senator and gave a slow, knowing nod.

After the crosswalk light turned green, the Sheriff continued down J Street. The Senator and Theodore strolled across the street, heading through the park toward the Capitol. It was late, but he would be expected. The Agency needed to wrap up the final loose ends before calling it a night. Besides, Theodore was getting cold. The Senator hadn't planned on staying out this late. Otherwise, he would have brought the dog's sweater.

* * * * *

Curt looked up the silent, dark street. There were no movements, no cars, and no pedestrians. He jogged to his house and peered through the kitchen window. No lights were on in the home. He glanced back over his shoulder before ducking into the side yard. He shut the wooden gate to give him better cover from any passersby.

He was careful as he pulled out his keys. Turning his butane lighter on high, he cupped his hand and used it like a makeshift flashlight. With patience, he rotated the back door handle, careful not to make any noises. It was no surprise that the Agency hadn't changed the locks. Presumably, only Curt and Melody had a set. They wouldn't be using theirs any time soon. The house was warm and stuffy. He wasn't surprised when he walked inside; everything he had was gone. Standing alone in his vacant living room, he recognized the finality of his situation. As far as the rest of the world knew, Curt Anderson didn't exist.

Entering his bedroom, he was hoping that the Agency hadn't found his secret closet room. Curt rotated the blinds to the window closest to the back of the room. As the slats rotated open, it allowed enough light from the neighbor's backyard porch to illuminate the room. Then he turned toward the closet door.

As he opened the door, he breathed a sigh of relief. The room had not been detected. Pushing his palms against the false wall, he slid it aside. The hum and heat of his computer and monitor screens filled his senses. He squatted into the closet and slid through the door and shut the wall behind him. Inside, he reached up to the green office lamp on top of his desk and turned on the monitors.

As the screens filled with images of his neighbors, he saw no activity. Curt began to boot up his computer.

The Spark

He sat exhausted in the closet. The hum from his computer fan and the low buzz from his desk lamp were the only noises. He saw the folder next to his teapot and debated whether or not to open it. It was his curiosity that had started this entire mess. The comforts of his surroundings gave him a different perspective, gave him courage. He yearned for a sense of normalcy. He turned to creature habits—a cup of tea and a cigarette. Curt was grateful that the electric power to the house hadn't been cut. Curt grabbed the teapot, a bag of green tea, his Oakland A's mug from the closet and headed for the kitchen. They were the only kitchen items remaining. They'd been stored in the closet, a fortunate result of his laziness. There was no substitute for real flame-boiled water in which to steep his tea.

The automatic starter emitted a repetitive clicking sound as it ignited the gas flame. A microwave cup just wouldn't do. He started to feel somewhat normal. He found the moment peaceful. No one knew he was alive. He had searched the Internet for the list of passengers on the United Airlines website. Both his and Melody's names were on the list. He allowed himself to accept the reality that he was now off the Agency's radar. He was dead. No more Agency and no more running. What next?

Curt slid open the patio door and enjoyed the feel of the evening sea breeze on his face. He fumbled with his Marlboro Ultra Light 100 cigarette, struggling to inhale as the butane lighter, still set to high, flashed. As he enjoyed his cigarette, his mind wandered back to the folder in the closet. He knew he was missing something. What had he missed?

The teakettle whistle broke him from his trance. Curt walked over to the stove, lifted the kettle, and poured the steaming water into his mug. The awaiting tea bag tumbled in the boiling liquid as it filled. As he turned the stove top knob to extinguish the flame, the neighbor's dragging a garbage can to the curb caught his attention. The sound echoed through the open door. The gentle breeze carried the noise into his vacant home, rebounding against the bare walls. Curt turned his head in the direction of the door. It was just enough of a distraction. The stove top knob stopped just short of completely closing. The flame was reduced to a thin blue circle. A breeze drifted into the kitchen with just enough force to blow out the tiny flame. The gas cooktop continued to emit gas, slowly filling the kitchen with natural gas.

Curt shuffled across the tile floor and eased the glass door closed. A soft metallic click resonated as the lock engaged. As he carried the mug back into the closet, his mind came back to the folder. He couldn't ignore it any longer. He eased into his rollaway leather chair and opened the file folder. In the other room, the soft hiss of escaping gas continued. It would take some time before enough gas accumulated to be detectable. The gas company had manufactured the gas to include a unique smell so that if the gas somehow escaped it would be easy to detect.

* * * * *

Curt pulled up the remaining names from the list through a *Yahoo* search. He wasn't surprised to learn that one of the remaining people had died in an apparent water skiing accident while vacationing in Arizona. The other two people still had future meeting dates. It would be the second meeting for the investigative reporter and the first for a young rising Congressman from New Jersey.

As Curt lifted the portable hanging folder, placing it back onto the desk, he noticed a single folded piece of paper peeking out from behind the last divider. As he pulled it out, he remembered dismissing it as erroneous and unimportant. His tea mug had long since been emptied, and it had been several hours since his last smoke. He felt the urge for a smoke break but decided to read the note first.

The kitchen had been filling with natural gas. As gas is lighter than air, most of it accumulated at the ceiling. Because the gas density was lessened at the lower areas of the room, the smell was still undetectable. Although the gas continued to fill the area, it accumulated in the upper kitchen ceiling and had not drifted back to the closet area. Curt had no idea there was a problem as he continued to read.

During his visit to the coffee shop, he had obtained Gina's username and password. With this information, he was able to access her *Yahoo* email account. As he scanned her emails, he found numerous messages that were obviously spam. However, one email, sent earlier that day from someone using a military domain, caught his attention. The person was easy to identify, given that her formal name was part of the email address. It was sent by Lt. Colonel Diane Klein. The email title was profound—"I'm So Sorry!"

Dear Gina,

    I am so sorry. If it wasn't for me, you would never have been recruited. If it wasn't for me, you would never have been on that assignment. You should never have been on the plane to Hawaii. If it wasn't for me, you would be alive! It is all my fault. I love you so much. Please forgive me. Ask God to forgive me.

               With all my love,

               DK

E. A. Padilla

Curt's face was frozen in disbelief as he read the message. This Gina person had been on the plane! He began opening other emails to see if he could find anything else about her. In a *Yahoo* folder titled Photos, he found one. It was a picture sent by one of her friends. The young woman was standing next to a convertible and bore a huge smile. The sender had titled the photo "Nice Ride!"

In that instant, Curt remembered that he had seen this woman before. As he recounted the week he surveyed the Agency building, it came to him. It was the attractive woman who had entered the building. Curt squinted as he studied the photo. He was certain it was the same person. He thought back, trying to recall if he had seen this woman enter the plane. He and Melody had been one of the first people to board. After several moments, he was certain she had not boarded. He had waited for all the passengers to board before he had ordered the drinks. He remembered wanting to look at the face of each person who boarded. He was certain hers wasn't one of them.

With no hesitation, Curt clicked on the message to reply to Lt. Colonel Klein. He began typing at a furious pace. "It was no accident. The Agency purposely took the plane down. They killed your niece." Instinctively, he moved the curser over and clicked Send. The message was instantly sent.

He pushed himself away from the desk and exhaled, exhausted. It was time for a smoke break. Out of habit, he walked out of the closet, making a beeline to the sliding glass door. He was a creature of habit, and he tried to smoke outside. Melody hated the smell of smoke. He pulled his cigarette lighter out and began to strike the butane lighter. As he exited the closet, the flame setting was on high. Curt still hadn't adjusted the lighter's flame back to normal; as the lighter ignited, the flame still stood tall. Curt entered the kitchen, inhaling to assure that the cigarette was lit. As he approached the confines of the kitchen, he released the lighter and the flame extinguished.

210

Pacing through the kitchen, Curt stretched his arms toward the sliding glass door latch. His face recoiled as his nostrils detected the strong acrid odor of natural gas. The cigarette was fully lit and his face was angled toward the doorway in the direction he was walking. The door slid open and Curt could feel the fresh cool outside air begin to rush inside. The combination of events caused a delayed reaction— the angle of his head, the height of the cigarette. It was a perfect set of circumstances. For a brief moment time stood still.

Curt glanced backward into the kitchen area, and for a brief moment nothing happened. But subconsciously, his brain began to process its surroundings and recognized the danger in the situation. A soft breeze entered through the open door-way and interacted with the burning cigarette. The increase in air flow caused the end of the cigarette to burn more intensely. The increase in oxygen caused the tobacco to burn hotter, emitting an almost white flame surrounded by bright orange embers. As the breeze continued into the doorway, a fleck of the burning tobacco separated from the cigarette and floated into the air.

Curt's eyes bulged as he saw the small fragment of red ember drift away from the cigarette and float into the kitchen. It drifted upward, floating deeper into his home, propelled by the outside breeze. His mind processed the danger before his waking consciousness understood its significance. Without thinking, Curt began to raise his armed to protect his face.

The gas at the ceiling ignited. An eerie mixture of lights, flames, and gas whipped into a storm cloud of flames. It smoldered and grew in an instant. The last thing Curt saw was a brilliant, all-encompassing blast of light, followed by super heat as the full reaction took effect. He never felt the pain of his burning flesh as the explosion threw him through the glass door. Both his arms broke as the blast wave forced his limbs back against his face. One wrist twisted backward, grossly extending his muscles so that the small metacarpal bones pierced his skin, causing multiple compound fractures across his entire wrist. As the flames hit his body, his clothes ignited in a flash of heat, melting the fibers into his legs and chest.

The entire house lifted off its foundation as the explosion expanded and increased in strength. The available oxygen entering through the doorway increased the magnitude of the explosion. The empty house acted like a cylinder inside a combustion engine, like an explosion that forces the piston downward. The blast could be heard by residents in the surrounding cities. When the resulting shock wave jolted the buildings, many residents believed they had just experienced an earthquake. The house was reduced to a heap of sticks. The explosion blew out the fire but still damaged every house in that section of the subdivision.

The calls began to pour into the 911 telephone emergency system. Meanwhile, Lt. Colonel Diane Klein had just received an email. As she read the name of the sender, her face froze in disbelief. It was from her dead niece. She looked at the screen. She didn't move a muscle and couldn't bring herself to open the message. The shock and guilt of her niece's death invaded her senses. Tears pooled in her eyes and a single drop slid down her cheek. Ignoring her tears, she gathered the courage and prepared to open the message. Her face flushed and turned red from her increased body temperature. *What does this mean?*

* * * * *

"I'm so sick of this!"

It was the week that the surveillance tapes were archived. It was an Agency ritual. All rookies assigned to the security detail had to pay their dues in archiving the surveillance tapes. It was a guaranteed six months of boredom. Although their job function focused on watching the compound twenty-four, seven, three sixty-five, there was something to be said for watching a videotape of events that had taken place thirty days prior. True, it was like watching a rerun, only worse, with no immediacy, no sense of urgency. Indeed, it seemed like an exercise in futility because, if a breach in security had taken place, its discovery would only document some event on an after-the-fact basis. Who wanted to watch surveillance tapes where nothing happened?

With any job, the initial days were exciting. A person learns new tasks, meets new people, learns new responsibilities, and trains on new equipment. Experiencing something different brings its own rewards. In the Archive Department, the boredom usually set in on the second day after lunch— watching the same views, seeing the same people doing the same things. After twelve hours, the boredom would start to overwhelm a technician's mindset. It was a natural phenomenon that the Agency had seen time and time again. For this reason, they restricted the compression and archiving to only one full week during any given month.

No one had ever discovered anything out of the ordinary. However, because it had become part of the standard training protocol, no director ever removed this task from the training procedures. Regardless of the fact that everyone deemed the manual review of these surveillance tapes as a complete waste of time, not a single director chose to remove the procedure, for fear of it coming back to bite them. The bureaucratic cover-your-butt decision was implemented and destined to be perpetuated generation after generation.

"When's that new guy from Monterey gonna take over?"

A loud electronic chirp echoed at the door as the new guy pushed the heavy steel door open. A sense of relief washed over the technician's face, and his shoulders drooped as the stiffness in his muscles began to relax. He had already been training the new guy for the entire week. It was tradition that the formal changing of responsibilities took place the first Friday after lunch. The senior technician's smile was from ear to ear. A childlike euphoria seemed to possess him. He had survived archiving. He was free at last.

The new guy strode confidently to the terminal and control panel. He was excited at this new opportunity. It was now going to be his signature on the archive records. It was now his opportunity to find something unusual, out of the ordinary. He had taken the sign-in logs and knew that the videos for the janitorial crew and copy firm technicians were coming up for review. He had also considered a potential source for espionage was during the delivery of gasoline from the tanker trucks. He had concluded that these events represented the best chance at discovering something.

This new rookie took on this challenge similar to how he'd approach a jigsaw puzzle. He had the patience. He looked back at his past accomplishments as president of his chess club in high school and college as proof of his past performance. He had become the top student in his language class by mastering basic Russian and German, as well as finishing in the top five percent at the famed Monterey School of Languages in advanced Spanish and Portuguese.

He didn't see the idea of archiving as boring or part of some institutionalized hazing ritual that he had to endure. This man took the task as a personal challenge to his pride. The assignment was viewed as even more challenging, given the abbreviated time constraints of the assignment. As such, he had been contemplating how a spy would attempt to infiltrate the Agency, and he focused his energies on those points of entry. Intuitively, he knew that spies truly existed. His task was to document their existence. His personal challenge was to find the evidence buried somewhere within the surveillance tapes.

It wouldn't take long. Curt's tape was only six viewing hours away from being archived. That videotape had already been pulled and sat cold on the archive table, waiting to be compressed and reviewed. It was just a matter of time.

* * * * *

Rule One Twenty

Across town, Curt's body had been excavated from the debris. He was still alive, but his body was charred beyond recognition. He was being strapped down on a gurney to be taken to O'Connor Hospital.

* * * * *

Diane's pulse fluttered. Her neck turned bright red from her increased blood flow. Pursing her lips, she almost bruised her index finger as she clicked the mouse to open the email that had been sent from her niece's Yahoo account. As Lt. Colonel Klein reread the message, her mouth dropped open and her heart skipped a beat. *How is this possible?*

* * * * *

The EMT readjusted the oxygen mask attached to the victim's face. Curt's features were unrecognizable. Most of his hair had been singed away; only the hair on the back of his head, just above the collar, remained. The skin on his face was blistered a bright pink, reflecting the interior lights of the ambulance off the clear fluid that had seeped out of his pores. The reflection was similar to headlights bouncing off water that had pooled on a wet street. A large splinter protruded from Curt's cheek. Both arms had sustained compound fractures. After cleaning the wounds, the EMT set Curt's forearms in a temporary Velcro brace and then looked down at the victim. He knew that if the man he was treating survived, he would have to endure many months of pain and countless operations.

The ambulance sped away, its red flashing lights reflecting off the houses in the court. The neighbors were standing on their front lawns and watching the ambulance speed out of the cul-de-sac. A young woman holding a child close to her chest stood motionless like a statue, mesmerized by the steam that rose out of the rubble. She awoke from her trance when she heard the clanking of a fireman's ax as it was reattached to the

215

storage area on a large fire engine. Her face was expression-less. She turned and reentered her quiet, lonely home and closed the door.

As the ambulance hurried toward the hospital, Curt drifted in and out of consciousness. He heard a distant siren and could distinguish a blurry red flashing light just in his field of vision. He felt swollen and puffy, with an intense numbness through-out his entire being. His ears were muffled and had a distinct high-pitched ring, but in only one ear. His body was in com-plete shock, with too many injuries to comprehend. His system did the only thing it could do and shut down all except its most basic functions: Those systems that controlled his ability to breathe and pump blood remained on line. As he lost consciousness, his brain began to swell. Without immediate attention, Curt would not survive.

The ambulance exited the freeway and began dodging surface street traffic, slowing only at intersections before crossing. The emergency room had already been notified, and a burn specialist was en route. The triage nurse lifted her head as she heard the siren approach. The waiting room television ran a live feed from a traffic helicopter reporter. The aerial view showed a black charred blot as if a smart bomb had made a direct hit in this otherwise quiet suburban neighborhood. The newscast cut to a ground crew that was recapping the events. They confirmed that a victim had been found and was being transported to O'Connor Hospital. The identity of the survivor was unclear.

The ambulance pulled into the ER back access area. As the victim was rushed into the operating room, the other patients could detect a distinctive smoky odor similar to that of a campfire. One of the patients stood and watched the person being wheeled past him in the hallway, and his nostrils recoiled at the smell of burning flesh. A man in the lobby heard the commotion but turned away and took his seat. He raised his hand to his face as he watched the live report continue on the lobby television. The unique smell lingered for several minutes after the victim was taken to the operating room.

Curt almost didn't survive his eight hours of surgery and had to be resuscitated twice. When the surgeon finally came out of surgery, he reported to the nurse that the victim's likelihood of survival was going to be hit or miss. If he survived beyond three days, they would reassess his prognosis. Assuming he survived, he would be moved from the recovery room and then placed in the intensive care unit. Without any identification and the fact that no one had come to wait for the victim, the patient's identity was unknown. His clipboard chart was identified as John Doe.

* * * * *

The new technician had the surveillance room reorganized the way he wanted. He had a fresh stack of sticky notes, the labels were neatly organized, and his working table and keyboard were still damp from a disposable Clorox wipe. He had a fresh Dr Pepper sitting on a coaster. He had been viewing the tapes and compressing the CDs with the required detailed labels. He felt a sense of accomplishment when he attached the first label that bore his name and badge number. This was his first work product for the Agency. It was his name.

He had already made a procedural change in his system. In order to view more tapes, he utilized the high-speed dubbing and fast forward. He would wait until he had copied one of the tapes onto CD and begin the second copy before he viewed the earlier copy. He would fast-forward the copy through the static non-action sequenced pieces. Using this technique, he was able to cover more hours of viewing time while still accomplishing his goal of copying and personally reviewing the surveillance tapes.

His focus and personalization of his task made the time pass extremely quickly. If his supervisor, Mr. Mills, hadn't dropped by to check on his progress, he probably would have missed his scheduled lunch. As he exited the room, the rookie looked forward to the next tape. Based on the log timeframe and date of the next tapes, he knew that most of the activity would take place there. The copy machine technicians were scheduled that day for their monthly maintenance of all of the machines. As such, the rookie knew that this would be an opportunity to evaluate the actions of the outsiders. He had reasoned that focusing on all activities of outsiders was his best chance.

Upon returning from lunch, the rookie copied the tape of the lobby camera first. As that tape was being copied he loaded the other four cameras that focused on photocopy machines. He was dubbing five separate tapes at the same time. When he asked the other technician who trained him why he wasn't making multiple copies at the same time, he was told that making the copies wasn't the issue; he still had to manually view each CD. He explained that it was a waste of time. The rookie disagreed and rationalized that fast-forwarding through the static portions was still meeting his directive of manually reviewing the tape.

As the copying was completed, he began reviewing them in sequence. Studying the lobby, he watched two men enter the room and be greeted by the receptionist. He toggled the magnification to get a close up of the outsiders. The lobby tape continued and he saw two other people enter. Based on their attire, he knew they were being interviewed. They were still outsiders, so he studied the figures and watched their every move. There was very little activity in the lobby area, and he fast-forwarded through that camera. He completed the labels, signing and dating them. He moved to the next copy and took a long swallow of his now warm drink. When he saw the copy technicians meeting in front of one of the main copy machines, he leaned forward in his chair, watching every move. One of the technicians left; the other remained to work on the machine.

The rookie's eyes bulged with excitement as he watched the copy guy open the machine, place a suitcase down on the carpet, and begin his work. The rookie adjusted his chair and decided he would watch this sequence of tape in real time. As he leaned forward into the monitor, the display showed an agent approach the copy machine area. He zoomed in and could see the copy guy look up at the agent from his crouched position on the carpet. The two men spoke, and then the agent left the camera view. The agent left something on the table next to the machine, but the camera was at an angle so the rookie couldn't quite make out any details of the object.

The rookie's face tightened as he concentrated on the monitor. The copied CD hummed on the player. The viewing area was quiet except for the high-pitched whines from the CD reader. The rookie continued to watch the monitor and saw the copy guy stand up from his crouched position and turn his head from side to side, as if trying to determine if he was being watched. The rookie blinked back in disbelief. He interpreted the copy guy's behavior as suspicious and out of place. He cursed the monitor, speaking aloud to no one in particular that he wished the camera was at a different angle than the view it was showing. He only had a view of the copy guy's back and an obscure view of the table and contents.

With the copy machine to the right of the copy guy, the man reached into the machine and detached a separate compartment inside the machine. Then, the copy guy reached in front of his body but out of the view of the camera and brought a stack of papers to the machine. He then fed them into the machine. Papers then came out of the machine. *Is he making copies?* As the rookie watched this sequence of events, he stopped the machine. Raising his gaze to the ceiling, he thought back to the same sequence of events that he watched during his training. When the other man worked on the machines, he hadn't copied anything or brought out any papers. *Did I overlook something before?*

It was unclear where the original papers had come from. The rookie pressed play and continued to watch. The monitor showed the copy guy feed a stack of papers into the machine.

In rapid succession, copies came out of the machine. The rookie's cheeks puffed out in contemplation. He was certain now that in all of his prior viewings of the other copy guy, this had never been done. The rookie's pulse quickened. He felt a sense of excitement and his curiosity grew. His concentration became even more focused. He hit rewind and replayed the entire sequence ten times. He reviewed it in super slow motion, in reverse, and at normal speeds. He was certain that the copy guy had been testing the machine to make sure it was functioning properly. Continuing his viewing, the rookie became more perplexed when the copy guy placed the copies into his briefcase.

The rookie jotted a note down to focus on the surveillance tapes of all of the copy machine maintenance that this new copy guy performed that day. His thoughts jumped to camera 43. That camera angle documented the hall traffic along the wall, giving a view opposite to the one provided by this camera. With some zooming and focusing in the upper area of that shot, he might be able to see what was going on from that angle. The rookie continued to think through how he could see where the copy guy had pulled the original papers. After spending forty-five minutes contemplating the situation that in real time took only four minutes and twenty-three seconds, he finally allowed the copy to continue to run forward. Then he saw it.

As he watched the copy guy place the copies into his rollaway briefcase and step away from the copy machine, the rookie could see an unmistakable agent case folder. It all made sense. The rookie's mind went into overdrive. The agent who had approached the copy guy had left his folder on the table. The rookie had missed it before because the agent and copy guy's bodies had blocked the camera's view. But now, there it was in plain sight. The rookie stopped the CD and sat motionless. His eyes darted up and down. *Is this something? Did the copy guy really copy the agent's folder?* As the tape ran, he watched the agent return to the now unoccupied machine, pick up his folder and make a single copy from the folder. The agent carried the folder away with him out of the camera's view.

The rookie didn't want to overreact. It was probably something that the new guy had been trained to do. *He didn't copy the folder, did he?* Before jumping to any conclusions, the rookie decided to pull all the tapes of this new guy. He probably did the copy deal on every copy machine. He finished off his warm drink and began to copy the other tapes. He didn't want to get behind his taping schedule. As the tapes were copied, he tracked down the cameras that focused on the copy machines. There were ten copy machines in the building. The rookie wanted to be one hundred percent sure before he brought this to anyone's attention. The last thing he wanted was to make a fool of himself.

As he continued with his copying of the tapes, he considered that the new copy guy might simply have been following a new procedure. It wouldn't take the rookie long to see the inconsistency in Curt's actions. He had only made one set of copies. He wasn't testing the machines. It was all there, documented on the surveillance tapes. It was just a matter of time.

* * * * *

Diane had read the email a dozen times. How could this be possible? She knew with one hundred percent certainty that her niece had been on board that *United Airlines* flight. She had called her home and cell phones on countless occasions following that incident. She had attended the funeral and laid a single rose over the empty grave. The guilt rushed into her mind as she recalled how difficult it was for her to make eye contact with her sister. Her sister had no idea that her daughter was working at the time of the accident. She thought that Gina had taken that long awaited vacation. Everyone who knew her niece recognized her ambition and dedication. Her friends expounded upon the years that Gina had prepared and planned for her future. She had it all—looks and brains.

After the accident, the Agency had a floor meeting where the director had explained that three of their newest agents were involved in a terrible domestic plane accident. He explained that they were on a training exercise in basic surveillance and were to be debriefed in Honolulu. It was a reward for making the cut and to get some R and R on the Agency's nickel. Each Field agent appreciated the grueling training that rookies would under go in the coming months. These reward missions had become a ritual that each seasoned veteran looked back on with fond memories. The director had even passed out memos detailing the bios of their fallen comrades in arms. Many tears were shed that morning.

Diane Klein—the citizen, not the hardened Lt. Colonel—stared out her kitchen window. She was just beginning the second week of her vacation. Marriage never entered her mind. It just didn't suit her lifestyle. The Agency and her career were her life. She had remained single. Her vacation was uneventful, with no particular plans. She just needed time to think things through. Her life had become complicated.

But now, after receiving the email, she didn't know what to think. *Who sent it?* And more importantly, *Why did the sender place blame on the Agency?* To help her understand what had happened to her niece, she had confirmed with the airlines and through her contacts that the cause of the crash was a reverse thruster malfunction. So it had been a mechanical malfunction, not an act of the Agency.

As she contemplated the circumstances, she thought of an old colleague, Glen. This man had a history with the Agency. He had retired and opened his own computer consulting firm. He was a Cal Tech graduate who loved anything and everything that had to do with computers. Diane opened the yellow pages and started dialing. If anyone knew how to track down what was going on with the email, it would be him. She was right.

* * * * *

Curt's surgeries went as well as could have been expected. The surgeon and hospital personnel had no one to contact on the victim's behalf. He came to them with no identification. Not a single inquiry had been made to the hospital regarding their victim.

He remained in the intensive care unit with his chart listed as John Doe. He remained unconscious and continued to sleep under deep sedation. His burns required his skin to be aggressively scrubbed clean. When he stabilized, he would be moved to the burn unit. Until he regained consciousness, it would be unclear whether he had sustained any brain damage.

It was almost certain that he would sustain significant hearing loss. The doctors expressed concern about his vision, but all of these questions would be answered only if and when he awoke. The amount of burning he sustained left no question that he was not yet out of danger. Although his hands and arms had snapped like a twig from the blast, they protected his eyes and nose in the process. There was a distinct singe burn pattern from the outline of his forearms. He had an unusual effect from the burn that was similar to the striping on a zebra. The obvious main difference was the color of the stripes. They were bright lobster red, not black and white. If the patient survived, he would undergo numerous skin graft surgeries.

As the nurse finished changing Curt's dressings and adjusting the IV needle, she studied his face. She couldn't help but feel sorry for the man.

No one had inquired about his condition. She pursed her lips and continued with her work. She checked his pulse and glanced at the monitors. As she closed the curtain, she glanced back one more time and wondered what he had looked like before the accident.

The patient remained unconscious for the next four full days, and even then he stirred only during brief periods. The room was quiet as the monitor emitted a weak electrical tone that mimicked his heartbeat.

* * * * *

The rookie was beyond excited. He knew with absolute certainty he had found something. What it was, he wasn't certain, but it was unusual enough to report to his superiors. He had copied and reviewed every tape recorded that day. It confirmed that once and only once had there been anything copied. Only at the first machine, and only the one time, had the new Copy Cats guy manipulated something inside the machine and then made copies.

The rookie had a separate CD that chronicled his findings. He had the specific incident copied at full speed, slow speed, and super slow motion at three different magnifications. He even had a two-part recommendation for future follow up. He was recommending an interview of the copy guy supervisor, having him view the evidence and then explain what had transpired. Then, he recommended obtaining detailed information about the copy technician's entire personal background.

The rookie sat peering at the still image of a man bent in front of copy machine. He continued to ponder the idea that this man was a spy. If he was, they didn't want to scare him away. With the approval from the surveillance superintendent, a recommendation could, with proper supporting documentation, order direct daily surveillance. The Agency would need to know to what extent the espionage had gone. The rookie began to focus on the technician's clothes, his shoes. *Who does this guy work for?* He was leaning toward the Russians, but the Chinese or North Koreans were still a possibility. *What was in that file, anyway?*

His excitement was in full bloom. His eyes were wide and his breathing elevated. He gathered his research and took a quick glance at his appearance in the window reflection. He reached the superintendent's office and walked in. Mr. Mills raised his head from a paper covered metal desk. The rookie stood in front of the superintendent without speaking. Mills raised his eyes, pressing his bifocal glasses with his index finger. As he widened his eyes, the rookie spoke.

"Mr. Mills, I think I found something."

* * * * *

"So how have you been? It's been a long time."

"I'm so glad I could talk to you, Glen. I've got an issue that I need some help on."

"Do you need me to come down to the Agency?"

"No, no. It's not related to that at all. It's a personal matter. I think my *Yahoo* email account was somehow compromised. I know you're busy, but you're the only one I trust enough to look into this matter for me. I'm really concerned that something bad has been happening."

A brief silence echoed over the telephone line as Glen digested what Diane was saying. He had too many years as an Agency operative to miss what wasn't being spoken. His personal relationship with Diane gave him a greater insight into the distress in her voice. He had been her first supervisor for the Agency, her mentor. During that brief telephone exchange, despite the four-year gap since he had last spoken to Diane, he could sense something was seriously wrong.

"Diane."

"Yes."

"I'll come to you right now. What's your address?" Before Glen hung up the phone, he had the address mapped out and the directions were being printed. It would take him eighteen minutes. As he walked out of his office, he instructed his secretary to clear his calendar for the afternoon and to hold all of his calls. He had a personal matter to attend to that would require the rest of the afternoon.

* * * * *

The surveillance superintendent had reviewed the CD with the rookie. At first, Mills expected the typical zeal he had seen from the other rookies. It was something everyone did, like clockwork. Each agent felt somehow compelled to find something. It was almost a science in human behavior—a foregone conclusion. It made the most sense. The newest agents assigned to the Surveillance Archive would never be more focused or enthusiastic than when they first entered the Agency. The boredom wouldn't have set in. New agents had that fresh energy, that laser focus. They were still open to the real possibility of a breach in security. However, until today, nothing of real importance had been uncovered. Today was different.

The superintendent felt his pulse quicken. This kid may have found something. "Get Copy Cats on the phone. I want their HR department to pull all the information on that technician. I want you to pull all subsequent dates forward. I want to analyze every single time one of those guys touched *any* of our machines, especially that new guy!" Mills voice had continued to rise with each word he spoke. As he finished his sentence, Mills almost sprayed the rookie with saliva.

"Yes, sir."

"I've reviewed your recommendations and agree." The rookie's facial muscles tightened with determination. He had found something. Based on the superintendent's reaction, it was something very important indeed. The rookie lifted his eyes, absorbing every one of Mills' gestures and innuendos. "Good job, rookie!"

The superintendent felt like a bear awaking from a long extended hibernation. He looked down at the papers on his desk and now viewed these reports as part of his past; a past that held mundane rote responsibilities.

His position over the internal surveillance of the Agency, although important, had never resulted in anything tangible. During his tenure, they had never uncovered anything of substance. After all these years, his sense of urgency and the perceived value of his department to the overall Agency enterprise had diminished.

Today was different. Intuitively, it was going to change for many years to come. This event was a wake-up call. Mills felt re-energized. As he pushed away from the desk, he couldn't recall the last time he'd had anything meaningful to discuss at the weekly department-head meetings. This week would be his. He had two days before that meeting. He wanted the information dialed with a solid recommendation.

"When can I expect to get the information on that Copy Cats guy?"

With confidence, the rookie stood and met Mills' stare. "It's already done. I'm waiting for a call back."

Mills' face changed. A broad ear-to-ear grin replaced a once defeated expression. It was the first time the rookie saw the superintendent's perfect teeth. Mills' cheeks were about to burst from the force of his muscles. With a quick nod of his head, the superintendent instructed the rookie to have the information faxed over.

"I want you to ride herd on this one, rookie. Place a call every hour. If we don't get it by 2:00 p.m. today, I want you down to their office in person. Got it?"

"Yes, sir!" It was 11:07 a.m. The Copy Cats Company had less than three hours to comply.

* * * * *

Glen and Diane sat at her kitchen table. The atmosphere was thick with confusion. The mood was almost manic. Their conversation would cycle from her niece's death to the accusation from the unknown emailer. The seesaw of intensity in the conversation was emotionally draining.

"I agree with you, Diane. There seems to be no doubt that your niece was on that flight. You've already checked her cell phone and there were no outbound calls. The last activity is just before she boarded the plane. I don't think we need to check her credit cards. So let's do as you suggest. Let's find out what computer sent that email."

"How do we do that exactly?"

"You said the email came from her personal *Yahoo* email account, not her military one; right?"

"Yeah."

"The security on those accounts is a joke. Has Gina ever used your computer?"

Diane thought back. It was several months prior to her interview, when Gina had stayed the night. They had a great visit and Diane had shared some exciting overseas adventures she had in her early years. She chastised herself as she remembered telling Gina those stories. More memories of how she brainwashed her niece into taking this job. Her shoulders had drooped and her head listed forward as the guilt sank deeper. She blinked back her memories and whispered her response.

"She did. She pulled up her emails after we checked for movie times."

Glen could see the pain in Diane's face. He swallowed and continued with his analysis. "If she accessed her email from your computer, then we have her email user name and password."

Glen pulled out his laptop and copied a file to a CD. He inserted the copy into Diane's personal computer. The program was used to access protected passwords. It was commonly used to apprehend hackers and child pornographers. In a few seconds, Glen had accessed the hard drive and the monitor displayed every person who had signed onto the computer and where the person had searched. On the screen, the username and password were clearly displayed.

"We now have her username and password. Let's look at her sent emails."

Glen opened the folder and found the email. As he opened the email, printed it, and opened other items, he immediately noticed different IP addresses.

"Diane, she sent emails from many different locations. Let's find out where she was when she sent the one you received." Glen made several calls to isolate the ISP address and placed a single call to his office. Within twenty minutes, he knew it hadn't come from a cellular or wireless device; he had the physical location.

"Diane, let's take a ride."

* * * * *

The rookie sat in front of the fax machine, organizing the information. He spoke to the new guy's supervisor and had scheduled a face–to-face meeting at the Agency. It was 12:46 p.m. The supervisor would be there at 1:00 p.m. sharp. He had some time to brief Mr. Mills and get his input on having the Copy Cats supervisor view the surveillance tape. He also had meeting room one set for full interrogation and video documentation.

The rookie gathered the last fax into the folder and made a beeline to Superintendent Mills' office.

"Mr. Mills." The rookie leaned his head through the open doorway. Mr. Mills was just finishing a submarine sandwich from across the street. With wide eyes and mayonnaise in the corner of his mouth, Mills finished his last bite and chased it with a furious inhale on his straw.

"Whatcha got?"

The rookie handed over the faxes and the folder. "The name of the Copy Cats tech is Curt Anderson. He was a new recruit who allegedly wanted to start his own copy firm. But interesting enough, he only made it to work for one day. After he came to us, he never returned. Don't you think that's strange?"

Superintendent Mills looked through the file. The scanned image from Curt Anderson's temporary badge had been printed in full color. Mills pursed his lips and nodded. He now had a detailed photograph of the intruder.

"What about the other guy, the supervisor?"

"I have him coming in at 1:00 p.m. I personally spoke to him. He's scared. I've got meeting room one ready. The interrogation protocol is in place. I really think we should have that supervisor look at the tape and get his reaction."

Mills smiled. "Good one. I want to know what those pricks were up to. Get the polygraph guys warmed up. We can ice this guy all week if we have to. Good job, rookie. Good job!" The rookie stood by as Mills reviewed the folder. Then Miller's desk phone rang.

"Sir, a Mr. Alex Moeller from the Copy Cats firm says he has a one o'clock meeting with you. But we don't have him scheduled for maintenance until Friday."

"It's okay. I need to see him. I'll be right out."

As Mills hung up the phone, he stared at the receiver. "Who was that?" Mills shrugged. "It must be a replacement. It didn't sound like Diane Klein. Follow me to the reception area." As they entered the lobby doorway, the security guard informed Mr. Mills that Lt. Bishop was working the front desk and that Lt. Colonel Klein was on vacation for two weeks.

With all of the unscheduled activity, the Agency personnel could sense that something was up. Even though neither the rookie nor Mills had discussed the case or their suspicions with anyone else, everyone had noticed. The change in normal routines—faxes, outbound calls, an appointment with a vendor, the rookie with the boss—everyone knew something was up. Everyone was on full alert and fully concentrating. Something was definitely going on.

As Alex Moeller waited for Mr. Mills in the lobby, he couldn't understand why a meeting had been called. He was confused, feeling vulnerable and somehow responsible for something. One of the machines probably went on the blink and damaged something. Moeller's mind started cycling through all the possibilities. He was wondering if it had anything to do with Curt Anderson. *What might I have exposed my father's company to?* He started to connect the dots and figured that Anderson's disappearance was no coincidence. The man that Moeller spoke to on the telephone had been more than demanding. He made him feel like he had no choice. The Agency was Copy Cats' biggest client. *Something must have gone wrong. Maybe Anderson did something, and that's why he didn't come back or answer his calls.*

As each minute passed, Alex became increasingly agitated. Nervous? That was an understatement. He was unable to harness his emotions; it was as if everything was out of his control. He continued to pick his fingernails and comb his fingers through his hair. As he looked up at the wall clock, he began to massage the back of his neck, looking for any relief. As he closed his eyes, two large doors burst open into the lobby. A loud metallic noise rang out, echoing through the lobby as the lock disengaged.

"Mr. Moeller?"

"Yes."

"Please come this way."

* * * * *

"Glen, do you really think we could find out what's going on? I mean, what are we going to do, even if we do find the location? Are we going to go up and ring the doorbell?"

Glen looked back at Diane. He had never seen her in such distress. Her eye sockets were gaunt with deep dark-colored circles underneath. Her normally pristine hair was somewhat disheveled. She looked like she hadn't slept for days.

"You know, a picture tells a thousand words. Let's go back to basics. We might just learn something from the house, his car, whatever. Is it an isolated home without any neighbors? Is the yard kept up? What kind of neighborhood is it anyway, the 'hood or an upper top-drawer lifestyle? You know the drill, Diane, the basics."

Glen continued to maneuver the vehicle and followed the directions. Diane felt a sense of embarrassment for acting so flustered. Glen had retired from the Agency years ago and he still knew what to do. He simply followed his training and did what came naturally. Diane's self-chastising was written all over her face. Her facial features twisted with disgust at her inability to stay focused. Glen knew it was one thing to analyze someone else's situation, but self-examination was one of the most difficult tasks to accomplish. The human tendency to evaluate a situation was contaminated by self-interest. It's always easier for someone away from a situation to be more balanced in their analysis. An uninvolved party has no stake in the outcome, regardless of circumstances.

"You're just too close to it, Diane. Just too close."

As the vehicle turned into the subdivision, they both reverted back to their professional nature and Diane's comfort zone. Without further prodding, Diane began to verbally report her immediate observations and opinions.

"An upper-middle-class neighborhood; looks to be white collar, judging by the vehicles. Also, notice the absence of cars on the streets or in the driveways. They're actually using the garage space for their cars, not as a storage dumping area. The lawns all neatly manicured, probably strict CC&Rs from the association."

Glen nodded in agreement. As they entered the cul-de-sac, their eyes focused on the obvious charred out ruin that had once represented a home. Although the flames had been extinguished days before, the deep charcoal-colored framing members piled in a heap dominated their view. As they read the adjacent house numbers it sank in with a powerful jolt. The address where the message came from had originated from the charred house. Diane's face contorted in disbelief.

"What the hell!" she gasped.

* * * * *

"What is Curt doing?" Alex's face sagged as his mouth hung open. He stared at the large flat-screen monitor as the CD replayed the tape. Alex closed his eyes and inhaled. He knew at that instant that he had been duped. This problem was all Alex's fault. He had found Curt and rushed through the interview and background clearances.

He watched the tape for a third time, this time in super slow motion, and recalled the innocent way in which Curt had approached him at the sandwich store. It was all a setup. Unable to meet the agents' gaze, in a monotone voice, with the energy draining out of his voice, Alex finally spoke.

"He's disabling the counting mechanism. And then he made copies from the file that the man left in the folder. There is no doubt in my mind. Curt Anderson had to have been a spy."

The rookie and Superintendent Mills sat motionless in disbelief. As the admission began to sink in, they turned their heads toward each other. They didn't have to say a word. Their eyes told the story. They had done it. Mills had waited his entire career for this. As the rookie watched Superintendent Mills stand, it finally hit him that this was beyond a big deal. It was huge. He followed Mills out of the meeting room. As the automatic lock engaged behind them, Mills instructed the lobby security guard to keep Alex Moeller on ice. The rookie followed Mills into his office like a dog waiting for a morsel of food from his owner. The rookie sat opposite Mills. A brief silence permeated the room. Mills bolted upright out of his chair and, almost yelling, barked orders at the rookie.

"Go get a car from Ad Services. We're going for a ride."

The rookie was startled into action. Eyes bulging from the sudden increase in blood pressure, the rookie ran out of the office.

* * * * *

Glen and Diane sat in the car, their faces frozen. The energy in the air inside the car stirred from all the increased brain activity. The skin on Diane's temples shook as her brain demanded more blood.

A dark green Mayflower moving van roared into the cul-de-sac, breaking their trance. It parked across the street from Anderson's house and the crew began opening the bay doors and rolling hand trucks and carrying boxes to the front door. A young Asian woman opened the door; she carried a young child in her arms.

As the workers invaded her home, she walked out to her front yard, staring at the burned-out shell that was once Curt Anderson's home. She appeared aged beyond her years, and her eyes betrayed a deep sadness. Like someone who had exhausted her energy reserves, she bent down and placed her child in a bouncy chair. As the baby began to rock his body, the woman stood, continuing to stare across the street.

* * * * *

"Let's see what the neighbor knows."

Diane nodded in agreement. They crossed the street toward the young woman. Glen took the lead and spoke first. He'd said "Excuse me" several times before she even noticed their presence.

"I'm sorry," she replied. "I just can't seem to concentrate. I space out all of the time. Can I help you with something?" The young woman's face flashed a smile that seemed out of place; a pose really, a social conformity.

"I'm sorry to bother you, but we're looking for someone who used to live there." Glen pointed his index finger at the burned out rubble across the street.

"What a tragedy. I heard from the realty company that— excuse me, are you family?"

"No, no, we're just friends. Well—"

"Oh, you know, every one was shocked. Curt Anderson seemed like a nice man. He recently died." Her voice was rapid, as if she hadn't spoken to anyone for a long time. As if she was trying to get as much conversation out of the encounter as she could. She seemed eager to hear someone else's voice. It was a reprieve from some unknown isolation. Both Glen and Diane exchanged inquisitive glances.

"How did that happen?" Diane pried.

"The real estate guy said he was involved in a plane accident. It was all over the news. He must have been going on vacation. The plane was heading to Hawaii."

Diane's head jolted backward from the news. It was as if the words had attacked her mind. She physically recoiled. She squinted as if to begin a full interrogation of the woman. Glen watched Diane process the information. Her eyes shifted from side to side as she contemplated the questions with which she was preparing to bombard the woman. On instinct, Glen turned his attention toward the woman and sidestepped in front of Diane. He reached behind his back, motioning with his hand for her to calm down.

"Was anyone hurt in the fire across the street?"

The woman paused and held her chin with her hand as if cradling it. In a slow, thoughtful response, the woman continued, "Yeah, there was. It was weird too. The home had been vacant. The relatives must have placed it up for sale. The firemen found a man buried under the debris. He was found outside of the home at the fence line. They were checking the neighborhood to see if anyone was missing. Originally, they figured he must have been some unlucky guy walking his dog. He was in the wrong place at the wrong time. But no one was missing. They just let everyone in the cul-de-sac know that they took him to O'Connor Hospital, just in case anyone came around looking for him. He was very badly burned. No ID."

As the woman finished her story, Alex and Diane had moved so that the three of them stood side by side, peering across the street. After a brief moment, Glen thanked the woman and led Diane by the hand back to the car. Diane was in shock and remained silent. She sat motionless in the passenger-side seat, looking out the front windshield. Glen closed her door and hurried to the other side. He fumbled for his keys and started the vehicle. After exiting the subdivision, he pulled into the first shopping center they came to and parked the car.

"Do you think it was Curt they took to O'Connor Hospital?"

Diane looked up. "It had to be him. Did you hear what she said? He was supposed to be on the same airplane my niece was on. This is no coincidence; the email blaming the Agency; the airplane; the home for sale. It has all the signs that the Agency was involved. Curt knew something. He knows what happened and why Gina died. He blames the Agency. She was on a training assignment. Curt—or whoever wrote that email—knows about her death. He knows something."

"Okay, okay. Let's be smart about this. As far as we know, no one knows that this Curt guy sent you anything—right?"

Diane nodded.

"Fine, then. No one knows he's maybe still alive. For all we know, it was a neighbor walking his dog. Let's do this: I'll go back to my shop, research the passenger manifest on the plane. You go to the hospital. Do you know where it is?"

"Yes. My sister delivered Gina there."

"Okay. I'll get as much information as I can on this Curt Anderson guy. We need to determine if the survivor even fits his age, ethnicity, or whatever. See if it could even be possible that it's him. We need to be as sure as we can about his identity before we bring anything up about the email. Wait in the hospital parking lot until I call you with what I've found. Then go see if you can visit the man they pulled out of the house."

Her energy renewed, Diane agreed. She now had something other than her grief to focus on. She had a mental distraction, a riddle to unravel. As Glen drove back to his office, Diane's determination gradually grew into anger and resentment. What if the Agency was responsible? If it was true, the government she had dedicated her life's work toward had murdered her niece. She opened her passenger window to feel the rushing air against her face. As she ground her molars, she found an intense focus of energy. Someone was going to pay. Diane was a woman on a mission.

As she exited Glen's car, she gave him a quick hug and almost sprinted to her car, yelling over her shoulder, "as soon as you get Anderson's bio, call my cell. I'm going to the hospital."

* * * * *

Superintendent Mills and the rookie parked their nondescript Ford Taurus. Neither spoke. From the front windshield, their view was dominated by the burned-out rubble that had once been Curt Anderson's home.

"We need to let the director in on the situation. I want you to work on an abbreviated report. I'll put a cover memo with my recommendations."

The rookie sat in the passenger's seat. He couldn't believe his luck. It was a dream come true.

"Yes, sir. It'll be on your desk before the end of the day."

* * * * *

"Diane, I've got Curt's information. I compared it with the information from the hospital. It's possible that their John Doe is, in fact, Curt."

Diane sat calmly in her car, listening to Glen's report. She had been waiting in the parking lot for his call. This was the only thing that made sense. Curt was involved in the Agency somehow. Maybe he was one of the independent contractors working for the A-Team.

"What room is he in?"

"Room 315." After a brief pause, Glen added, "Diane, be careful."

She walked into the hospital and went to the gift shop. She paid cash for a large bouquet of flowers and then proceeded to the elevator. Hiding behind her large sunglasses, with her hair tucked under a baseball cap, she pushed up the sleeves on her large jacket. The sleeves bunched up at her elbows, making it difficult to hold the flowers in front of her face. Keeping her head facing the ground, she entered the elevator and depressed the elevator button with her gloved hand.

* * * * *

Superintendent Mills sat in the director's front office waiting area. The secretary had hand delivered his report to the director himself. He was almost finished with a meeting with one of the senior agents. She had confirmed with the director the importance of Mills' visit and made sure he knew he was waiting to discuss the matter.

Mills couldn't remember the last time he had been so involved and preoccupied with his career. The last few days had renewed his energy and his interest in his department. This discovery and subsequent investigation into Curt Anderson had changed his perspective. In a strange way, Anderson's actions, although treasonous, had forced Mills to re-evaluate the importance of his own role. His presence was significant. Upon reflection, his appreciation for his department grew; his efforts were in fact honorable and very important. It was as if he had forgotten this at some point, but recent events had awakened that memory. In a twisted way, Mills was thankful for Curt Anderson.

Mills felt different now. He found himself sitting up taller and carrying himself with greater confidence than before. He had been making more eye contact with other personnel. He was awakening from his bureaucratic slumber. His job was important. His efforts were important. He was important. His life had meaning.

Mills glanced up at the director's secretary and exchanged a soft confident smile followed by a gentle nod of his head, in acknowledgement that he understood and appreciated how she handled his important matter with the director. She made a mental note that she had some how misjudged Mr. Mills. He was a much more positive person than she remembered. He

238

was probably a good manager. Rebuffing herself for her initial assessment of his character, she settled into her work and began to type a memo the director had dictated earlier that morning. Mills sat, waiting for his turn.

* * * * *

Behind closed doors, the director was concluding his face-to-face meeting with the senior agent. This assignment was especially complicated, given the magnitude. Not only did the assignment involve countless victims, but it involved agents—his agents. Given the inexperience of the three rookie agents, combined with the directive to immediately and permanently resolve the matter, it had been his decision alone to take the plane down. Containing the leak and the existence of his Agency and undercover agents was of top importance. The dubbing of the *CNN* report of the bust that was shown to Curt and Melody was a piece of art. It was amazing what could be accomplished through computers and the right motivation.

"John, this was a difficult case. I don't know how that Anderson guy had access to all of that data, but it looks like it's all over."

The director continued to read the 102-page report detailing all the events leading up to the clearing of Anderson's personal belongings and the forging of documents. The report always included with exact detail how all physical evidence was resolved. Much time was spent verifying the destruction of each piece of evidence that had any possibility to bring attention back to the Agency.

"Now what's this about no computer? That's weird, isn't it? I mean a computer science major from Cal Berkeley, and he doesn't have a computer?"

"We thought so too, but the agents at the airport had visual confirmation that Anderson carried his laptop onto the plane. We searched high and low, so we're confident it went down with the plane. As such, it's in pieces, resting at the bottom of the Pacific Ocean. We tracked his Internet usage and all known email accounts. As protocol dictates, we continued to monitor all of his financial accounts up until yesterday, when I closed the file. It was silent. No activity at all. No safe deposit boxes, no unusual parcel charges on his credit, debit, or by check. He could have paid cash, but we hear nothing on the telephone taps of all his known associates. We have all of his potential contacts on tap. Only the regular chatter—discussions about poor Curt, bad luck, etc. Nothing's popping up unusual."

The senior agent sat silent, waiting for the director to look up, anticipating any additional questions. The director continued to leaf through the thick report. Knowing that this case had followed protocol, the director closed the file and reviewed the closing facing sheet. Every box had been checked. It was already signed off by the senior agent. It was time for him to ink it and formally close the file.

"Well, that's that."

The director opened his top drawer and pulled out a large rubber stamp and his red-colored ink pad. He jammed the stamp deep into the ink pad, rocking it back and forth to assure that it was fully engorged. Pounding the stamp resonated in the director's office as he slammed the impression onto the cover page, transferring the image onto the front page. He glanced at his wristwatch and recorded the exact time of his signature. The inked impression confirmed the director's authority through his signature and the embossed seal that the case was now formally closed. He then placed his right thumb into the ink pad and pressed his thumb below his signature before looking up.

"Make sure it's DIRECTOR ONLY security filed. No copies. This is only the second one of these I've handled," instructed the director.

"That other one was mine, too, Director."

Pursing his lips and nodding his head slightly, the director remembered. "That's right. I want all the taped conversations, real estate dealings, and any and all other items pertaining to this case on my desk this afternoon. I have to personally secure this one away in the DIRECTOR ONLY safe."

"It'll be here by 4:30."

The agent stood to leave. "Hey, Bill." The senior agent was startled. The director never used first names. He turned and faced the director. "This one was ugly, real ugly. Good job."

"Thank you, sir. I appreciate it."

As the senior agent exited the office, the director placed the file on the corner of his desk. Then he glanced at his in tray. It was the last report of the day. Earlier, his secretary had interrupted his meeting. It must be important enough for the superintendent of internal surveillance to wait outside his office. The director wondered what could be so important that Mills wanted to discuss the matter face to face. As the director opened the folder, the first heading made his blood pressure jump. It was captioned "Certain Security Breach." As he read on, the name and picture of the person of suspicion caused a physical reaction. The director moved his hand to his face and gasped. Curt Anderson's name and a full-face picture stared back at the director. Under his breath, he muttered, "What the hell?"

* * * * *

In the director's lobby, the intercom buzzed. Using the phone, she said, "Yes, Director?" After a quick exchange, the woman's facial expressions changed. Her face tightened and her lips pursed tightly together. "I'll get him in there right away, sir!" She hung up the phone and turned to Mills.

"Yes, the director needs you in his office right away."

Mills was startled by the sudden burst of energy from the secretary. The sense of urgency and pitch of her voice said it all. The director must have just looked at his report.

"Superintendent Mills, please go inside. The director is waiting. Another senior agent from A-Team will be joining you shortly."

Mills clutched the gold-plated doorknob to enter the large double doors. He couldn't have imagined that the A-Team would become involved. As he opened the door, the director stood and waved him inside. It was Mills' first visit into the director's inner sanctum. He was beyond impressed at the furnishings and vast space. Mills couldn't help but compare his office to that of the director. It was in complete contrast to his own glorified enclosed cubicle.

"Superintendent Mills. Please sit down. I've got a senior agent coming as we speak. Right now I need you to give me an abbreviated version of what you found out about this Curt Anderson character."

As Mills was about to begin, the door burst open and an agent from the A-Team entered. Catching his breath, he sat in the chair next to Mills. "John, Superintendent Mills was just going to tell us about a breach of security that his department uncovered." As Mills began to recite his tale, both John and the director exchanged looks of utter disbelief. It was as if this Anderson guy would never go away.

The Awakening

Diane walked down the sterile hallway and looked into the intensive care unit. She could barely see anything as she peered into the unit through a small glass window. The duty nurse glanced up to see someone at the double doors and stood from her chair, waving toward the woman. Before entering, Diane pushed her sunglasses against her face. Taking a deep breath to calm herself, she pushed the heavy double doors open and walked into the ICU.

"Can I help you?"

As controlled as possible, she approached the nurse and spoke. "Yes, I have been trying to contact my brother and was told he may have been taken here. His name is Curt, and he was somehow involved in an explosion at his house. It happened several weeks ago. Is he by any chance here?"

The nurse broke into a huge, ear-to-ear grin. "We do have a patient from an explosion, but we had no identification for the man. He has been doing much better. You are the first visitor he's had!"

"I went to his house, and a neighbor told us what had happened. I called ahead and was told he was in room 315." Diane kept her face hidden behind the bouquet and turned her head down the hallway. She was certain that the nurse never got a good look at her. Diane peered down the hall and could see into only the first couple of rooms. The rooms were divided by glass walls so that the staff could look directly into the room. The construction design increased the likelihood that the nursing staff could notice a patient in distress for situations that the monitors were not designed to detect.

The nurse understood the woman's preoccupation and constant glances into the adjoining glass rooms. She empathized; the poor woman was still trying to track down her brother's whereabouts. She might be able to positively identify the man and, with that information, they could track down his insurance company. The hospital administrator had already started calling their desk to see if anyone had come forward with his identity. She was certain that getting even his basic information would help the hospital recover its expenses.

"Let me take you to his room." The nurse led her down the hallway before making a turn. The front door was open to room 315, but a doctor and nurse were in the room. The duty nurse turned back to Diane and explained she could visit the patient to see if it was her brother after the doctor and his nurse had made their rounds.

"It looks like Dr. Braisher is making his rounds. You'll have to wait about a half hour. Will that be okay?"

Diane pivoted away from the doorway. She didn't want anyone else to see her in the hospital. As she walked back to the entrance of the ICU, she replied "Sure, sure. No problem."

"On the main lobby floor there's a cafeteria. The food is actually pretty good. Did you want me to hold your flowers for you while you eat?"

Diane reluctantly handed over her camouflage prop but did so only after she had tilted her head downward and away from the nurse. Diane pivoted on her heels to face away from the nurse and hurried out the doors of the ICU. Before the doors closed, she almost yelled back through the swinging doors that she'd be back in forty-five minutes.

The duty nurse was eager to tell Dr. Braisher that they may finally have John Doe's true identity. As she placed the flowers on the end table, she heard the other nurse telling the doctor that during the night the patient had shown signs of gaining consciousness. His pain medication had also been reduced.

In this way, as he came to, he'd be better able to communicate with the doctor. They were out of the woods as far as the patient's surviving the ordeal, but they all knew that he had many skin-graft and plastic surgeries in front of him at his next stop in the burn center. Once he fully stabilized, he would be transferred to the Burn Unit at Stanford Medical Center.

"Nurse?"

"Yes, Doctor."

"I'm not sure, but I have a feeling our Mr. John Doe may finally become fully conscious sometime today. Even a brief period of wakefulness would give us the opportunity to see which of his senses have been affected. He had three separate stirrings just last night. If his sister shows back up, let her stay with him at his bedside. Given his physical condition, I'm not sure she will be able to make a positive ID. At the earliest, he probably will not become conscious until later this evening. I don't see any harm in letting her stay with him; it couldn't hurt." With a shrug of his shoulders, Dr. Braisher updated John Doe's clipboard chart and continued making his rounds. As the duty nurse closed the heavy glass door to room 315, she glanced back at the patient. His forehead and eye were covered with a gauze bandage. His breathing was deep and strong. He was looking much better today. With a satisfied smile, she returned to her desk.

* * * * *

Mills was just concluding his verbal recap of events. Both the director and senior agent sat motionless and awestruck. Could Anderson have somehow survived the plane crash? Might he have returned home and then been involved in that gas explosion? Their faces became tight, and the stress of this new information cut deep furrows into their wrinkled foreheads.

"Mills: No word of this to the general population. Is the rookie the only person not on the A-Team who knows?"

"Yes sir, but our department personnel know something's up. We still have the Copy Cats supervisor locked up in room one."

"Keep it that way!" shouted the senior agent. The director's brain went into overdrive. "We need to know if anyone was in that house when it caught fire. John, I want three A-Teams assembled, ASAP. We need to know if anyone was transported to a hospital from that location. We need to speak to every single neighbor. We need to revisit all known associates of Curt Anderson—family, friends, and co-workers. First priority is ambulance services. John, I want you on the lead for that task."

"I'm on it!" snapped the senior agent. He bolted upright and jogged out of the office. Before he exited the director's lobby, he had pulled his cell phone and was talking to someone. John ordered the three most experienced teams to an immediate meeting. He grabbed the box full of the documents he had prepared for the director's safe. That would have to wait now. As he carried the box into the A-Teams' largest conference room, he began to divide some of the documents from the box into three separate stacks, placing them into neat piles on the expansive table. Men began to enter the room. Once all the team members were present, John instructed everyone to turn off all cell phones, pagers, and any and all other electronic devices on their persons.

He then walked over to the audiovisual control panel and entered a security code. This system activated a high frequency scrambler to interfere with any and all known electrical devices to prevent any possible transmission, copying, or eavesdropping from inside or outside of the room. The last time such measures had taken place was when Hinkley had attempted to assassinate President Ronald Reagan. John stood rigid at the lectern, both hands gripping the corners of the wooden pedestal. His clenched fists caused the tendons in his knuckles to bulge. He elevated his head and addressed the group.

"We have suffered a breach in security. I've separated the available documents into three categories. Each team will pursue single-mindedly your specific assignments. Do not bother yourselves with the details peripheral to your assignment. There will be time for that later. The single most important goal of this assignment is that we need to know if in fact this man still exists." The senior agent turned on the overhead projection screen. In full color, blown up on the screen, was Curt Anderson's temporary security badge from the Copy Cats firm. Each team member studied the image with a burning intensity.

"My personal directive is to determine if anyone was found dead or alive at this suspect's last known residence. If any survivors were found, where were they transported? Alpha Team. I want every possible conveyance considered. The most obvious is by ambulance, but consider any and all means of transportation possible—taxi, limo service, shuttle bus, even bicycle. We know that the location was recently destroyed by fire. I want to know all about that fire; When? How? Who responded? Were there any survivors? What was the cause? The origin? Was it an accident?" The senior agent gulped for breath before continuing, "Bottom line, did anyone, I mean *anyone*, survive that blaze?"

With bulging eyes and a strained face, John glared at those in the room, daring anyone to utter a sound. The intensity of the situation was electric. The sense of urgency was beyond obvious. The importance of the situation was raised to the highest level any of the agents had experienced, second only to 9/11. A sense of panic and disbelief dominated everyone's minds.

"Alpha Team, you got it?"

The five members of that team stood and nodded their heads in unison. "Then go, now! I'll meet up with you there. Alpha Team, what are you waiting for? Go!" The Alpha Team stormed out of the conference room almost running to the adjacent main-floor open area to begin their work. The last agent from Alpha Team almost dropped the documents as he hurried through the doors.

The senior agent glared at the two remaining teams. "Team Bravo! The immediate neighbors adjacent to Anderson's last known address. I want every single neighbor interviewed. What do they know? If they're not home, where are they? If they're out of town, when and where did they go? Flash your badges and push everyone hard. The kid gloves are off. Scare them, intimidate them. If you think someone's hinky, full court press: credit ratings, home phone calls, place of employment; everything is fair game. What do they know about Anderson?"

The Bravo Team didn't hesitate. Once the senior agent stopped speaking, they rose from their chairs, gathered their documents, and stormed out. John continued with Team Charlie.

"Now your assignment is all known associates. You have the most tedious task. I want to start with Anderson's telephone calls, computer, same for all known associates. The bastard was supposed to have died on Thursday, August 30th. Everything should have gone silent from that day forward. As with any incident, any inkling of activity from anyone, in any form, will be a concern."

Before Team Charlie could storm out of the room, he deactivated the frequency scrambler, grabbed his cell phone, and dialed out to the Alpha Team. He walked toward the door and froze in the doorway. His face distorted as if he had just inhaled straight ammonia.

"You're fucking kidding me!" The senior agent paused in deep thought before proceeding out of the conference room. "Meet me in the director's office now!" He snapped his cell phone shut and hurried back through the building. Charlie Team members couldn't remember if they had ever seen their boss in such a state. They gathered their documents and began their assignment in earnest.

The director had just sat in his high back leather chair when he heard John return to the reception area outside his office and ask to speak to him. Before his secretary could announce his arrival, the director stood and opened the door. The senior agent's face was ashen from the stress he was under. His eyes were wide with excitement and disbelief. They entered the office and slammed the door closed.

"What is it?"

"Someone survived the fire," the senior agent replied. "He was transported to O'Connor Hospital. The team has confirmed that a John Doe is recovering in room 315. The patient has started to come back into consciousness. He was in a coma since the fire. What do you want to do?"

The director knew what protocol dictated. If somehow Anderson had evaded the plane accident, as incomprehensible as it seemed, he had to be eliminated—now. There was no time for elaborate planning. The Agency term for such situations was Snap Shot. The translation was an immediate elimination. The director glanced at his family portrait on his desk. Gathering his thoughts, he turned his attention back to his most senior agent.

Knowing what was about to happen, John organized his thoughts. He knew the next assignment was going to be his. It was his initial case. Anderson was his problem. As the director made eye contact, John, without waiting for him to speak, mustered his confidence and spoke.

"I got this one. Regardless of this guy's identity, it's the *One Twenty Rule.* It's an urban issue. This guy, whoever he is, was definitely in the wrong place at the wrong time. If it's Anderson, well then, he has it coming anyway."

John blinked back his eyelids to clear his thoughts. The director was still amazed at his agents' abilities to transform from office paper-pushing bureaucrats into highly skilled professional killers in a single breath. The director allowed John a moment of silence to fully organize his thoughts. With a final deep inhale, John pushed back from the director's desk and stood.

"I'll make a full report tomorrow morning."

With no further discussion or hesitation, John exited his office. The director opened his back armoire to reveal a panel of monitors that showed the views in crystal clarity of the interior and exterior areas of the Agency building. After a short delay, the senior agent's image was documented on the surveillance camera as he exited the building. The director deduced that John must have stopped off in A-Team's supply room for some necessary supplies.

He saw a dark figure with a familiar stride. The man had covered his eyes with dark sunglasses and was wearing a baseball cap. He was also carrying a large jacket tucked under his arm. As the figure cleared the view of one camera monitor, the image reappeared from a different angle, captured by yet another camera. The director continued to watch the figure open the door of a nondescript, tan-colored, four-door sedan. The director adjusted a knob on the console, causing the view to zoom in.

As the monitor image refocused on the zoomed view inside the vehicle, he focused on the GPS mounted on the dashboard. The figure in the vehicle interacted with the GPS, and the director could see the small screen illuminate street grids with directions. The device brought up the destination coordinates in large, bold script. It found the location and identified it as O'Connor Hospital. The instructions indicated that it would take the driver approximately forty-five minutes. It had accounted for traffic.

The director turned away from the armoire and closed its solid wood doors. He locked his room and set the key pad sensor alarm securing his office. As he walked through his office lobby, he spoke.

"I'm calling it a day, Sandy. See you tomorrow."

"Good night, Director."

"Good night."

* * * * *

Curt's muscles began to stir. He could remember brief periods of consciousness. He thought back and recalled a sense of fear, extreme pain, a surge of heat, a blast of air, and then nothing. His brain started to retrigger, and for the first time in weeks he began to reorient himself into an awareness of his surroundings.

Although he hadn't yet reached a clear, conscious state, his senses began to tingle back into the present. A sterile odor dominated his senses. The smell of antiseptics, ammonia, and medicine all wrapped up in a distinctive combination that filled his nostrils. For a brief moment, he came into full consciousness. He reconnected with his arms, legs, and back. His joints and vertebrae felt stiff with a deep soreness. The medications pushed his body back to sleep.

But his mind was starting to churn through what he had experienced. It was like a computer rebooting into its startup mode. His mind began to categorize the events. It was formatting his memories so that its keeper could make sense of his surroundings. Curt would survive. The first step was to awaken. But the human spirit, the tenacity of our nature, was to do more than exist. Curt's entire being was preparing for the fight of his life.

* * * * *

Diane had walked outside. The crisp, cool air filled her lungs. She was amazed at how crystal clear the air was. The surrounding hills seemed almost artificial because of the clarity; they seemed close enough to reach out and touch. The skyline and buildings appeared crisp and fresh, in sharper contrast than usual. It was as if no pollution existed.

She glanced up at the side of the building. The glass window of Curt's room was in clear view. She admired the view one last time before she went back into the hospital. She had become familiar with her surroundings and decided to take the service elevator. It would bring her up where Curt was located. She entered the elevator and depressed the button. She knew

Curt would be awake today. She had a lot of questions that needed to be answered. The door closed and the elevator began to rise.

* * * * *

The senior agent sat in the parking lot. On his drive to the hospital, he had formulated a plan. He would visit the target in room 315 and inject liquid caffeine into his IV. The purity and concentration of the chemical was a standard supply item inside the Agency's arsenal of death. He had taken some from the Agency supplies before he left. His only concern was being seen by any hospital personnel. He wanted to minimize the possibility that anyone could later identify him.

He would leave no physical evidence at the scene, except for the liquid solution inside the victim's veins. With the trauma from the fire, John knew Anderson would already have a large amount of other chemicals floating in his system. It was probably a miracle that he had survived up to this point. If an autopsy was later performed, the presence of a natural substance such as ordinary caffeine would probably go unnoticed. It was unlikely that a medical examiner would suspect foul play. It would appear instead to be a simple case of cardiac arrest, which was typical for victims who undergo such terrible accidents.

As John entered the main lobby elevator, he dropped his head toward his chest to keep his face from appearing on the elevator surveillance camera. He depressed the button and waited for the door to slide closed.

* * * * *

Curt could feel the gauze bandage covering his face. He could detect pressure from the IV tape at the crook of one arm. One of his eyes was uncovered and exposed to the open air. He could feel a soft breeze from the air conditioning vent as the air flow caused his eyelashes to flutter. He began to notice light pressure from the weight of the sheets placed on his body.

He was stiff and sore from his toes to his ears. He noticed a muffled puffiness around one of his ears. It was as if one side of his body was numb, almost as if his normal senses were missing from one side of his body. He tried to move the fingers on the numb side of his body. He was surprised that they moved. He felt a sense of relief that if he was paralyzed, it wasn't complete. He knew that he had limited control over his body. His eyelids were heavy. From the lack of use, a thick crusty film had accumulated at the corners of his eyes. He urged his body to focus all of his energy and strength to open his eyes, but he could feel a soothing wash of exhaustion dominate his body. His pain medication was kicking in. Curt drifted back to sleep as his body continued to awaken.

* * * * *

John exited the elevator and could see the large double doors of the ICU. The lettering above the doorway clearly marked the area as the Intensive Care Unit. He peered through the small glass window. The reception area was vacant. He kept his head down as he pushed the doors open and walked across the hallway, looking for room 315. The heels of his black wing-tipped shoes resonated with a staccato click as he searched the hallway. He had already loaded the liquid caffeine into the syringe and held it deep in his jacket pocket. He turned the corner and saw the room. Glancing in both directions, he reassured himself that no one was in sight. Glancing up from the ground, he noticed that the rooms were made of a clear transparent material, probably a thick plastic. He finally saw the room. Without hesitating, he pushed the door open.

As the door closed, he turned his attention to the bed. A man was lying down, and an electric monitor reported the steady heartbeat of the patient. The only other sound was the man's breathing. The senior agent glanced at the clipboard chart. The patient's name was listed as John Doe. He glanced at the metal stand next to the bed and located the IV stand. With professional efficiency, he walked to the bedside.

He had performed such a maneuver before. He removed the syringe from his pocket and inserted the sharp needle into the tube inserted in the man's hand. The liquid caffeine mixed with the medicinal fluids. From experience, he knew it would take several minutes for the mixture to reach the bloodstream. He also knew that the high concentration would have an immediate effect. The reaction would be instant and lethal.

Without fanfare, John wiped the plastic tube with the bedsheet to remove any fingerprints. He replaced the syringe needle's protective plastic cover and dropped it back into his jacket pocket and then turned and left the room. The entire process took less than ten seconds.

As he headed down the hallway, he heard another elevator bell ring, announcing someone else's arrival at the ICU. John increased his pace and pushed on the large double doors. No one knew anyone else had visited the ICU. Only a review of the hospital surveillance tape could have proved otherwise. But, in this case, that would never happen. John entered his elevator. As he watched the elevator doors close, he could see a figure pass the ICU doorway. No one would ever know what he had done.

The elevator doors slid closed, and John felt a sense of relief and accomplishment. This was only his second Snap Shot. As the elevator descended, the soft ding that resonated in the steel capsule acted like a checklist in his mind. John had done everything right. No one saw him. He left no physical evidence. The target would die at any moment.

This event was like a personal graduation, an accumulation of all his Agency experience. As the senior agent, he couldn't help but feel a sense of pride. His work was difficult. Few people could accomplish the tasks he was asked to perform. When the elevator doors opened on the ground floor, he maintained protocol. Ducking his head, he exited the building.

He could assure himself that this Curt Anderson issue was finally a closed case. The Agency no longer had to worry. As he drove out of the parking lot, a Code Blue was being called out from O'Connor Hospital's ICU.

* * * * *

Diane exited the service elevator. She was growing accustomed to the hospital environment and walked to Curt's room. As she opened the door, she could hear the monitor report his steady, strong heartbeat. She walked to his bedside and looked down at his peaceful expression. She knew his face only from his driver license photo, and his burned face looked nothing like what she remembered. She looked forward to being able to speak to him. He would have a long road to recovery.

After a brief silence, she sat in the soft chair next to his bed. She opened the magazine she had purchased at the gift shop and read the Hollywood gossip for the moment. She was going to wait until Curt regained consciousness.

* * * * *

The duty nurse had returned from the filing room. She was distracted by the other charts waiting on her desk, still needing to be filed. She walked through the hallway to make a visual round of the patients. The doctor had just completed his rounds, but protocol required this walk-through by the receptionist once every half hour. As she passed room 315, she noticed a visitor inside. She looked at the woman and exchanged a brief smile. She would complete her walk-through and then return to check out the situation.

* * * * *

Diane heard Curt's breathing change. A soft cough and gurgle echoed in the quiet room. She focused her attention on Curt's face. His nose moved as if he were trying to scratch an itch. His exposed eyelid struggled to pry itself open. A faint groan resonated from his raspy throat. Diane could swear that Curt was speaking German. She contemplated why his first words would be spoken in another language, but then she turned her attention back to the magazine and continued her wait.

* * * * *

The nurse returned to the front desk and entered her notes, documenting the time she completed her walk-through. She glanced down at the monitors and confirmed each patient's vital signs. Everyone was stable. Before she could relax, though, her trained ears heard the distinct Code Blue alarm blare. The light over room 315 began to flash. The nurse arose and headed toward another crisis. Her efforts would be hopeless.

* * * * *

Curt felt himself becoming fully conscious. It was like a surge of freshness expanding throughout his body. His mind began to catalog the most recent events that he had unwittingly experienced in his unconscious state. He began to recall hearing someone enter his room. He had heard footsteps and had the feeling at this moment that someone was very close to him, as if they were next to where he was lying down.

His strength had returned. A sense of urgency flooded his thoughts. He was desperate to leave this dreamy state of consciousness and re-enter the world of the living. He forced himself to push past the desire to go back to sleep. With each breath, he seemed to gain strength. His eyelids felt heavy, as if they were glued down. As he stretched the muscles in his forehead, he could feel his eyelashes flutter as his eye muscles came to life. His exposed eyelid opened a little more with each breath he took. Once his eye was fully exposed, he found his vision blurred, as if a thick coating of mucus covered his cornea.

He blinked several times before his vision cleared. In full view, a face he recognized stared back at him. As he studied her features, he had the impression that he knew her, but no name came to mind. For some reason, the woman triggered something inside him. That first image of her as he returned to consciousness elicited a sense of fear.

Curt recoiled from what his eyes had revealed, and his instincts took over. He pulled his shoulders away from the direction of the person in his room. The IV tubes and monitor wires shook as he pulled back. A loud electrical noise began to sound; it was a constant tone, the flat-line alarm. In an instant, the duty nurse burst into the room. With a shocked look on her face, she and the visitor both looked at Curt. He was definitely awake, but something was wrong.

* * * * *

The nurse saw the patient's monitor displaying the flat line. As she deactivated the monitor alarm, she could hear Code Blue being announced on the intercom. She noticed the wide-eyed female visitor standing at the bedside. Another ICU nurse entered the room, followed by a doctor. The woman was escorted out of the room and told to wait in the ICU lobby area.

The doctor began to administer CPR, and the nurses readied the defibrillator. In disbelief, the woman stumbled to the lobby area. The last thing she heard before she passed out was the doctor ordering the nurses to "Clear!" The distinctive sound of the electrical surge echoed from room 315, and the woman collapsed in the hallway. The patient in room 315 never regained consciousness and was pronounced dead fifteen minutes later.

* * * * *

The doctor looked down at the patient's clipboard chart. Puzzled, he began to question the duty nurse.

"What's this John Doe chart still doing here?"

The duty nurse hadn't noticed that the old chart for room 315 was still on her desk. It hadn't been filed because it was unclear whether an insurance company needed to be listed. "I'm sorry, Doctor. When we transported the other patient last night, we must have left his chart." She took the old chart and pointed to the opposite end of the desk.

"Mr. Hardy's chart is over there. He came in last night from a car accident on the 880. He didn't look that bad then."

The nurse watched the doctor return to the man's room and then walk toward the ICU lobby area. She never understood how doctors learned to deal with meeting family members to break the bad news. She re-entered room 315 and covered the patient with a sheet. She secured the toe tag, pulling the wire tightly around Mr. Hardy's big toe. After drawing the curtains to conceal the area, she glanced back at the lifeless body. Then she closed the door to make another walk-through.

* * * * *

The nurse looked at Curt's startled face. She tilted her head and saw that his vital-sign monitor wires had become detached. She reconnected the hook ups and the annoying constant blare was replaced by a peaceful steady heartbeat, although at a quickened pace. The nurse felt Curt's pulse and smiled.

"Welcome back! I'll get the doctor to come in, now that you're awake. You're so lucky to have such a nice sister." The nurse touched Diane's hand as she adjusted the window blinds before she left the room.

Curt was beyond confused. He knew that he didn't have a sister. He also knew he had seen this woman before but had not yet made the connection. Diane continued to watch Curt.

His heartbeat slowed back into a normal rhythm. She waited a few moments before speaking.

"The Agency was going to find you sooner or later. The hospital had no information about you. I was the only person who visited you, and I had to move you as soon as possible." She paused. In an awkward, shy manner, she finally asked him: "You are Curt Anderson, aren't you?"

Curt didn't know what to say. He blinked his exposed eye as he nodded his head. Diane exhaled in a wash of relief. At the hospital, she had no time and made an instant decision. She had worked for a large bureaucratic machine for most of her adult life. During her initial visit, the duty nurse had asked if John Doe had health insurance. She considered the concern the administration office had placed on the expenses for his care. She knew that even a large hospital had economic considerations, and the cost to keep Curt alive must have been outrageous.

She had hoped that she could get this done without any documentation, but this situation involved an unidentified individual facing mortal injuries. As such, hospitals were prepared to deal with enhanced legal protocol requirements. A total separate set of procedures existed if the actions of the health provider may have contributed to the injury or death of a patient. Health care providers called it a Sentinel Event. This protocol required that the legal authorities be involved in documenting the actions taken to identify John Doe cases.

This process was automatic and inflexible. It made sense, given the legal disposition of that person's assets should he pass away. It made sense that all efforts were made to properly identify each person. Religious considerations could also be involved, which made immediate notification of next of kin an important issue.

Hospitals always did what they could to avoid any potential PR fiasco. From a legal perspective, the issue concerning foul play also had to be ruled out. Countless questions were typically raised and had to be addressed. As such, hospitals were always mindful and compliant with regard to adhering to these duties. Whenever a legal authority did step forward to acknowledge and accept jurisdiction over the situation, hospital management would breathe a collective sigh of relief. Hospitals in particular relished the fact that a potentially large case could be ruled in their favor in terms of protocol and the quality of care provided. Getting paid was important, but avoiding lawsuits was equally important.

After contacting Glen, Diane provided an abundance of fictional credentials to convince the hospital that the transfer was legitimate. False documents were created, and they even required the hospital administrator to sign the documents to further authenticate the situation. The charade was detailed and would have convinced any seasoned administrator. The transfer out of state further convinced the administrator that the Feds, rather than the local PD, were involved. It all made sense. The Feds had the jurisdiction. In their eyes, the matter was resolved.

Every item was considered. Diane was even able to have the video surveillance tapes copied to the Feds and then wiped clean from the hospital data base. They explained that this was protocol for this type of situation. When Diane provided a cashier's check and an address for billing the balance, the hospital administrator had bent over backwards to complete the paperwork. The unusual nature of the transfer and Federal involvement raised suspicions, but Glen's people remained proactive, initiating the signing of forms and providing copies of signed documents.

The entire process had been well rehearsed and seemed authentic. The only downside was that the unusual nature of the event was one that everyone involved would remember. The talk at the water cooler speculated on who this John Doe was. What was he involved in? Why did he get such a VIP treatment? Who was this guy who not only had the involvement of the Feds but had relatives capable of producing large amounts of cash, and no health insurance? It was strange—strange enough that people would remember this event. But it would be years before anyone looked into it. Those years were enough, though.

After they left the hospital, with help from Glen they acquired a private ambulance service to transport Curt. They used fake names. Given that they paid cash, no one asked any questions. If Curt didn't come into full consciousness within the first week, they were prepared to move him again. Diane had purchased a private mailbox at a Postal Annex. She did everything over a pay phone or by fax. No one had seen her. O'Connor Hospital billings were directed to that mailbox. Curt had been transferred to Las Vegas.

* * * * *

"How long have I been out?"

"It's been three weeks since your accident."

Curt's eyes seemed to focus more clearly. It finally hit him who this woman was.

"Why did you send me the email from Gina's Yahoo account?" Diane asked.

"After reading your message to her, I had to do something. That Agency got away with murder, but it wasn't your fault, Lt. Colonel Klein. They were after me. They dropped the plane to try and kill me. It wasn't your fault."

Diane's eyes began to well up with tears. Her mind flooded with conflicting emotions. Her chest began to ache from the loss of her niece. A stinging hot sensation began to resonate within her chest as her guilt blossomed into anger. It all came back to the Agency. She again felt responsible for Gina's death. If Diane hadn't glorified her past experiences with her niece, she may never have pursued a career in the Agency, and she might still be alive today.

Curt began to relax. He was safe. He was away from the Agency. No one knew he had survived. For all he knew, only Diane knew.

"Does the Agency know I survived?"

Diane wiped her eyes. Curt could see her transform before his eyes. Diane's jaw line tightened as she ground her teeth. With focused, steely eyes, she returned Curt's gauze.

"I've devoted my life to the Agency. I knew we did things that no one could know of. I always believed we were special. We kept the country safe. We protected lives. We only existed to preserve our American values." After a short pause, she continued. "I was wrong."

Diane's face remained rigid and determined. In a soft whisper, she turned away from Curt and stared out the window. "Someone's going to pay. Someone's going to pay."

THE END

Prologue

Things are not always as they seem, especially when it comes to human thought. Many times, people do things on a regular basis and view their world a certain way. Humans seem to have the innate need to understand why things are the way they are. Humans seem to have a deep need to form a rationale. Everything, from religion and science to philosophy must be explained.

History has shown that mankind, when faced with the unknown, has a tendency to formulate its own opinions and conclusions. Whether the facts support such conclusions is unimportant. Not to have an opinion on how every single entity and concept came to be is a crime to the mind. Consequently, it is better to rationalize a hypothetical justification, however absurd, than to have no opinion.

It is interesting how history has shown that every single scientific fact that was widely accepted as truth had later been proved to be wrong. At one time people knew the Earth was flat. At one time, people believed the center of the universe was the Earth. At one time, people believed that it was impossible to travel beyond the speed of sound. All these beliefs were later proved false.

Likewise, throughout America's history, a cycle of trust, expectations, and societal needs for belief systems has vacillated from the extreme positions of good and evil. The factors that determine whether a position is good or evil depends on who you are and how it affects your life, combined with the prevailing public opinion. America's changed reality had its roots early in its infancy and persisted throughout its history. From the Boston Tea Party, slavery, and the construction of interstate highways to the creation of the FBI and the CIA, society has forgotten the real truth, the real reason that these beliefs, these institutions, came into existence. And it is this need for rationality that keeps society perpetuating these beliefs as true. Yet, upon reflection, we must ask ourselves: Have my beliefs become distorted and somehow manipulated for another's cause? In fact, is my belief even rational? Does it deserve to be held as truth and perpetuated into the psyche of the next generation?

For example, in the twenty-first century, Americans may simply believe that they prefer coffee as their hot beverage of choice because of its taste. But is that the real reason? Or has society simply been repeating behaviors that represent cultural prejudices and altered motives? A strong argument can be made that this beverage preference was forever changed based on many complicated factors that ultimately resulted in the Boston Tea Party. It may be that this event had more influence on the American preference for coffee than did aromas, tastes, and free choice. Another plausible answer could be found in analyzing how the early Colonists expressed their dissatisfaction of taxation without representation rather than their palatable preferences: They vandalized an entire tea shipment from England. Prior to this event, tea had been the hot beverage of choice.

Over the centuries, Americans have evolved their initial rebellion into a complex boycott of English customs by doing the opposite. A modern version of this rebellion can be seen in such simple demonstrations as installing steering wheels on the opposite side of the car.

This same altered and selective memory can be said about the creation of our roadway system. To understand the roads is to understand the American way of life. The advent of automobiles, combined with the ideology that defines freedom, has to some degree been molded by the evolution of this technology. The multitude of interrelated industries that support the concept of automobile travel using this vast network of roads ultimately defined the American psyche. As the roadways developed and expanded, the powers that made such decisions for society were forced to justify the use of so much land and resources to the development and maintenance of this never-ending network of roads.

Ironically, this evolution also affected the boundaries of the country and its territories. Ultimately, regional distinctions arose. These distinctions literally divided the most populated state, California, into regionalized quadrants defined by its beltways, freeways, and interstates. These man-made boundaries began dictating and indirectly encouraging growth that maximized the network, when in fact, the original motivation to construct the roadways was a direct response to the Japanese invasion of Pearl Harbor in 1941.

In response to the nation's newly recognized vulnerability, the U.S. government wanted the means to quickly move its armed forces from coast to coast. The interstates were designed not only to handle the tremendous weight of tanks, but also to be capable of landing the largest military bomber aircraft. Such over-engineering allowed America to immediately establish makeshift airports throughout its lands.

The primary motivation was simply to properly defend itself. And to achieve this rapid deployment of heavy machinery, the interstate freeway roads were designed to handle large carrier vehicles loaded down with tremendous weight. More importantly, the roads were designed so these vehicles could travel at speeds of at least eighty miles per hour, without the fear of overturning. Rapid deployment was the primary objective. Consequently, these goals dictated the design. The only predesign was for particular military-based communities and cities to become connected through this roadway system. The most obviously bicoastal connection is the Nation's Capital and California's Capital; Washington DC and Sacramento—

Interstate 50. The byproduct of these roads created their own tendencies—a natural evolution.

The roadway system evolved to the point that everything surrounding the driving experience redefined more than just transportation. Cars and roadways became "self evident." Using them became an inalienable right. Freedom began to be defined not only by one's individual physical ability to think one's own thoughts, but also by the perception people held about their access to boundless travel.

The only apparent limitation to travel became the lack of these roadways to certain areas. So as the roadways grew and expanded across the nation, Americans began to experience an apparent endless opportunity to explore their country. America's great physical size and the fact that it literally spans the width of the entire North American Continent, combined with its philosophical origins of freedom established by the rebelling founding fathers, fueled and accentuated the American psyche. The construction of the roadway system enhanced the entire concept of freedom. Its effect on the American society, when examined in its entirety, became the differentiating factor between it and the society of any other country in the world.

As society enjoyed the freedom of travel and its side benefits, people began to forget the original reason the roads were created. The roadways were not created to enhance the experience of freedom. It was a response based out of *fear of invasion*. It was this fear that justified its construction. The original motivation to construct this network was based on *paranoia*. It was an ever-increasing concern and fear of being exposed to some unforeseen invasion by another warring nation. It was fear of the unknown and the need to prepare at all costs against an unforeseen enemy. It was a desire to never again be caught unaware, unprepared, and vulnerable. This paranoia shaped how our society thinks.

The American psyche was defined more by the Japanese invasion of December 7, 1941, than anyone would have thought. It was that sequence of events, the creation of fear and mistrust, the loss of human life and dignity, and vulnerability on the world scene that forever changed the framework of this society.

The construction of this roadway system had become the single most expensive civil project ever undertaken. But the side benefits of this roadway system have, over the years, clouded our recollection as to what motivated its creation. All Americans have enjoyed the benefits of this great creation. It undoubtedly enhanced our freedom. The impetus grew rural towns into cities and enhanced commerce. The byproduct of commerce was not only enhanced trade, but also the establishment of niche market industries that grew out of the need to service the users of this roadway system. The fast food chains, convenient gas stations, restaurants, motels, trucking, and busing industries became the symbols of success. Such names as McDonald's, Chevron, Shell, Denny's, Motel 6, Mack Trucks, and Greyhound became everyday name brands within American society.

This *perception of freedom of choice* is interesting. To what degree does freedom truly exist? The motivation for constructing these roadways had nothing to do with expanding our individual rights to be free. Rather its creation was ultimately to protect our country's existence by making it better able to defend itself. Even though these roadways created a side benefit of easier access by the citizens to explore and interact with previously isolated communities, one must also ask: *To what degree does this perceived individual freedom truly exist?*

An example of the fictional Agency in reality can be found in the factual and real life attempt to overthrow President Roosevelt. Today, the following events are considered fact. In 1933, some of America's richest business owners were afraid that President Roosevelt was going to redistribute wealth from the rich to the poor. To prevent this from happening, these wealthy business owners plotted to recruit General Smedley

Butler to lead a military coup and establish a fascist government.

These business owners believed that because they controlled the newspapers, and because General Butler controlled the military, their plan would work. However, General Butler identified with the troops and not the elite. Consequently, General Butler went along with their plans in order to gather evidence to stop the elite. After collecting enough evidence, he went public with the plan. A Congressional Committee was formed but whitewashed the public version of its final report and deleted the names of the most powerful elite that were involved. Given the elite's influence in Congress, the story became watered down, resulting in only rumors and hearsay.

Although this novel, *Rule One Twenty*, is pure fiction, looking back at what has been proved to be reality, one must wonder what types of secret agencies exist not only in the U.S. government but also in the governments of other countries.

About the Author

E.A. Padilla was born in a small town in Northern California, the youngest of four children. Many of his writings reference his home town, Red Bluff, California. He had a knack for mathematics and entered UC Irvine as a Physics major, later graduating from CSU Sacramento and changing his major to Economics with a minor in Psychology. During his younger years, he had the desire to write. Some of his writings were published in his high school publications.

After graduating, he continued to write as a hobby. He felt compelled to secure his financial future first in the banking industry and ultimately in the insurance industry. During those years, he continued to write procedure manuals as well as corporate documents that required detailed processes, as well as the reporting of facts, including legal analysis and case law. Producing large corporate documents allowed him to hone his skills in the written word. Unfortunately, he was unable to concentrate on his novel.

Once he had achieved a successful business, he began enjoying writing for pleasure. Consequently, he was able to re-engage his efforts to finalize his first novel, *Rule One Twenty*. He is concluding his second novel, a psychological murder drama titled *Michaso* (the Korean word for crazy).

His third book is a political drama surrounding a family split between North and South Korea and centers around an American Officer tasked with military protocol and human suffering that a family endures when it has become separated by an artificially imposed border created by the powerful countries who won World War II. This book is titled *Tunnels,* which details the real life existence of huge tunnels dug underneath the countries and used by North Korea to invade South Korea.

The sequel to *Rule One Twenty,* titled *Sentinel Event* will be completed the last quarter of 2016.

Made in the USA
San Bernardino, CA
14 November 2015